The
Glass Wives

The
Glass Wives

—— A NOVEL ——

Amy Sue Nathan

St. Martin's Griffin
New York

THE GLASS WIVES. Copyright © 2013 by Amy Nathan Gropper. All rights reserved. Printed in the United States of America. For information address St. Martin's Press, 175 Fifth Avenue, New York, N.Y. 10010.

www.stmartins.com

ISBN 978-1-250-04016-9 (hardcover)
ISBN 978-1-250-01656-0 (trade paperback)
ISBN 978-1-250-01657-7 (e-book)

St. Martin's Griffin books may be purchased for educational, business, or promotional use. For information on bulk purchases, please contact Macmillan Corporate and Premium Sales Department at 1-800-221-7945 extension 5442 or write specialmarkets@macmillan.com.

First Edition: May 2013

10 9 8 7 6 5 4 3 2 1

To Zachary
For understanding that books are my baseball

To Chloe
For understanding

When the glass shatters,
who will be there to pick up the pieces?

The
Glass Wives

Chapter 1

EVIE PICKED UP A SMALL, silver-framed photo and wiped away invisible dust. The groom towered over the groomsmen, his hair windblown without any wind, his smile slightly askew, big blue eyes staring and pensive. She knew it all too well, but the tug of familiarity was not déjà vu. Evie had been there before, decades earlier, with the same groom. But in this picture she was not the bride.

No one noticed Evie put back the photo or swish her hand on her pant leg, pretending now to wipe off the nonexistent dust. She walked through the crowd toward the floor-to-ceiling window. No one noticed her do that, either. Burgundy velour curtains tied back with thick, black tassels framed a six-foot, imitation pine tree. Hallmark ornaments masquerading as heirlooms dangled from its branches. Gold tinsel fringe and shiny red balls sparkled. It all seemed out of place, yet Evie knew it belonged. Probably more than she did.

Evie shook her head to clear an internal fog. It didn't work, but certain thoughts were clear no matter how few hours she'd slept, and no matter how her head throbbed a low, steady beat. Her ex-husband had died. Her children had no father. And if she were still married, she would be a widow.

Evie had accepted that she and Richard no longer shared the same happily-ever-after, but she'd assumed that they would move forward with grace and goodwill. So what if the grace was all her doing. She and Richard would share their children's bar and bat mitzvah, proms, graduations, weddings, and grandchildren. They'd have different partners, of course—different homes. They'd be positioned at opposite ends of the same long holiday tables, but they would continue to share Sam's and Sophie's milestones. After their divorce three years ago, it took Evie a full year to find her footing, twelve long months, to believe deep down she had a strong enough foundation to create a new, full life. And then, she created it.

Now the building blocks were scattered again.

She looked across the room at Nicole, who, within four years, had been Richard's mistress, his wife, and now his widow. It wasn't hard to imagine how she felt. The blood would have left her extremities. Her stomach would be in her throat. Her heart would ache for touch as her head searched for answers. No doubt she'd be nursing a cocktail of anger, sadness, and shock. Evie knew all this because she had mourned the same loss, but she had done it when Richard was alive.

Nicole sat barefoot on a low, wooden bench customary for sitting shiva. She slumped, arms at her sides, hair in disarray. Her daze extended beyond her personal space and touched everyone else in the room. Nicole was thirty, fifteen years younger than Evie, but the circles under Nicole's eyes stretched to midcheek. She wore no makeup and her skin was sallow without the benefit of foundation or blush. Every mirror in the house was covered with a white sheet. Shiva was for mourning, and prayer, and, yes, food, but vanity was forbidden. And while Nicole wasn't Jewish, she was respecting Jewish customs in the home she'd shared with Richard. Evie hated to admit it, but she admired the effort, despite the plastic cranberry-and-popcorn garland hanging above a stack of yarmulkes.

Evie sat on the couch, a black leather casualty of divorce, and stroked the worn cushion with her thumb until it burned. During the young married years, the couch was the only furniture in Evie and

Richard's living room. During the young parenting years, she and Richard sat on the couch, legs intertwined, each holding one of their twins. During the recent turbulent years, Richard sat at one end of the couch, Evie at the other, each leaning toward the farthest wall, two arms' lengths and vacant miles between them. Why had she let Richard take the couch? The couch was a timeline, a testament, a tribute.

Or maybe it was just a couch.

Evie's stomach growled. The shiva food remained untouched. Soon the pickles would lose their sheen, slices of lox would curl at the edges, and the tuna salad would sour. So people hovered, waiting for some official signal that it was Time To Eat. Only then would they soothe their psyches with the time-honored Jewish death fare.

"Everyone, please have something to eat," Nicole said through a sniffle, and the crowd began grazing. She lifted six-month-old Luca from his bouncy seat and drew him to her chest. Nicole's words and motions were fluid, as if rehearsed.

Sam and Sophie stood shoulder to shoulder, or shoulder to arm. At ten, Sophie was still taller than her twin brother, although Evie suspected that that wouldn't last the year, since every week Sam's pants and sleeves were getting shorter. She scooted to the middle of the cushion and the kids sat on either side, their thighs touching hers. The kids hated getting dressed up, yet here they were, in starched and pressed clothes usually reserved for Yom Kippur. Tomorrow Evie would let them wear sweats. After all, when the rabbi explained the ancient custom of *kriah,* tearing of clothing—or a black satin ribbon—and wearing it as a symbol of grief for an immediate family member, he never said they couldn't wear it on a hoodie. Evie had clenched her jaw and swallowed baseball-size sobs when she'd first heard the satin ribbon rip. Then she held her breath as the pins poked through her babies-who-were-no-longer-babies' shirts, making holes that would never truly be mended. Richard had once been Evie's immediate family as well, but the space over her heart remained empty.

As people passed on their way to the buffet, some glanced at Evie. Most never looked at or spoke to Sam or Sophie, but some closed their eyes and nodded as if it made her fatherless children invisible.

Was that the point?

A brave few extended their hands and said or mouthed, "I'm sorry." Others patted one twin's head or the other's. Richard's Uncle Abe pulled a quarter out from behind Sam's ear, and then Sophie's. They were too old to be dazzled, but they smiled and so did Evie.

Sidestepping the hungry mob, Nicole inched her way to Evie. With Luca in one arm, Nicole rustled Sam's already-messy blond hair, touched Sophie's chin with her fingers, held the baby's back, and bounced. Nicole stood six inches from Evie's knees, abrasive electricity between them.

"Can we go watch TV?" Sam asked. He cocked his head to the side and smiled, wrevealing his overbite, inherited from Richard.

"Please?" Sophie said, wringing her hands as if she wanted to download more songs onto her iPod or have extra minutes on the computer.

"Are you sure?" Evie said. Her instinct was to tighten her grip on their arms.

"Yes," the twins said, nodding.

"Oh, okay, go!" Evie said. She squeaked in an effort to match their enthusiasm but her voice quavered.

Sam and Sophie stomped down the stairs to the rec room Richard had built for his second family, unlike Evie's unfinished laundry-room closet and the half-built shed in her backyard. She felt light without them touching her. It was a welcome reprieve, but laced with yearning.

Evie looked up at Nicole and patted the warm, indented cushion. "Do you want to sit?"

Nicole shook her head. "I just wanted to say . . . I'm glad you and the kids are here. I wish it were different, but we should be together at a time like this."

Just two more days of shiva and Evie's *time like this* was over. She ached to escape the sights, sounds, and smells of death by rinsing them away with lavender bath soap in her oversize tub, holding her breath, dipping below the surface, bubbles dissipating around her, each *pop-pop-pop* taking away a little of the day, the weekend, the sadness. The scene wouldn't play out that way if she were home, but the daydream seemed harmless. Sam and Sophie had sobbed when Evie mentioned going *home* early. Richard's house may have been their every-other-weekend house, but the beige-brick Georgian held the most recent dad-memories under its vaulted ceilings. They needed to be inside this house and inside this life for a little bit longer—two days longer. Evie needed those days to figure out what was next for all three of them.

"I wanted to thank you for coming," Nicole said. "And for organizing everything. There's so much food, and I heard more is coming tomorrow. I hope you'll take leftovers."

Evie wouldn't take anything, but nodded to be polite. Nicole twisted at the waist over and over again, as if stretching to exercise. It made Evie dizzy.

"You don't have to worry about the food, everyone chipped in," she said, in case that was causing the twisting. She diverted her eyes to the half-empty lox tray on her limited horizon. A lot of food was left, but Jews fed people. *That's what we do. It's written somewhere in an ancient scroll: "Thou shalt not let anyone leave thy house hungry."* "Everyone chipped in." Evie knew it was a mitzvah—a commandment—to console the bereaved. And nothing was more consoling than nova.

"That's so generous." Nicole stopped swiveling but now shifted from one foot to the other as if she needed to use the bathroom. The fidgeting made Evie want to find Nicole's off-switch. "This is sort of like a wake in reverse," Nicole said. "Wakes come before funerals and there's usually an open casket, you know?" Nicole's cheeks appeared sucked in and hollow; her eyes drifted to a spot on the wall.

Evie squinted and searched for a smudge, a spot, a spider. Nothing. She had nothing else to say.

Baby Luca popped his head from Nicole's shoulder. He blinked and turned his face toward Evie with one creased, pink cheek and watery eyes. With the palm of her hand, Nicole traced a zigzag on his back. She kissed his sweaty head. "Can we talk more another time?"

"Okay." Evie said. *If we must.*

In the kitchen, the Shiva Brigade rallied. Evie watched with awe as they took the reins. Her next-door neighbor and best friend, Laney, played traffic cop—arms flying, fingers pointing. Laney turned away from the food and gathered her long, auburn curls into a ponytail. She preferred her hair down around her shoulders because it balanced her hips. Laney with a ponytail meant serious business.

Beth shimmied through the crowd. She lived on the other side of Evie and boasted a short, brown bob and petite frame. Her penchant for Lilly Pulitzer and Miss Manners anchored the best-friend trio in suburban sensibilities, which was annoying *and* endearing. Beth hung winter coats in the closet but arranged the furs by color and length over the oak banister. She primed the non-Jewish guests on shiva, officially the seven-day mourning period, although they'd condensed it to three. A martinet for protocol, Beth put her hands on her knees and whispered in the ears of anyone who sat on the wooden benches, and they moved to softer ground. She had positioned Laney's teenage daughters inside the front door to ensure that guests, upon approaching the house, washed their hands outside, rinsing away death. The pitcher of warm water had already been refilled twice. While on the move, Beth whisked her smartphone out of her quilted purse and used the voice recorder to note the names of everyone who entered with food, whether homemade or store-bought, and the few names of those who brought nothing, unless their names were included on the list for the lox tray. She did all this while combining cream-cheese containers and arranging a plate of kugel.

Evie read Laney's lips from across the room.

"You never go to a shiva house empty-handed," Laney said to Beth as she stacked bakery boxes on Nicole's kitchen counter.

Laney saw the world in black and white. Right and wrong. Good and bad. Evie's life was shades of gray. Like her hair.

Evie's almost-black, wavy hair with its questionable roots hung past her shoulders in an attempt-to-be-trendy array of scattered layers. Her sweeping bangs weren't doing any sweeping, they were just hanging.

The kids were smart to hightail it out of there. Evie didn't want to talk to anyone either, but she *was* content to people-watch. Richard's cousins from Cleveland huddled in the corner; the older aunts and uncles who migrated to Florida sat in a semicircle talking louder than they should. Neighbors Evie last saw on Halloween and their mutual grad-school friends who were strangers outside e-mail mingled with Pinehurst College faculty and Richard's Ohio State fraternity brothers he had not seen since graduation. Why did they come? For themselves? Richard? The kids? Nicole? For memories? It didn't matter. They were equal when gathered for sadness. But their presence was also akin to a gapers' delay on the tollway, where everyone slowed to see the pileup and then floored it to get away.

"Not exactly the scenario *she* planned when she snagged herself a married man and had a baby," Laney said behind a sesame bagel. She eyed her husband. Herb furrowed his brow and sucked in his lips, trapping his words. Laney winked at him and a smile broke through Herb's full lips and mustache. He put his arm around Laney's waist. Evie squelched a gasp. This was normally where Laney would feign an itch on her ankle and step away, but she didn't move, except closer to Herb. Evie watched her friends and counted.

One, two, three. She gave it more time. *Four, five, six.* Flabbergasted, Evie continued. *Seven, eight, nine.* And with a deep breath—the finale . . . *ten.* Laney did not move away. Richard's death had initiated a truce.

Evie watched Laney as Laney watched Herb. He kissed Laney's head and walked away. Laney then moved to the couch close to Evie, even though Laney could have claimed a whole cushion for herself. She was protective; almost possessive. Beth sat on the other side of Laney, bagel-less, a more suitable space between them. Beth put her arm around Laney and extended it, patting Evie's back.

"This is so sad," Beth said.

Laney sat taller, even though she was already the tallest. She flared her nostrils in disapproval. "Don't you dare feel bad for *her.* What goes around comes around," Laney said with a bagel bite in her mouth. Laney's shoulders relaxed and she glanced from Beth to Evie. "At least you don't have to deal with her anymore. Or the baby."

Evie hadn't been thinking about Nicole. She'd been thinking about her kids without a father. Herself without an ex-husband. How dare Richard leave her to raise the twins alone—not just sometimes alone—and to juggle a half brother and a stepmother and a Christmas tree! But was Laney right? Was *that* the silver lining? Would Sam and Sophie even have a stepmother? It would make things easier if they did not. But only easier for Evie. *Damn conscience.*

"Your kids will be okay no matter," Beth said, as if reading Evie's mind. That possibility was comforting as well as disconcerting because Evie craved more than okay. Evie craved normal.

Laney turned ninety degrees, faced her friends, and pointed at Evie, which startled her out of her daze. "Ms. Evie Glass," she said as if taking attendance, "you are now a divorced mom with a dead ex-husband. JDate will never be the same."

Beth hung her head and, without looking up, smacked Laney's

finger. Evie didn't need JDate and Laney knew it. Evie had been dating Scott Miller every other weekend for the past six months, and when the kids were with Evie and she couldn't see Scott, they e-mailed, texted, and talked on the phone late at night. They'd just come back from a weekend in Michigan. That meant something. Evie just wasn't sure what.

After the rabbi led the evening *minyan* and finished the service with the traditional *Kaddish* prayer, Beth and Laney wrapped their arms around Evie in the tightest group hug three people could give. The rocking motion enveloped her in safety, staving off death and Christmas folderol. Then, a shadow blocked the overhead light. The jumbled group separated. There stood Scott with a plate of rugelach.

From that angle, he looked tall to Evie, but he was Jewish five-nine, which meant *five-seven*—something Evie learned quickly when she started online dating. He held a Christmas paper plate filled with Evie's favorite—the two-bite, flaky, rolled cookies filled with chocolate bits or raspberry jam or nuts or apricot preserves. They had been her grandmother's, *Bubbe*'s, specialty.

Though sweets seemed counterintuitive for mourning, everyone reached into the plate. Evie reached instead for Scott's other hand and noticed his nails, clean, trimmed and buffed as always. He was her man of the moment and foreseeable future. The *boyfriend* label seemed childish, and the *significant other* moniker seemed, well, too significant.

"This is Beth and Laney," Evie said, pointing with her chin so she didn't have to let go of the rugelach, or of Scott. For three years—The Divorced Years—Evie had kept her random dating escapades distant from her kids, her friends, and her pristine Chicago suburb of Lakewood. But the best-friend trio had agreed—it was time for Beth and Laney to meet Scott. He was a gentleman, a banker's banker with a receding hairline, an ex-wife in California, but no kids. He made Evie laugh and think and he was great in bed. Evie pointed to the last rugelach, but he shook his head. *Such a mensch.* Any man who gave up the last rugelach must be a keeper.

Evie smiled up at him and squeezed his hand. He smiled, but he didn't squeeze back.

"This is Scott," Evie said, releasing the plate onto her lap. She didn't know what else to say.

"We met at the funeral," Beth said. "Nice to see you again. Well, you know what I mean."

Laney nodded in agreement.

"Sure, same here," said Scott, taking his place on a separate cushion, keeping his physical distance, but watching Evie, never averting his eyes. He looked as if he were in a trance, so that meant he was either riveted or bored. To Evie, everything and everyone was tired-blurry. She blinked hard in lieu of rubbing her eyes, even though she had on no makeup. Evie pointed out her parents and sister. Laney named each Lakewood friend and foe. For Laney there were always foes.

"Where are your in-laws?" Scott said. "I mean, your *ex*-in-laws?"

"Richard's parents died young," Beth whispered. She mouthed the word *cancer.* "He was an only child."

"That's his great-aunt and -uncle over there," Evie said. "I don't think I've seen them since the wedding." *That wasn't very nice. They were old.* She and Richard should have visited them. Or invited them to Lakewood. Paid for the plane ticket. Yes, they—*Richard*—should have done all those things and much more.

"Which ones belong to the widow?" Laney said.

That was a good question. Where was Nicole's family? Evie knew almost everyone. Where were the strangers? The other side of Richard's new family? The new friends that went with the new life? Evie shrugged. "No clue."

"They must be here somewhere." Scott looked around the

room without moving his head, his eyes appearing to follow a bouncing ball.

"I don't think so." Evie scanned the crowd in more of a tennis-match movement, quick and side to side. Frantic to find the missing members of Nicole's family, Evie looked around the room. Had they been there all along, lost in the crowd, unseen because they weren't being sought? No. There were sitters and standers and leaners. The real helpers, the pretend helpers, and the ones who had no intention of helping. The grazers, the pilers, the pickers. The Christmas sweaters. The Christmas sweaters might be Nicole's family, but then why weren't they cuddling Luca or bringing Nicole cups of grief tea? A subtle awareness tugged at Evie as if a memory, or facts, were just out of reach. She pushed aside the thought. She could ask Nicole about her family later, if Evie remembered.

As the shiva crowd thinned, Evie's parents and sister carried wooden kitchen chairs and placed them near the couch, joining the elite group of leftover mourners. Shirley, Evie's mother, looked at her watch and then raised her eyebrows. Laney then looked at *her* watch.

"When are you going home?" Laney said to Evie.

"Later."

"You've done enough, Evelyn," Shirley said, shaking her head. "You don't need to be here any longer."

"I'll stay till the kids are tired. They want to be here."

"It's time for you to go home," Evie's dad, Bob, said. "This doesn't make sense, staying here, helping out. Enough is enough." He remained standing and crossed his arms.

"We'll come back with you tomorrow, promise," Lisa, Evie's sister, said. She was only eighteen months younger, but Lisa was a divorced, no-kids D.C. attorney with a town house in Georgetown who wore yoga pants *only* to do yoga and washed her hair even if she wasn't leaving the house. She scoffed at the well-married, luxury-minivan-driving, stay-at-home soccer moms of Lakewood, but never lumped Evie into the same category.

"The kids just want to stay longer." Evie dumped her empty plate into a passing trash bag carried by one of her neighbors. Maybe she should have used a doggie bag, but instead she checked her fingers and lap for rugelach crumbs and popped a few sweet escapees into her mouth. "Please don't make this harder for me."

Evie's parents and Lisa left for Evie's house. They'd take care of the dog and stay up late discussing her fate, which they'd undoubtedly share with her in the morning. She couldn't wait.

As if lights had blinked indicating it was time for everyone to go, neighbors hugged Evie good-bye. Acquaintances touched her shoulder. Strangers nodded in her direction. She was glad to have them all graveside and then back at Nicole's; the hum of their voices and their buzz of activity kept her thoughts in the present. She knew that for most, a death gathering mirrored a one-night stand—gratifying, brief, and tinged with regret. Evie envied their right to keep moving when her own feet were stuck to the floor. Tomorrow other families might be ice-skating in Millennium Park and then searching the *Cloud Gate* sculpture—*The Bean*—for their frozen, bundled reflections. Her family would not.

Her family. For three years, Evie had defined *family* as her and Sam and Sophie. And for Evie, that still held true. But the shape and breadth of her children's family had changed forever. Nothing for them would ever be the same, which meant nothing would be the same for Evie. Again. She inhaled deeply, the air snagging in her lungs, then exhaled to make sure she could.

The twins walked to the couch and in silence took their designated places on either side of Evie. They leaned their heads on their mother's shoulders and wrapped their arms around her torso, and each other. When the twins were babies and toddlers, they both climbed into her lap at the same time. Evie knew if they did that now, her lap would still have been the right size, because a mother's lap is always the right size. She kissed each of them on the head, and simultaneously each child took one of her hands, squeezed tight, and held on, as if they might fall.

Evie needed to find her footing again and find it fast. Because if she stumbled, they all *would* come tumbling down.

A cold wind whipped into the living room. A chill sped down Evie's spine as if a snowball had struck the back of her neck. She shivered, turned her head, and noticed Scott leaning by the open front door. His camel cashmere overcoat buttoned to his neck, hands in his pockets, his head tilted and resting on the doorjamb in a classic *GQ* pose. Scott winked at her. Evie smiled and closed her eyes in silent gratitude.

When she opened them, he was gone.

— Chapter 2 —

WHEN SHIVA ENDED, SO DID the catered meals and constant company.

Evie was a mixed bag of glad and sad when her parents and Lisa had flown home the day before. They'd done the driving, the consoling, and the laundry. For Evie, those were equally important. But without them there was no worrying about Lisa's part-time vegetarianism or her parents' bouts with acid reflux. Her family came, they comforted, and they conquered the kitchen by filling the pantry with boxes of cereal and granola bars, stocking the freezer with ice cream cones, and loading the fridge with bags of apples, oranges, and containers of homemade meals. But Evie knew her kids best—so tonight they would forgo Shirley's pot roast, Bob's turkey burgers, and Lisa's veggie chili, to cook hot dogs in the fireplace. Evie's mantra of the day: *Nitrates and carcinogens in moderation never hurt anyone.*

After dinner, showers, and check-in phone calls to her parents and sister, Evie read aloud to Sam and Sophie from their well-loved book *Freckle Juice*. It didn't matter that it was the twins' favorite three years ago. There was safety and familiarity within those pages. And they always laughed. A silent mom-prayer went out to Judy Blume for images of Andrew Marcus drawing freckles on his face with a Magic Marker. Evie would much rather have her kids dreaming of freckle-juice-drinking monsters than of a limousine ride to a cemetery.

Sam and Sophie snuggled into sleeping bags and listened, or pretended to. Evie read until her tongue felt thick with words she said but didn't hear; until the twins' eyes flittered shut and mouths dropped open, their winter complexions lit and warmed by the dwindling fire.

Sam's head rested on the padded arm of the sectional, his legs curled against his chest. He was gangly for a ten-year-old. Richard and Evie always remarked on the twins' long limbs, glad they inherited that trait from Richard's side of the family. One day Sam would reach things on the top shelves, while his mother—all five feet four of her—would still have to hunt for the step stool. Sophie was tall too, and Evie could see the outline of her daughter's long legs under the blanket as she lay on an air mattress at the other end of the couch. If she stretched, Evie could reach down and twirl her fingers in Sophie's long, light brown curls that were just like Lisa's.

Cuddling up alone in a static-ridden White Sox blanket, Evie reveled in the silence, marred only by the occasional crackle of the disintegrating logs. To entice sleep, she tried replaying her favorite movies and TV show episodes in her head, the chatter from three days of polite conversations filtered through her personal reruns.

She'd long ago settled into a coveted place of indifference with Richard—that convenient cubbyhole that had emerged after the hatred had dissolved. But now, bad memories bubbled to the surface. Evie pushed them back. She and Richard hadn't bickered in years. Their lives were pleasantly linked by the twins—and legally linked by automatic support payments—but not by emotions or broken promises. They tag-teamed for soccer games and cochaperoned field trips.

Then, she saw Richard's face. Not just ex-husband Richard's face, but the face of the twenty-five-year-old she'd fallen in love with. She couldn't deny Richard's good looks even postdivorce because Sam looked just like him. Yes, she'd focus on that, as it had been a long time since she'd thought of Richard's face as sweet *or* kind.

Evie flipped from one side to the other, struggling to find a comfortable spot where she didn't feel a gap in the cushions against her lower back. Her eyes burned but she couldn't sleep, probably because it was ten o'clock. With the blanket wrapped around her shoulders, Evie tiptoed into the kitchen and by the glow of her cell phone called Scott. Voice mail. He was probably in the shower or reading a book he couldn't put down until the end of the chapter. She tried his landline. Voice mail again.

"It's me," she said. "I tried your cell too . . . just wanted to thank you for the other day. For coming to shiva." *You don't thank people for coming to shiva.* Evie didn't know why, but she knew it was a Jewish faux pas, one of those things Bubbe had mandated. Scott probably knew that rule too. "I mean, I just wanted to touch base since we haven't talked since shiva. Well, okay, call me when you get this . . . um . . . talk to you soon . . ." She stopped short of adding, "Love ya."

What if it had been Scott who died instead of Richard? Evie's hand smacked her mouth and it stayed there.

When her cell phone buzzed, Evie's heart leapt, her face exploding into a broad smile. She held her phone tight with both hands and looked at the screen. Her mood sank when she saw Richard's number. *What did he want now?* Then burnt hot dog lurched into her throat, coating it with reality. It couldn't be Richard. It had to be Nicole. Evie tapped DECLINE.

Evie tried to fall asleep for another hour. She'd have to go upstairs to get any rest with the twins' resonant snoring. The sound was in direct contrast to the way they looked when they slept—peaceful, cherubic faces, fluttering, long eyelashes, and twitching, drooling smiles. Such sleep belied her tweens' fondness for video games, anime, basketball, and soccer. Mothering was easier when they loved *Dora the Explorer* and zwieback toast. Goopy, slimy zwieback toast. When a baby wipe cleaned every mess, kisses healed every hurt, and when a pinkie-swear sealed every promise.

Light trickled in the window and poked Evie in the eye. She was on top of her comforter and propped up on three pillows. Her eyes focused on Sam and Sophie, back-to-back at the foot of the bed, playing handheld video games on silent. Evie hadn't even felt them climb on.

She cleared her throat, and the twins wiggled over to her. They fell into a family hug. "You'll be okay," she whispered, reassuring herself and, by default, Sam and Sophie. "I promise with all my heart." She alternated her words with light kisses on their ears.

She had said the same thing more than three years before, on a day Evie prepared for with military precision. With the word *divorce,* the twins' shrieks of terror had ripped through her. Yet they had made it through okay—not great or amazing, but okay. But with no warning, no court dates, no list of pros and cons, there had been no way for Evie to prepare herself—or Sam and Sophie—for Richard's death. It had been a dark, snowy December night in northern Lake County when his car slid on black ice during a sharp turn and smashed into a guardrail.

"He couldn't have seen it," the police officer said.

"On impact," the doctor added.

Impact, indeed.

A week's worth of mail stuck out of the basket hanging on the kitchen wall. Evie reached, then pulled back her hand. The mail could wait. She wasn't going to ruin her coffee refuge by opening bills. With the kids still tucked in her bed and glued to their games, she just wanted a little peace and quiet and coffee. She'd sort through the mess later with a fully caffeinated tank on board. In the meantime, Evie pulled out a few catalogs and tossed them into the recycle bin. It was less daunting without the bulk.

As if on cue, Beth tapped on the back door. Still locked—which was unusual. Evie let her in. Beth patted the tops of Tupperware containers and foil-wrapped plates as if she were playing bongos, which would have been a sight in her North Face jacket and leather gloves. Evie smiled so wide her cheeks stretched.

"People dropped off more food at my house for you," Beth said, stacking them on the kitchen counter.

Death was horrifying enough, but death and hunger would be a *shanda*, a disgrace. The amount of food delivered was directly proportional to the level of fear engulfing each Lakewood family. The more they cooked, baked, and delivered, the less likely this would happen to someone else they knew. At this rate, Lakewood residents would live forever.

"Let's sit," Evie said, as if it were a novel idea.

Laney emerged from the front hall. Thank goodness for a friend with her own key. Any other day she'd have come through the back door, and any other day she'd have been stunning. But this day Laney wore mismatched sweats with a clip holding a clump of her curls.

Dead ex-husband and frumpy, front-door Laney—Evie's personal apocalypse.

"Where are the kids?" Laney asked.

"Upstairs, why?"

"We need to rehash shiva."

"No, we do not," Beth said.

"Being there was enough rehashing for me," Evie said.

"Nothing bad, just, well, a lot of people showed up every day. It was nice. As nice as a shiva can be, I mean."

Beth opened a box with more force than was needed. "Why are you surprised? I know you had a problem with Richard, but not everyone did. And, anyway, people do what's right in a situation like this. You did."

"I did it for Evie and the kids."

"So did I." Beth was annoyed, put her hands on Evie's shoulders, and shifted her away from Laney.

Laney drummed the side of a box. "You need to get out of here."

"Out of where?" Evie turned, opening her eyes wider than was comfortable.

"This house."

"Right now? I don't really feel like going anywhere. . . ."

"No, I mean, in general. You need a new place."

"You want me to move?"

"No, I don't *want* you to move, but maybe that's the best thing. A change of scenery always helps put things into perspective."

Who the hell needs perspective? I see everything clearly. "This is my home. This is what I need."

"A smaller place would be easier to manage," Beth said.

"I've been managing this house on my own for over three years, in case you've forgotten. It's not like Richard moved out yesterday." Evie cringed at Beth's and Laney's suggestion that this house wasn't her forever home. She held her hair off her face with one hand and fanned herself with the other. Her eyes shifted left as she counted. "I've lived here for more than a dozen years. I'm not moving. Ever."

"Take a deep breath," Laney said. Evie did. "Are you finished? It was just a suggestion," Laney said in a timid, un-Laney-like voice. "Your parents just thought—"

"You're in cahoots with my parents?"

"And your sister," Beth confessed without making eye contact.

"This is where I want to be," Evie said. *This is where I need to be.*

"Of course we don't want you to move. But can you afford to stay?"

"How can I afford not to stay?" Evie threw her arms up into the air. Her friends were being ridiculous. She and the kids needed stability. Even moving across town would be disruptive. And they'd had enough disruptions.

"We mean *afford*," Beth said.

Evie froze. She'd been so busy experiencing the emotional reverie of Richard's death that she hadn't considered the financial consequences. Without his support check adding to her commissions from her part-time job at Third Coast Gifts, how the hell *was* she going to pay all the bills this month? Or next month? Or ever? The mortgage was due in two weeks. No, sixteen days. Considering Richard was alive one minute and dead the next, and that in the past week they'd had a funeral, shiva, visitors, and a cookout in the living room—sixteen days seemed like a long time. But it wasn't. Maybe she *had* to move.

"We should go," Laney said. "But just think about calling your parents and sister to talk about it. There are nice, new town houses on the other side of Lakeview."

"Don't go," Evie said. "I can't move. *That* is one thing I'm sure of." Evie didn't know how she was sure of anything without a real meal or a normal night's sleep since when? And it was what day? It was Wednesday. Maybe. "The kids would have to change schools. They'd have to make all new friends, they'd have new teachers. I can't ask them to do that. I won't."

"Kids are resilient," Laney said, picking at the pilling on the front of her sweatpants.

"When it comes to the twins, I think I've cashed in my resilient chips."

Evie had heard it a million times since the divorce—kids *are* resilient. Hers were proof. But you could stretch a rubber band only so many times before it snapped. Plus, *she* didn't want to move. This was the home where she'd recalibrated her definition of *family*, accepting that she and Sam and Sophie were complete—not a unit with missing parts.

"Your parents told us they'd consider moving here," Beth said.

The words tumbled in Evie's heart. Her parents couldn't live in Lakewood; they'd waited their whole lives to leave Wilmington and become full-time Floridians. But Evie wasn't really thinking about them. She was thinking about herself and Sophie and Sam. What she wanted. What she wanted for her kids. Which was for things to remain as normal as possible. Maybe it was selfish to stay, rely on friends, grasping at ways to make the newest new life make sense. Maybe the best way for a new life was to leave the old one. Maybe she should move to Palm Aire so the kids could be near their grandparents. It might be nice with its sunshine and pools and shuffleboard tournaments. And of course there were those early-bird dinners. Yes, it would be nice—when she was eighty. Until then Evie would revel in deep snow and winters that lasted until June, a center-hall colonial with a red door and black shutters that needed a coat or six of paint. She wanted the backyard with the swing set no one used and the kitchen door that squeaked a familiar tune even with squirts of WD-40 that would make the Tin Man sing. She wanted the house where she'd memorized the cracks and crevices, where the twins had learned to walk, where *she'd* learned to stand on her own.

The house where she'd learn that all over again.

This old house in Lakewood, with its mud patches in the backyard, with its drafty, double-hung windows and dated pink-and-black-tiled bathrooms was hers, quitclaim deed included. She'd gotten it in the divorce, knowing the planned renovations would never happen. She didn't care. It suited her in its simple, dated grandeur. It was best for her and the kids a few years ago, and it was better than best for them now.

Unless she couldn't pay the mortgage.

Chapter 3

FOR THE THIRD NIGHT IN a row, Sam and Sophie fell asleep watching a movie in the living room. The thought of rallying them into bed via a normal routine did not appeal to Evie. It was winter break in Lakewood. She knew their routines would be redesigned, but not just yet. Right now she existed just a little bit in denial. It was a safe and comfortable place.

The phone rang. The kids didn't budge—the blessing of exhaustion. Evie reached to answer without looking. It had to be Scott. She'd left messages for two days. He'd have some explaining to do. Who was she kidding? She'd just be glad to hear his voice.

"Hey, handsome," Evie whispered, cupping her hand around her mouth.

"Evie, it's Nicole."

Evie straightened and her cheeks grew hot.

"I'm in your driveway."

"You're where?"

"I'm in your driveway." Evie wasn't deaf, just dumbfounded. "Can I come in? I was driving around and noticed the glow from your TV."

What were they? Sorority sisters? What made Nicole think a late-night chat—at Evie's house—was good or even acceptable? What happened to old-fashioned, ill-timed, hastily composed e-mails strewn with typos? Was nothing sacred?

Evie clicked the phone off. Mouth agape, she walked to the front door.

There was Nicole, in all her inappropriate splendor—a pink, fuzzy robe that looked three sizes too big wrapped all the way under her arm. Her hands were tucked up into her sleeves and she hugged herself. Nicole looked like a swaddled newborn, secure with the wrapping, unsure what to do with arms, limbs, and emotions.

"Who's with Luca?"

"He's in the car, sleeping."

Evie pointed to the idling sedan. "You can't leave a baby in a car. In December. Why don't you call me tomorrow?"

"Since you're still awake, could we talk now? I'll go get him."

Evie, bitch-slapped by Nicole's gall, still didn't want to fight. Not with Nicole. Not at ten-fifteen. Not while she was waiting for Scott to call. And not with the kids asleep in the next room.

"Fine. Get the baby."

This better be good. Evie had had her fill of bad. And Scott would probably call any minute.

Settled in the corner of the dining room, on Bubbe's reupholstered wing chairs, as far away from the twins as they could get, Nicole leaned over and laid her hand on Evie's leg, piercing a force field Evie had thought was impenetrable. She leaned over and scratched an imaginary itch in order to wiggle her leg back inside her armor.

"We're family now, right?" Nicole said.

"Who?"

"You, me, the twins, Luca . . . we're a family."

"I never thought of it that way," Evie said, searching for tact. Her senses had been dulled by the memory of burnt bagels, pine-scented room deodorizer, and the throbbing reality of a dead ex-husband. *This is what Nicole wanted to say?*

"Well, I *have* thought of it that way. I know Richard wouldn't want me to take Luca away from them," Nicole stage-whispered. "I wanted to brainstorm some ways we can make this easier. On all of us."

"Easier? I don't think this is going to be easy no matter what we do."

"I know. That's why we should help each other."

"We who?"

"Us. You and me."

Evie and Nicole had never been an *us*. "And how would we do that?" Evie asked.

"By spending more time together."

Does this ten o'clock visit count? "Well, sure, we can plan some playdates."

Nicole played with her fingers, as if she were counting. Or stalling. "I was thinking more than playdates."

Evie tapped her foot instead of slapping Nicole's hands away from each other. "It's late. I'm tired. Can you just spit it out already? What do you want?"

"I don't know."

Evie ignored Nicole's opaqueness. "It's still winter break, I'm sure we can figure out something." Evie stood and inched her way to the door. "Maybe we can go downtown to the Children's Museum one day next week." An outing with Luca might be good for Sam and Sophie. A new memory to glue-stick into an empty scrapbook.

"I guess I should go," Nicole said.

You shouldn't have come.

Nicole giant-stepped to Evie, leaned over, and hugged her with one arm, the other cradling Luca, still sleeping. *Like a baby.* "We'll figure out the best thing for all of us," Nicole said. "We have to. That's the way Richard would want it."

Evie didn't *have* to do anything, yet she hugged back spontaneously and patted Nicole's back. The duet of compassion and indifference edged her toward kindness and then yanked her back. "Talk to you soon, I guess." Evie didn't know what else to say.

Evie climbed back onto the couch. Who knew the kids snored in unison? She wondered if it was a twin-thing or an exhaustion-thing or a grief-thing. Evie lifted her hair from her neck, pulled the blanket to her chin, and tucked it around and under her. Safe in an unlikely cocoon, she closed her heavy lids, but words scrolled inside as if she were reading from a teleprompter. Her ex-husband's widow—the same woman whom Richard cheated on Evie with—wanted to spend more time with her. The idea was ominous. No, it was insane.

Evie didn't even know if she wanted Nicole to visit again—ever. She smiled at the premise. *No Nicole. No Luca.* No step-anything. No half-anything. How simple life would be. For Evie. Yet, she admitted to herself, how sad for Sam and Sophie. Evie's thoughts deflated as her insides tumbled to and fro from a maternal tug-of-war. Her load would lighten without Nicole or Luca, yet Sam and Sophie would bear the weight. She couldn't do that to her own children. Could she?

She nudged the kids off the couch and they sleepwalked to their rooms, Evie behind them. Ascending the stairs, Evie relented. The best way to heal the gaping wound in Sam's and Sophie's hearts was to keep Nicole and Luca in their lives, maybe every other weekend. Could Evie cope with a regular dinner date with Nicole and Luca? Weekend field trips? Birthday parties? Heading into the no-snore zone of her bedroom, Evie knew she would do anything for Sam and Sophie, but a woman had to have boundaries. Especially a woman with her very own widow making house calls.

Evie reached for the wand of the miniblinds to block out the light from outside. Light from outside? At eleven-thirty?

She had her very own widow, indeed. *Still in the driveway.*

Evie backed away from the window and climbed into bed. About ten minutes later, when she heard a car drive away, Evie closed her eyes and primed for sleep. But future scenarios wound through her thoughts like a tapeworm. She tried to avoid them, but Nicole's visit broke the dam. No more child support—the financial kind or the father kind or the every-other-weekend kind. How was she going to pay the mortgage? She'd ask for more hours at Third Coast. How would she spend time alone with Scott? Whether she wanted to work or to play, Evie would need to hire a babysitter. *Do almost-eleven-year-olds need a babysitter?*

Sam lay on his bed, nose to wall, atop the *Star Wars* comforter he was really too old for but begged Evie not to donate, trash, or hide in the attic. She obliged and just kept washing it.

"Some of your friends are downstairs," Evie said. She sat next to him without disturbing the muddle of pillows and floppy stuffed frog *she* didn't want to throw away.

"My friends?" Sam rolled toward her.

"Your friends. Remember? It's winter break. You invited them over this morning? To play video games?"

He rubbed his eyes, lifted his head, and laid it on Evie's knee. "Mom?" Sam stretched the syllable and his voice rose, adding an extra question mark at the end. Evie held her breath. Sam blinked and looked up at her, wide-eyed. His chest rose as he inhaled. "Do we have any bagels? I'm starved."

"Uh-huh." It was all Evie could muster as she exhaled. The sickening instant of not knowing what came after "Mom?" drained the blood from her limbs. Relieved, Evie turned and looked around the room. Except for the bed, Sam's room was tidy from Evie's every-other-weekend cleaning extravaganzas. Her routine: The kids left for their dad weekends (first with just Richard, then with Richard and Nicole, and then with Richard, Nicole, and Luca), and Evie dusted, scrubbed, and straightened the twins' rooms for thirty minutes. Each. She changed the sheets, rearranged the books, toys, trophies, and knickknacks so they could come home and start their week in peace, recover from the Disney-Dad effect, and ease into real life, the one without monorails, cotton candy, and pancakes for dinner. Now Evie looked at the dust-free shelves and searched the floor for dog hair tumbleweeds, marbles, or Pokémon cards—for any sign of Sam. But, no, she had transformed his boyhood sanctuary into a furniture-store model room. Evie didn't ask Sam to straighten the bed, and for good measure she toppled the books on the desk before leaving. A tidy room was no longer a priority.

She poked her head into Sophie's room. No Sophie there. Evie checked the bathroom. Her pace quickened as she tiptoed down the hall. She was not in the mood for a missing child but couldn't emit panic.

"Hey, kiddo," Evie said. Sophie was lying on the floor next to Evie's bed with her long arms wrapped around Rex. "Your friend Isabel is downstairs waiting for you. I think she's in the kitchen with Beth and Laney poking through boxes of cookies."

"'Kay." Sophie stood and moved within an inch of Evie. "Where are *you* going to be?"

"I'll be down in a minute." *Or six.*

"Why not right now?"

"I have to pee."

"I'll wait for you."

"I promise, Soph, I'll be right down. Don't leave Isabel with a roomful of grown-ups and boys!" Evie crossed her eyes.

Sophie smiled and hugged her mom long and hard before letting go. "Comin', Issy," Sophie yelled. She turned and looked at Evie, who nodded slowly. Sophie breathed deep and left the room. Evie heard her daughter run down the steps and jump the last few and land with a thud.

Evie did not want to go back downstairs into the death-and-cookie zone. She smoothed her bed, tightened the comforter around the corners, punched the pillows, and stepped back to admire the floral bedscape. She needed *something* in her life in order. But Evie knew the oasis was nothing more than a mirage. She stared a moment longer, then closed her eyes and shook her head from side to side—her *wish-I-was-magic* movement, akin to Samantha Stephens's nose-twitching on *Bewitched*. The past week resembled a nightmare, and she wanted to open her eyes and have it all disappear.

It was the opposite of what Evie had wanted when she woke up the morning after Richard proposed. She had skipped to the dresser, fingers crossed that the black velvet box with a ring was still inside the top right-hand dresser drawer. He chuckled at her from his side of the bed. She closed her eyes, shook her head, opened her eyes, and, yes: the box, the ring, the fiancé—it was all real.

This time when Evie opened her eyes, she saw Rex gnawing on a rawhide bone.

"How did *last night* go?" Laney said, sitting on the arm of the recliner and sliding into its depth.

"What do you mean?"

"What do I mean? I mean Nicole pulled into your driveway at ten o'clock, that's what I mean. And then after she left—she came back!"

"Are you spying on me?"

"I'm not spying on you, I was awake. Well, Herb was awake and he woke me. You should have called. I would have rescued you."

"I sleep through *everything*," Beth said. "Was she okay?"

"Was she okay?" Laney scrunched her eyebrows together. "There is nothing okay about showing up uninvited on someone's doorstep."

"It was fine, no rescuing necessary. She just wanted to talk."

Laney squirmed.

"She's having such a hard time," Beth said. "It was nice of you to talk to her."

Nice had nothing to do with it. "I'm not going to turn her away," Evie said, although she wasn't sure why that was true.

"Why not?" Laney barked.

"It's called empathy," Beth said without looking at her friends.

"I don't know what it's called," Evie said. "I just know that as much as I'd like to say it's over, I know it's not."

"Why do you have to go through losing Richard again—and with that woman?" Laney asked. "You've been there, done that, bought the T-shirt."

"It's not about her, it's about the kids. Right, Ev?" Beth asked, hopeful.

"It's about doing what feels right at any given moment."

"Even if it seems crazy?" Laney asked.

Evie just nodded.

The alarm clock buzzed and buzzed and buzzed. Evie reached for the snooze button but her hand patted something cool, slick, open, round, and . . . wet. A coffee mug? She opened her eyes. She wasn't in bed; she was on the couch, lodged in the corner, magazine open on her chest, drool on her chin. The best part about having friends like Beth and Laney was that Evie could ask them to leave without offending them. And she had. That noise again. It wasn't her alarm clock. What was that noise and why wasn't someone shutting it off? The doorbell! Evie waited for someone to skedaddle through the house on tiptoes not wanting to wake her. Who was she kidding? Beth and Laney had gone home, and the kids didn't answer the door unless you screamed or they were expecting a pizza. The doorbell rang again, so she mindfully stretched, ran her fingers through her hair, and prepared to play hostess to whoever was bringing a bakery box of whatever deliciousness the person determined would get her on *the good list*. Evie wiped the midday sleep from her eyes and put on a tired but neighborly smile.

She peeked out the sidelight, rubbed her temples, counted to three, and opened the door.

Luca, in his baby bucket, dangled on Nicole's arm. Next to him was a tapestry suitcase. It stood straight like a proud, saluting soldier at the end of a long trail of squashed snow next to Nicole's footprints. Evie wanted to turn and shut the door, pretend she hadn't heard the doorbell.

"You're back?" Evie said, looking at the suitcase, at Nicole, at Luca, at the suitcase. The suitcase.

"I figured you wanted to stay home today," Nicole said, stepping into the house, baby and luggage in tow. "So I brought Luca here to see the twins."

"What's in the suitcase?" Evie did not have time for mysteries *or* uninvited guests.

"Some of Richard's things. For the kids."

"It's too soon," Evie whispered, shaking her head and pushing the suitcase to the wall. "Take off your coat." She motioned to Nicole to hurry and draped it over the suitcase handle.

Sam and Sophie and their friends stampeded in from opposite sides of the house. The twins each took a side of the baby-seat handle without being told. Or asked. Nicole let go and the twins carried Luca between them, rocking him ever so slightly.

"Oh, okay," Evie said. "You guys take him into the living room. For a minute."

Evie whispered when the kids rounded the corner, "You can't keep showing up at my door, Nicole."

"You said 'talk to you soon.'"

"I meant on the phone." *Actually she hadn't meant it at all.* "I guess you can come in for a few minutes, but next time, call first."

"Last night I called first."

Nicole untied an itchy-looking scarf from around her neck. Evie half-expected Nicole to push up her sleeves, ready to fight. Instead, Nicole poked up her eyebrows, her eyes ablaze with questions. "You said we'd have playdates."

"It's just not a good time."

"If I had called, you'd have told me not to come."

"Then why did you?"

Nicole touched Evie's forearm, then drew back. "I had to get out of that house. It echoes."

"I'm sorry, I truly am, I don't think I could be any sorrier—but I can't *take care* of you and Luca." *I don't even know how I'm going to take care of us.* Evie took Nicole's coat and scarf and laid them over the arm of the bench in the foyer, the same bench the kids had waited on for Richard to pick them up on Wednesdays, and every other Friday. Anything or anyone on the bench did not stay for long.

"I don't want you to take care of us. I want us to take care of each other." Nicole's eyes filled with tears. "I just figured—us being family and all—it would make things easier."

The tears were not going to work on Evie. She wanted to morph into Laney and say there was no room at the inn, but she channeled Beth and threw out a blanket of kindness instead. *A thin blanket.* "If you want to stay for an hour to visit, that's fine."

Evie patted Nicole's upper arm, the one with the tattoo. Nicole wore short sleeves that covered it, even in summer, but one humid day at a soccer match she'd tucked those sleeves above her shoulders for just a moment. "Nice tattoo" had been all Evie could think to say. It had been three and a half years and a lifetime ago, and Evie had been close enough to discern that the tattoo was a rose. She could see a name or a word or letters surrounding the rose, but couldn't quite make them out. And she didn't want to. Evie did not want to see her ex-husband's name seared into human skin.

So, not only were Nicole's jeans riding extra-low on her hips; she had a tattoo. Nice *Jewish* girls didn't get tattoos. You can't be buried in a Jewish cemetery with one, and nice Jewish girls were always worried about where they'd be buried. So Nicole only arrived in Sam's and Sophie's lives bearing a tattoo, not to mention chocolate Santas and Easter baskets. The cultural sway still made Evie seasick.

She touched Nicole's arm and left her hand just a second too long. Nicole looked down and Evie retracted it as quickly as if she'd burnt her fingers on a hot pan. It sent a mixed message of advance and retreat.

As if someone had pressed fast-forward, Luca was out of his baby seat and lying on an activity quilt in the middle of the living room. Teethers and rattles surrounded him, and Sophie and Isabel were on their hands and knees, their faces over his, making him laugh. Evie sat with Sophie. Nicole plopped on the floor next to her and wiggled into position with her legs crossed. She looked comfortable. The kids on the blanket served as a mini-Switzerland.

Luca smiled when Evie scrunched up her nose at him. He wiggled in place the way six-month-olds do. Evie's phone rang.

At least she knew it wasn't Nicole. Was it Scott? She glanced down.

"It's my sister," Evie said without really owing an explanation. Last week Nicole probably didn't know Evie *had* a sister. Evie walked into the hall bathroom, flipped on the fan she always thought was too noisy (until now), and shut the door.

"Great timing, Sis. Nicole's here."

"She's at your house?" Lisa said as if English were not her first language.

"Yes, and I don't know how to get rid of her without being mean."

"Be mean."

"I can't be mean, her husband just died."

"You and I both know it wasn't such a big loss. She just hasn't had time to figure it out."

"Stop!" Evie said. "Please, don't make this harder for me. I'll call you later."

"Yes, you go back to being the hostess with the mostess," Lisa said as she hung up.

By all accounts, being a good hostess was at the top of Evie's list.

"Sorry about that," Evie said, stepping back into the living room. The kids were gone. Beth sat on the floor, and Laney sat on the couch, as if they'd been there the whole time.

"When did you two get here?" Evie asked.

"When you were hiding in the bathroom," Laney said.

"Do you want us to go?" Beth said, her voice whispery and apologetic. She motioned between herself and Laney, who crossed her legs the way tall people do, at the knees with her left leg bouncing against the right. Evie knew Laney wasn't leaving.

Nicole hugged her legs against her chest and rested her chin atop her knees. At least she was humble enough to know she was under scrutiny. Could Evie even get into that position now? Could she ever? Luca stuck a teething toy in his hand, his mouth, his hand, his mouth.

Luca would not know the pain of losing Richard, but he would share the experience with his siblings of growing up without a father. Were Evie's kids better off because they'd have their own memories of Richard, documented by mountains of photos, videos, and corroborated and even enhanced—perhaps embellished— stories told by Evie? Who would tell Luca stories about his dad? In the long run it would be Sam and Sophie, but for now it would be Nicole. And if Evie allowed it, it would be her as well.

"So, Nicole," Laney said.

"Yes?" Nicole cocked her head to one side.

"What are you going to do now? Move back near your parents? To Idaho, right?"

"Iowa." Nicole looked at Evie. "But I want Luca to grow up near Sophie and Sam."

"They're moving," Laney said.

A look of panic befell Nicole.

"I'm not moving!" Evie barked. Laney's impertinence was exhausting.

"Okay, maybe you're moving. Maybe to another house, maybe to another state, I'm just saying . . ."

"Of course, *we* want her to stay right here." Beth to the rescue. "And luckily that's what you want too, right, Ev?"

Evie glowered at Laney. "Yes. I'm staying here, because it's my home." Evie played with Luca in lieu of strangling her best friend. Babies—the great equalizer. Mothers could unite over spit-up and night terrors or cherub cheeks and teething woes, no matter the situation.

Except for Laney, who checked her Rolex. "I promised Jordyn and Jocelyn we'd go out for a sushi lunch. Anybody want to come?" Laney stood and looked at Beth and then Evie. Laney did not look at Nicole.

"What's Herb doing?" Evie asked.

"He has patients until one, and then he's meeting us." Laney smiled the oft-whitened smile of a dentist's wife, the same way she did when she discussed her chi, her yoga, or her newest vintage piece of jewelry. In her faded jeans and oversize sweater she was still put together, which is easy when your casual clothes come from Neiman's, not a big-box store.

"That's great," Beth said. "But I'm just going to hang out here for a bit if that's okay." She looked to Evie and Nicole. They nodded.

Evie walked Laney to the back door. "Chill," Evie said as she hugged Laney through her coat.

"It's a good thing Beth and I are next door." Laney pulled back, but held Evie's arms. "I saw her bring that suitcase inside. She's cozying up to you because she has no one. I'm suspicious of people who have no one."

Laney could be suspicious of people with a vowel in their name.

"Thanks, Lane. I appreciate your looking out for me, but I'm okay."

With Laney gone, Evie stood under the arch that separated the kitchen from the living room. Nicole was still on the floor with Luca. Beth sat within the parameters of their personal mother-baby space.

Nicole looked up at Evie. "I thought the kids would want to play with Luca more. I don't know why they didn't stay."

"They're with their friends. You know . . . being kids. It's not Sam or Sophie's job to take care of Luca," Evie said.

"I didn't say it was their job." Nicole's voice rose. "I just thought—"

"It's nothing against Luca." Evie did not add *or you.*

In truth, the twins' attention span with Luca was sincere but short-lived. They were just getting used to having a sibling, and now things were different. Again. During the day the twins wanted to be busy, they needed to be busy. Busy distracted them. Their friends distracted them. On the floor cootchie-cooing with a baby and their father's widow wasn't busy. It was a reminder.

"I don't think your other friend likes me very much." Nicole pointed her chin in the direction of Laney's former position.

Evie ignored Nicole's complaint. *If it is so bad, why does she want to spend more time here?* Evie attributed the negativity to Nicole's grief, new motherhood, and an absentee family.

"Don't mind Laney," Beth said. "She's just very protective of Evie. Like I told you, just give it time. Laney will come around."

Like I told you?

Nicole's mouth twisted. "I'm not going to do anything to Evie." Her tone matched that of a kid caught lying—a cross between guilt and belligerence, with a twinge of adolescent *I'm not stupid.*

"No one said you would *do anything* to her." Beth stared at Nicole until Nicole looked down between her knees. Was Beth defending Nicole or taunting her? Was Beth defending Evie or disregarding her?

Evie reached across their circle of three to help Nicole unload the diaper bag, sending another mixed message.

It was the only kind of message there was.

"Let's eat," Evie said.

They sat quietly around the kitchen table, but arms flying for turkey and rye, corned beef, coleslaw, potato salad, and leftover kugel. Evie found the contained bedlam soothing.

Nicole's plate held one piece of white bread and a golf-ball-size blob of potato salad.

"Aren't you hungry?" Evie needed to temper the maternal inclinations but the words had already escaped.

"I haven't eaten much since . . ."

"You have to eat," Beth said. "You have to keep up your strength for Luca. Remember what I said earlier."

Nicole nodded, said nothing, and fumbled with plastic keys on the high-chair tray.

"She's right, you know," Evie said. "Try the kugel."

Evie couldn't wait to slip under the covers and feel the warm flannel sheets. She shut off the living-room lights and double-checked the locks on the front door.

Nicole's scarf still hung on the bench.

Evie whipped her head around. The suitcase was gone from the corner. Then she felt a niggling sensation and opened the front door.

Women's intuition was a bitch.

Nicole's car idled in the driveway, lights on. It wasn't more than ten degrees outside. Nicole ran to the door. Evie opened the storm door but didn't invite Nicole inside. She rubbed her arms and bounced, and Evie wondered if she'd had the heat on in the car.

"Luca couldn't sleep, so I was driving him around. I saw the light on and thought maybe you were awake and would know what to do."

"Why can't he sleep?" Evie felt an unexpected stomach twist.

"I don't know, but he won't stop crying. Driving him around usually settles him, but tonight it's not working. I've been out with him for over an hour."

"You should probably keep driving, then, right?"

Nicole shrugged, pulled her hood onto her head, and ran to her car without a word. Evie watched Nicole wiggle into the driver's seat and buckle. Evie shut the door but didn't move. She leaned back to make it extra tight. And she waited. She waited for the motor, the bump of the tires over the uneven driveway. She counted to twenty, then opened the door again. Nicole was still there.

Evie grabbed her coat from the hall closet and slipped on shoes by the heating vent, a momentary source of warmth and comfort.

Before Evie reached the car, Nicole's window whizzed down. Luca was crying. Screaming. No, that particular sound was wailing. That was not a normal I-need-to-cruise-around-the-neighborhood fussiness.

"Does he have a fever?" Evie asked.

"No."

"Is he teething?"

"I don't know."

"Bring him inside."

Swabbed gums and a bottle of water put Luca to sleep.

"Take this," Evie said, handing Nicole the tube of Baby Anbesol. Evie hoped it had not expired. "You should probably stock up."

"I can't believe I forgot about teething. I could have avoided this whole thing. I'm so sorry. I'm not good at doing this alone."

"Mothers have been doing this alone for centuries." Evie raised one eyebrow and smiled in a flash of maternal bonding. "I bet you won't forget about teething again." She put on her tight-lipped, no-nonsense face, tucked a blanket in around Luca, and pushed his blond wisps off his sweaty face as if it were baby-business as usual. Luca resembled Sam. Evie's heart tugged—but for just a second.

"Richard was always home to help me. And now the house is empty all day long too. If he wakes up again tonight . . . I don't think I can do this." Nicole touched Evie's forearm as if trying to find a pulse.

Thoughts of what Laney and her sister would say flipped through Evie's head like an old-fashioned Rolodex. She slammed the imaginary lid.

"It'll wake Luca if you try to take him home, so, so . . . you should stay here." Evie said it fast before she could suck back the words, but then she slowed her pace and said, "Just this once."

"I've been meaning to ask you," Evie said as she piled blankets and pillows on the couch for Nicole to arrange herself, "where are your parents?"

"My mom couldn't make it. But I've talked to her, of course." Nicole's lips pressed together as if blotting lipstick.

"Of course," Evie said, knowing the conversation wasn't over. "Is she sick?" *Every person you're related to couldn't make it? To your husband's funeral and three days of shiva? They've all got what? Shiva flu?*

"Well, if you must know, my mother never wanted me to marry Richard, and my brother is stationed in Afghanistan."

Evie chose to ignore Nicole's brother, the hero. She was getting her dander up. The mystery mother didn't think Evie's ex was good enough for her daughter? Evie knew that, even eighteen years Nicole's senior, Richard was the quintessential catch if someone ignored that he was married, which Nicole obviously had. Evie banished the conflicting feelings and watched Nicole fiddle with her fingers and scrape at her clear nail polish, pulling it off in small bits. "Why didn't your mother want you to marry Richard? Because he was so much older than you?"

"No. She didn't care about his age." Nicole rubbed her arms as if warming from a chill.

"Why then?" Prying was now essential, and Beth was not there to stop Evie. She knew Richard's faults inside out and sideways, but that was after years together and years apart. What could someone who'd never met him have against Dr. Richard Glass, the Jewish college math professor? His title alone had mothers lining up to give him their daughters' numbers, even when she and Richard *were* married. Plus, criticizing Richard was Evie's turf. She never bad-mouthed him in front of the twins, would never undermine him as their dad. She tolerated it and even reveled in it when Lisa and Laney slammed him. But when a stranger disparaged the father of her children it defied the convoluted, unspoken Evie Glass Code of Good Divorce.

Nicole looked at the floor and drew lines in the carpet with her bare left foot. Evie couldn't help but think of her as a scared teenager who'd just gotten caught slipping in after curfew. "She thought I married him for the wrong reasons, that's all," Nicole said, wiping her nose with the back of her hand. She punctuated *reasons* with an audible sniff. "She didn't like that he was Jewish either. I don't want to talk about it."

"Oh." There wasn't a lot of anti-Semitism around Evie, or not any that was thrust in her face. But Nicole wasn't from a suburb like Lakewood or a city like Chicago. "But it didn't bother you. The Jewish part." Evie didn't know, or care to know, about the wrong-reasons part.

Nicole wrung her hands and shook her head.

"How about your father?" Evie said, still organizing the couch.

"He left when I was three."

Evie stepped away and motioned for Nicole to sit. "What do you mean, 'he left'?" Evie wasn't sure she wanted to hear the answer.

"He moved out. I don't know the details. I never asked because I wasn't sure I wanted to know."

"You never saw him again?" Evie said it before she could stop herself.

Nicole sighed and shook her head. "Do you mind if we drop it?"

Evie resisted the urge to push Nicole's hair off her forehead, to tell her she'd be okay. Nicole had no father. Like mother like son. Nicole had no father. Like Sam and like Sophie.

Evie wished this unforeseen bond wasn't there, for so many reasons. It was the time for loosening ties, not strengthening them—although Evie seemed to be doing that despite herself.

"Where in Iowa are you from?" Evie asked, as if she knew one Iowa town or city from another. "Do you think you'll go back?"

"I'm from Green Ferry, but my mom lives in Iowa City now." Nicole shoved her hands into the pockets of her robe. "And no, I'm not moving back to either place. I can't."

A trailer park sitting off the edge of a lonely highway flashed in Evie's mind, then was replaced by a subdivision full of postwar tract houses. She preferred the trailer-park vision and switched back. "You don't have any family here. Wouldn't it make sense to go back?" Evie wiggled herself straighter, but kept her gaze transfixed on Nicole.

Nicole's eyes opened wide and she stood, removing her hands from her pockets. "We have *Sam and Sophie*," she said, her voice rising until Evie put a hushing finger to her own lips. Nicole unfurled the blankets and bunched them up at her feet. She untied her robe to reveal fleece pajamas, a step above Evie's sweats, for sure. No holes. Cotton-candy pink.

"You're our family too," Nicole said.

Evie pretended she hadn't heard that last part. "Let's go to sleep. I'm sure Luca wakes up early."

"Yes, he does. Babies always wake up early, don't they? Good night," Nicole said, a touch of hesitancy to her voice, as if she had something else to say but thought better of it.

"See you in the morning." Evie almost reached to smooth the blanket, tuck it in tight. She clasped her hands behind her back and walked toward the stairs.

"Evie?"

"Yes?" She stopped and turned toward Nicole.

"Thank you."

"No problem." But Evie had a feeling it would be.

Chapter 4

Evie's bedroom was dark and her eyes were closed, but she felt Sophie's gaze from the doorway as if her daughter had lassoed her.

BD (Before Death), Evie had turned off her sixth, seventh, and eighth senses every other weekend. Now they were on autopilot. *Always*. During her marriage, Evie had known the kids were crying before Richard ever heard a sound. She knew when they were sneaking a cookie, watching TV on mute, or if they'd fed Rex their veggies under the table. Evie relied on her maternal instincts, the switch that flipped when the twins were born. But at some point her *marital* intuition went haywire. Perhaps it was easier knowing her kids were climbing on the kitchen counter than to accept the unstable nature of her marriage.

Evie peeked with one eye. Nope, she hadn't lost her touch, a relief as much as a burden. Sophie stood straight, eyes pried wide against the lure of sleep, her arms clutching a medley of stuffed bears, kittens, and dogs. Evie patted her bed and folded down the blanket: Sophie's cue. Up she climbed and over she scooted, right next to her mom. Evie welcomed Sophie's warm body with a leg hug and drew her daughter close and inhaled the light scent of baby shampoo. *Are the twins too old for baby shampoo?* Sophie draped her arm across Evie's shoulder, and the duo Eskimo-kissed and giggled.

Nothing was funny, but it was familiar and comfortable when so much was neither.

"I heard a baby crying," Sophie said.

"Yes, you did. Luca is teething. It's nothing to worry about." Evie said it as if she believed it.

"A sleepover?!"

Okay, they could call it a sleepover. "Yes, just one night, and you will see them in the morning. Did you have a good day?" Evie asked out of habit and to change the subject, even though she knew exactly how Sophie's day had been.

"Uh-huh."

Evie pressed her lips to Sophie's cheek and led the elephant in the corner into full view. "It's pretty sad without Daddy, huh?"

"Yeah." Sophie looked for direction, permission to continue. Her small body stiffened.

Evie kissed Sophie's nose and she squirmed, relaxed, and melted in. "It's going to be sad for a long time." Evie didn't say *forever*. Forever was too long for a ten-year-old. Forever was too long for a forty-five-year-old. "How about tomorrow we find some pictures of Daddy you can put on your desk?"

"You mean here? In this house?"

"Yes, here, honey. This is *your* house." Evie pulled back and looked at her daughter. "You can even put pictures of Daddy in the living room. Doesn't that sound nice?"

Nice? It would be strange. The day Richard moved out, Evie had packed away the wedding photos and replaced them with images of the twins and herself. The past belonged in the past. Until now, of course, when all the parts of Evie's life were mixing together like cookie dough in a bowl.

Sophie nestled her head onto Evie's shoulder and fell asleep. That arrangement worked until Evie heard loud sniffs—a mother's alarm clock, no sixth sense needed. She wanted the sound to be coming from a TV, from Nicole or Luca, from anywhere else but Sam's room. She just wanted to sleep. Evie slid out of Sophie's sweaty embrace and tucked pillows around her daughter. Evie had only been asleep for an hour but sat at attention. Her brain was awake. Her body, not so much. She arched her back and it cracked. She rubbed her hands together to get the blood circulating. Maybe the sounds would stop, maybe it was her imagination, maybe Sam would sleep all night. It was not her imagination that she ached for sleep. When the twins were little, all it took was a drive around the block in the car and they were zonked out. Now Evie waited, hopeful that he'd fallen asleep. They both needed the break. But there it was, another sniff. Off she went to intervene in Sam's nightmare.

Sam looked at her with red, wet eyes. Evie rubbed his head until he turned into the wet pillow and let out a muffled yet bloodcurdling scream that sounded as if it came from the bottom of his soul. She didn't know such force existed in his eighty pounds. Her hand on the mattress, she felt the vibration. Sam lifted his head, lurched forward, and Evie leaned back, but not far enough. Sam threw up all over Evie, and all over the bed.

Off came the sheets in one fell swoop while Sam went into the bathroom. Evie made up the bed again as quickly as she could, removing her clothing, soaked through with regurgitated pot roast. And ice cream. Maybe part of a hot-dog-with-corn-chips lunch. When she heard the water running in the hall bathroom, she knew she had time to change clothes and wash up. In the master bathroom, with the door closed to safeguard Sophie's sleep, Evie scrubbed the ends of her hair and cursed Richard for leaving a legacy of barf. *And squatters.*

Sam walked back into his room and fell into his bed, broken, ashen, withdrawn. Evie wrapped her arms around him. For the next two hours he lay on her lap, his clean tears soaking through her nightgown, spreading as if she'd dumped a glass of water on herself. But she sat still. He was a little boy, not even yet a young

man. And now he was half-empty instead of half-full. He was de-
pleted and overcome and Evie had no control over any of it. She
hated having no control. At least when Richard was alive, they
could argue. *Too much soccer, too much basketball, not enough violin.
Hair too long, up too late, too young for a cell phone.* Familiar arguments would have been a blessing.

Sam was a volcano of raw emotion, his grief flowing like lava.
For the moment he was at rest, but no telling when he'd blow again.
It was all becoming real. Richard wasn't coming back, and alone in
the night there was no place for the feelings to go. Evie knew
it would take time. She rubbed Sam's back and wiped his forehead in a sequence of patterns and motions employed to focus her
attention away from the clock. The minutes ticked by in place of
hours.

"I want Daddy."

"I know."

"You don't know anything." It was accusatory but with no
venom behind it. And he was right. She didn't know. She had never
been a ten-year-old boy, let alone one whose father had just died.

Sam crushed himself to her tighter. "Don't go away. Promise
you won't go away."

Evie held her son. "I will take care of you until you're old enough
to take care of yourself, okay? I'm not going anywhere, ever."

She crossed her fingers as she had every night for the past week
and a half. She crossed her toes too.

When Sam started snoring, Evie watched him for a few minutes. He deserved a peaceful sleep. She hoped his dreams were
sweet, but not of Richard. Then, Evie untangled herself from Sam's
embrace, walked to the hall bathroom, locked the door, flipped on
the fan, and sat on the side of the tub.

It was the first time she cried.

Morning arrived long before it should have. Rex breathed into Evie's face. She rolled Sophie off her, tiptoed through the bedroom, and slipped on her once-periwinkle terry-cloth robe.

She walked down the steps into the dark foyer. Like a film strip from elementary school, a scene played in front of Evie's eyes: Richard, his face an inch from the grandfather clock in the foyer inspecting it as a possession he'd left behind even though it had belonged to Bubbe. Richard had stepped away when he saw Evie watching him, with his hands up as if under arrest. Evie had made a point of leaning forward from the bottom step and wiping his nose print off with her sleeve.

Evie wished she could clean the glass now and wipe away her reality.

She led Rex by the collar through the living room and out the back door. New house rule: Never wake a sleeping widow. So, instead of snuggling into her spot on the couch, Evie turned on the light over the stove and started a pot of coffee. A piece of rugelach called to her from inside the box. Who was she to argue? The stale rugelach was a clear sign the bakery runs had slowed, like the phone calls and visits. Winter break was over in less than a week, and everyone who wasn't on vacation before was away now. The people who stayed local were carousing at indoor water parks and piggybacking playdates, not stocking Evie's pantry.

Evie sat on Beth's favorite stool and swung her legs, willing the coffee to drip faster, ignoring Nicole's snores wafting in from the living room. What Evie couldn't ignore was the pile of mail she had thrown on the desk a day ago. Even with her back to the desk, she could see it—damn those eyes in the back of her head—and she felt the weight of it in her hands and remembered the solid thud when she dropped it.

The bills were always paid on the first of the month, coinciding with her once-a-month deposit from Richard and her own from

Third Coast Gifts. Evie couldn't do math in her head before her first cup of coffee—*drip, drip, drip*—but she knew there wasn't enough in the checking account to pay the mortgage and the bills and take care of every other expense next month. With extra hours around the holidays last year, her own paychecks had allowed for the extras—the trip to the Wisconsin Dells, Evie's one-month love affair with knitting, a few trendy outfits, treating Scott to dinner for his birthday, and the requisite, yet yawn-inducing, Moms Night Out. That was the deal she and Richard had struck and then signed. Her checks did not cover gallons of milk or two pairs of gym shoes per child, new cleats, basketball uniforms—or the electric bill. That was all paid for by Richard. Evie had spent her last paycheck on Hanukkah presents. Soon there would be orthodontics for Sam and ice-skating for Sophie and basketball and soccer and, oh, a gallon or two of milk.

Forget losing Nicole and Luca in their lives, the twins couldn't lose their house, their activities, or any residual sense of normal. They needed security even when Evie wasn't wrapped around them. Jeez, she needed that coffee. She also needed something sweet, but not a stale memento of family tragedy.

Evie walked past the bills. They'd still be there in forty-five minutes, which was strangely reassuring. She plucked out a manila envelope. Midwest Mutual Life Insurance. Richard's policy! It was part of the divorce, to make sure the kids could go to college if anything happened to Richard. And anything had. There were papers for Evie to sign marked with arrow-shaped sticky notes and lists of documents to include when she sent it all back. She'd compile and sign and mail as soon as the post office opened. The twins would have money for college, and maybe there'd be a little left over. Then she saw another official-looking paper with tear-off edges. Social Security Administration. She ripped open the envelope without following the directions and then pieced together the letter. She clutched it to her chest like a love note. Her kids would get Social

Security until they turned eighteen. That money would replace some of Richard's child support. How awful, yet how awesome.

Evie opened the cabinets one by one, closing them without a sound, gathering ingredients by the glow of the oven light. She lined up everything on the counter and retrieved bowls without a clink or a clank. She measured, poured, cracked, and scooped. But the stand-up mixer would not be the household's alarm clock. She'd do it as in the olden days, with nothing but prairie determination and a wooden spoon. With neglected muscles, Evie put everything into it, counted every stroke. Then she counted dollars. She would have to count every penny even more closely than when she and Richard were both in graduate school. She didn't know how much the Social Security would be, but it would help with the daily expenses of raising Sam and Sophie. She would get Social Security too. That was her booby prize for sticking it out and putting up with it all for sixteen years. But would it cover the mortgage? Dog food? Clothes? How would she make up the difference without leaving the house and working full-time, turning their lives upside down even more? She loved working for Millie at Third Coast, selling one-of-a-kind table linens, custom-made jewelry, and designer baby bootees to the North Shore's finest shoppers. But she needed a career, not just a job. Maybe Third Coast needed a new manager. No, Millie had owned and managed the store for years. Could Evie find something professional in the middle of winter with a gap in her résumé the size of Lake Michigan? She needed extra income right away—and then next month she could be cool, calm, and calculated, if she didn't implode, or explode, from too many cookies.

Then, as Evie slid the cookie sheet into the oven, it hit her. The why-didn't-I-think-of-that-before? moment. *Shared marital assets.* A legal term had never given her warm fuzzies until the day she saw the bottom line of her and Richard's joint savings account over three years before. She'd received half of what they'd saved during their marriage. It was just half, but it was *Evie's* half.

Alan had set it up as a long-term investment. After all, with maintenance, child support, and her job, Evie had enough for the monthly mortgage, upkeep, bills, everything she and the kids needed, and some of what Sam and Sophie wanted. Sometimes she even had enough for a splurge on herself.

Though the savings was an invisible part of her life, it gave her a sense of security, like Spanx. When she allowed herself, she dreamed about a suite at the Drake, and a weekend filled with bubble baths, room service, and lake views. She also considered that the money might one day pay for an Israel trip or a South American cruise. When she was being more practical, she knew it could be a hefty down payment on a non-minivan hybrid. But that kind of thinking would have to wait. Those dreams were a luxury Evie could no longer afford. Her hard-won nest egg for the future had to save them right now.

"When did you bake these cookies?" Sam asked. He was still groggy from his restless night, with the red eyes and bed head to prove it. He held a stack of three cookies in one hand and a glass of milk in the other. Apparently, crying and vomiting works up an appetite. Sophie just stared at the plate.

"Early this morning," Evie said, putting her forefinger to her lips. "We don't want to wake Nicole." When Luca had made morning noises, Evie had scooped him out of the Pack 'n Play and played nanny. *God, I love babies.* He was busy with a bottle when the kids walked into the kitchen. The rare, picture-perfect mothering moment could only be more complete if she were wearing a shirtwaist dress, pearls, and an apron. And if her ex-husband's widow weren't asleep on the sectional.

Strange as it was, the vignette gave Evie a sense of accomplishment. She—they'd—made it through another night. Her kids were awake, vertical, and one of them was eating cookies right out of the oven. Although to be honest, these days she got the same feeling from showering and by making her bed before noon. Or at all.

"Will you make more?" Sam asked with his mouth full.

Evie let it go this time. Manners could be important tomorrow. "Sophie promised to help me make cookies, didn't you?"

Sophie shrugged.

Sophie never shrugged away a chance to bake. Evie knew the kids would change, it had only been about a week, but when everyday moments shifted, she quaked, unable to find an internal balance.

Sam was quiet, chewing quickly, swallowing loudly, refilling his fist for the same reason Evie filled her cookie jar—just so it wouldn't be empty. During the day Sam was composed, almost serene. With his friends he let loose all the good stuff, the laughter with his head thrown back, the shrieks of catching video villains. But the real villains came out to play at night.

"Morning," Nicole said from the doorway. Unkempt and unaware, as if she belonged to the house and the family, she walked to Luca and lifted him into her arms. She cradled and nuzzled him as if she hadn't seen him in a week, then leaned and kissed both Sam and Sophie on the tops of their heads. "You've been busy," Nicole said to Evie.

"Just passing the time," Evie said. "Help yourself."

She really had to be more careful with her words.

Evie poured a capful of pine cleaner into the toilet and flushed.

"Are you kidding me?" Laney said.

"It took you longer to get here than I thought it would," Evie replied. "I think it's almost ten."

"Very funny. Would you like to tell me this story somewhere besides the bathroom?"

Laney followed Evie into her bedroom, where in tandem the

friends pulled and tugged and smoothed the bed in silence. Then they climbed on top of the covers, creating personal divots Evie would later fix. Laney crossed her legs like a pretzel—or like an Indian if Evie were being old-fashioned and politically incorrect.

"Well?"

"Luca was teething. He was screaming. I had Baby Anbesol."

"There's a twenty-four-hour drugstore right on Western Avenue," Laney said.

"I felt bad. It was about Luca, not about Nicole. I wasn't going to let him be in pain to make a point."

"And they slept here because?"

"Because they just did. I don't have any other explanation."

"Okay, but don't say I didn't warn you." Laney climbed off the bed and readjusted the comforter and pillows. Evie did the same.

"Now what are you warning me about?"

"You don't want to do this alone and you're going soft. You don't want her help, you don't need her help. You'll figure out how to do this on your own."

"I've been doing it on my own," Evie said.

Parenting alone was nothing new. But having someone to talk to and share a cup of coffee with while she made the kids breakfast, that was something new. It was true that being the only adult in the house hadn't bothered Evie, it had empowered her—walking around the dining-room table while the kids worked on homework, bouncing from bedroom to bedroom at bedtime and when it was time to wake and go-go-go. She chose vacations and meals and wall colors. It would have been nice to have help, but it was also nice to not have anyone looking over her shoulder. And with the Divorce Days came the every-other-weekend respite not only from single-parenting, but *all* parenting. It wasn't lackadaisical; it was essential. Evie loved her kids ferociously and ached with the need to protect them, especially now. But she also needed to love and protect herself. How would she do that now? For three years Evie had been granted time to relax and play and refill the well of patience from which she constantly had to draw. Now, instead of having weekends to herself, she would have to restore and regroup between loads of laundry while fending off Nicole in the driveway like a suburban ninja.

Back in the kitchen, Evie doled out the snacks bought by Lisa: a box of organic raisins to Sophie, and a carob-chip granola bar to Sam. Evie offered them to Nicole too, and she accepted. Laney stared, her mouth open wide enough to catch flies. *No, a small aircraft.* Evie put her fingers beneath her own chin and pushed upward. Laney closed her mouth and headed for the counter to her stool of choice, next to the coffeepot.

"I'm ready to go," Nicole said.

Evie followed her and Luca to the door.

"We make a good team," Nicole said.

Team? As far as Evie knew, Nicole didn't do anything except ask for help and receive it. Teamwork implies give-and-take, not just take.

"We could make this work," Nicole said.

"We could make what work?"

"*This . . .*" Gesturing as if to embrace the house. "The kids loved having us here this morning. I'm a neat freak, I wouldn't interfere with anything. And I saw the pile of bills on your desk. You work at that little gift shop, but without Richard's support checks, will you be able to even stay in this house? Remember, I was his wife. I knew everything."

Evie bristled. If there was one thing she was sure of, it was that Nicole did not know everything. That was also part of the deal, just like the monthly checks.

"Think about it," Nicole said while strapping Luca into his carrier. "I can help with the twins, pay room and board."

Evie poked up her eyebrow so high it hid beneath her morning bangs. "You want to live here?"

"Don't worry," Nicole said. "I can afford it."

Evie squirmed to shake off the innuendo. "You're kidding, right? You have your own house and your own baby and you want to live in my house with my kids. And me."

"We'd be a family. And neither of us would have to do it alone."

Since when did Nicole care that Evie was doing it alone? She'd been the only adult in the house for over three years, and now Nicole thought that was not ideal? And what made her think Evie needed help with the twins? Why was Nicole contemplating Evie's bank balance? Even she didn't want to do that. Not yet.

"I'm fine," Evie said. She opened the door and propped it with her back. *Don't want the door to hit the widow on the way out.* Evie kissed the baby on his head and patted Nicole's back as she walked past. "Hey, where's the Pack 'n Play?"

Nicole called from halfway down the path, "I left it in the closet for next time."

"What do you mean she left it here for next time?" Laney said, dipping her hand into the cookie jar.

"She'll be back. She knows it. I know it. I saw no reason to deny it."

"You're crazy."

"So I've heard."

"Well, at least you're rockin' that robe," Laney said.

Evie ignored the style dig. So what if it was Week Two of the Clothing and Makeup Strike? There was no need for jeans and sweaters or mascara and blush. No need for shoes when memory-foam slippers would do. Evie wasn't going anywhere. She would probably never go anywhere again. It had been six days with no call, text, or e-mail from Scott, which was fine, considering she would probably never again have the energy for a night on the town or in his bed. Right now all Evie craved was eight, no, seven—even six— hours of uninterrupted sleep. Just thinking it, she yawned. Maybe

Laney would watch the kids while she napped. No, she wanted to hang out, be a good friend. She couldn't lapse into emotional oblivion, she had to be alert and awake and available. This demanded much more coffee.

"Kids!" She waved her mugless hand like a magic wand. "Go upstairs or downstairs—if you need me I'll be right here." Sam leaned in for a kiss. He did that all the time now. Sophie leaned in too but shook her head at the offer of cookies.

"Let's sit in the living room," Evie said. She needed a change of scenery. She also needed a change of subject. Anything but death or her affection for terry cloth.

"What's going on with you and Herb?" Evie asked. "Tell me everything."

"You sure you want to hear? Let's talk about you and the kids."

"No!" Evie snapped.

Laney cackled. "Okay, okay. You don't have to yell!"

"I just want to feel normal for a few minutes. Humor me."

Laney lay back on the couch and looked at the ceiling, dreamy-like. "It just hit me." She popped herself on the forehead with the palm of her hand. "How I would feel if all of a sudden, out of nowhere, Herb was just *gone*. I know I joked when he left for work and traveled, but it overwhelmed me that it could have just as easily been him—and not Richard." She looked over and put her hands on Evie's, who slid from the touch and picked up her mug with two hands. The coffee was warm. She drew it in through her teeth, pretending it was hot with a slurping noise. She abhorred being the poster child for "things could always be worse."

"Right there in the middle of the night after Beth called, I made him promise not to leave me," Laney continued. "I was crying and he was crying. We were hysterical. I honestly don't know if we were crying about Richard or about us. But things have been really great since."

"Must be nice. So Richard dies and you use that as a lesson to appreciate your husband. Great. Anything else I can do for you to make your life happier? Fall down the steps? Bite the inside of my cheek? Throw myself in front of an oncoming Metra train? C'mon, you can think of something."

"Don't be mad at me for having an epiphany."

Evie raised and lowered one side of her nose. "Whatever."

"I felt so disconnected from Herb, you know that."

Evie was ashamed she took solace in Laney and Herb's arguments—in their distance from each other—but it was a welcome departure from the on-screen love affair of Beth and Alan.

"Look, I don't begrudge your happiness." Evie didn't know if it was true, but it was the right thing to say. "Kind of sucks that this is what it took."

"I think everything happens for a reason."

"What did you say?" Evie asked, incredulous.

"Just that I think everything happens for a reason."

"Are you kidding me? Are you fucking kidding me? You're telling me that Richard died so that you and Herb could find your way back to each other?" Evie turned away and inspected the couch. Her kids' loss seemed a steep cost for Laney's gain. Evie wished she had time for a personal epiphany, one that would tell her what would become of her and Sam and Sophie. But if she knew what was next, it might be more intimidating than not knowing, so Evie would march forward without the comfort of foresight. The enigma sparked hope. Evie tasted it for a second, then swallowed the optimism with lukewarm coffee.

"That's not what I meant . . ." Laney said.

"Yes, it is."

"Okay, it is, but it doesn't mean I'm happy about Richard." Laney reached her hand toward Evie, who took it in hers.

"I'm sure Beth is tickled pink that things have picked up between you and Herb." Evie looked at Laney and rolled her eyes. She was not in the mood for more bad feelings.

"Beth is a romantic." Laney twirled her loose curls around her finger. "She can't fathom the reality of a bad marriage. How alone it can feel. How desperate."

"Well, I have a new definition of *desperate*." Evie deflected from Laney's fairy tale with reality—every kick, every vomit blast, and every tear—right down to opening the door and seeing Nicole in the driveway and baking the cookies. "And then there's the money situation," Evie said, cookie lodged in her throat. She'd promised herself she wouldn't mention that to anyone.

"You're okay, right? Richard left you all taken care of, didn't he?"

Who kidnapped Laney and replaced her with an optimist? Evie got the stack of bills from the kitchen and fanned them out on the couch. "Welcome to the new game show—*Which Bills Get Paid This Month?* Pick a bill, any bill!"

Laney's face changed from annoyed to concerned, scowled to soft.

"There is Social Security," Evie said. *After I fill out the paperwork, sit at the Social Security office for a day and a half, and prove sixteen times I am who I say I am.*

"What about life insurance? He had life insurance. Ev, tell me there was life insurance."

"Yes, there was a mandated policy for the divorce, and I have everything ready to mail back to them. But it's for the kids, Lane. For college."

"They're ten! And there are grants and loans, and by then, who knows how kids will be paying for college educations. What about the house? Can you pay off the mortgage or use the insurance in place of child support? Camp! The money can pay for camp so the kids have something to do this summer!"

Evie was tired of Laney's well-meaning barrage of questions and suggestions. How many times did she have to say that the insurance money was paying for college?

Laney's voice dropped an octave. "Evie, I'm so sorry. Please don't hate me for rambling on about Herb and me, but this is shit. Leave it to Richard to not have enough insurance. Figures. He always was cheap." Laney knew the last part wasn't true. The only thing not uptight about Richard was his wallet when it came to his kids. But at least the real Laney was back. "What are you going to do?"

"Get a full-time job?" Evie phrased it as a question because she didn't really know what she was going to do.

"Are you going to ask for more hours at Third Coast? You haven't worked full-time since the twins were born. Do you really think this is the time to leave them?"

"No, I don't, but what choice do I have? When the life insurance pays out, it's for the kids. A little bit will be left after setting up a 529 plan, and that will definitely help, but it won't be the amount Richard paid in support every month. I can't even figure out what kind of job I'd want or be qualified for, even with a master's in American history." Evie hadn't thought that far before that moment. It was true. She worked at Third Coast because the hours were good and the pay was fair, especially earning commissions. Plus, Evie liked being there. But Millie couldn't pay her a real salary or provide health insurance for the kids. Next month she'd have to pay COBRA to keep the twins insured.

"How are you getting by now? I know it's only been a couple of weeks, but still. What's going to happen when there's no check next month?" Laney's eyebrows bunched up. She was ignoring potential lines in her face. Laney was a true friend.

"I'm going to use my retirement savings."

"Your South American cruise fund?"

Evie nodded.

"You need Plan C," Laney said.

"The new job *is* Plan C." More like Plan Q.

"No, Plan C is a second husband." Laney counted on her fingers.

"The father figure, romance, and money problems solved in one ingenious swoop. Let's work on Scott."

Laney started toward the computer. Evie grabbed her arm. "No!" Laney sat with a thud and crossed her arms as if foiled again. "I wasn't on a husband hunt before, and I'm not about to start one now." Evie waggled her finger at Laney, who uncrossed her arms and held both of Evie's hands.

"I know that's not what you want—or at least that's not how you want it. I just thought . . . I assumed you got insurance money and were fine. I mean, not fine, but okay, at least, financially. God, I feel so stupid for not asking. I'm supposed to be your best friend but I'm an ass."

A little self-deprecation went a long way. Evie cut her friend some slack. "Assumptions are funny things."

"So when do you get the insurance money? I thought that happened, like, the day after someone died."

"I don't know. I've mailed all the paperwork but haven't heard anything from Midwest Mutual."

"Okay, so, what about Scott? Call him, he's a financial guy. Ask him for help."

"I did call. I left messages. I'm done." Tired of Laney's inquisition, Evie raised her shoulders to her ears and then smirked. She was devoid of energy for an explanation or a confrontation with Laney or Scott. "If he wanted to help, he would be here." When she allowed herself the luxury, Evie missed him. Maybe she should call him for help—at least with navigating some of the financial waters. He would feel needed. Men liked feeling needed. Maybe Scott was just backing up, making room, giving her space. She certainly needed space—she just wasn't sure how much or for how long.

"I'm sure he doesn't know what you want or what to say," Laney said.

"That makes two clueless people because I have no idea what I want except to wake up and find out all that isn't real."

Evie pointed again to the stack of insurance papers, govern-ment forms, bills, death certificates, and photos. One-stop shop-ping. But Laney was right. Scott didn't know what to do, so he did nothing. Maybe it was his way of being considerate. Maybe it was his way of being a jerk. Evie wouldn't know until she actually talked to him.

Even with no partying in her, Evie did have to eat. Lisa would like her rationale and love that Evie was thinking like a mercenary dater. So Evie would reach out to Scott, only for a meal, not a meal ticket. Laney perched on her stool for support, beaming with pride as if Evie were her daughter who'd just earned a spot on the U.S. Olympic Dating Team. Evie picked up the phone, dialed Scott, looked at Laney, and then put her finger to her lips. He never seemed to mind calls at work, although she had rarely done that. She said a si-lent "let him be busy" prayer so she could leave more than just a hello message.

Finally—a prayer answered.

"Hey, Scott, it's me again. I'm wondering if you still want to have dinner with Laney and Beth and their husbands next weekend. Let me know, okay? I hope you've gotten all my other messages." One dig, and then, click.

"What do you think he'll say?" Laney asked. "He seemed like a great guy. He'll probably know what you can do with your retire-ment accounts too."

"He was a great guy. I mean, is." Evie wondered which part of her statement was true. As for talking to Scott about finances, she wouldn't do it. Why was it okay to share your bed but not your bank balance? Some things were just *too* personal.

What Evie didn't tell Laney was that until Laney mentioned Scott, Evie hadn't thought about him much—a clear indication that her mental in-box was reaching capacity.

Laney checked her watch. "Let's get you dressed."

"Dressed?"

Laney took Evie's mug from her lap and set it on the coffee table. No coaster meant Laney was distracted. She led Evie through the house to the foot of the stairs.

"You love doing your hair and makeup and spending an hour finding that perfect casual 'I just threw this on' outfit," Laney said. She was right. Laney had sat on Evie's bed many Saturdays when Evie chose date outfits that ranged from sporty to sophisticated.

"I'm not getting dressed up to . . . do what?"

Laney swung her hair behind her shoulders in lieu of a response. "Well, at least put on some cover-up and change into sweats. No matter what else you do, the terry cloth has to go."

Evie drew lines on her face with a basic beige cover-up stick. If the makeup were black, she'd have looked like a football player. She moved her ring finger—weakest finger, strongest contender for cosmetic application—upward and around. She blended and patted. Camouflaging under-eye circles was easy. If only there were a concealer for uncertainty, something enclosed in a blister pack, hanging on a hook at two for six dollars. Evie dragged a brush through her hair and added a spritz for imaginary lift. A treasure trove of cottony warm-up suits from the workout days stuffed Evie's bottom drawer. She fluffed out the gray set and picked a plain black tee. Smooth and zip—she was dressed. But she drew the line at real shoes and slid her feet into slippers. The fuzz was matted but the padding was thick, providing a soft, quiet step. Before heading downstairs she stood straight and pulled back her shoulders. Her back cracked.

Laney had yanked Evie out of a funk when Richard moved out and was now kicking Evie's self-image ass once again. "It all starts with looking good," Laney said. "Then you'll feel good too. Eventually." Laney was right three years ago, and Evie wanted her to be right again—right this minute. "I feel better," Evie said, curtsying.

"Told you so," Laney said. "You look like you! And now I'll get going, and if you're not going to talk to Scott about your finances, you should call Alan and get this money stuff figured out. I'm sure you'll be fine. Things have a way of working out."

Did they?

"Oh, and your cell phone rang while you were upstairs."

Evie's heart dropped. *Scott.* "Don't go yet."

Laney took Evie's hand and they walked into the kitchen, away from the kids' ears and interest. Evie pushed the button on the phone to hear the voice mail.

"Hey, Ev, I got your messages. I was thinking . . ." *Thinking isn't necessarily good. Thinking is definitely bad. Anytime I think too much there is big trouble.* "You're busy and have a lot to deal with. I'm going to let you settle a bit, you know, get into your new routine. Call me when things get back to normal, okay? I miss you. Really. Talk to you soon." Click.

Normal? Scott wanted her to call when things got back to normal! A dead ex-husband, a widow, a baby, grieving twins, and no weekends off. *I'll show you* normal, *bucko*. Plus, "I'm going to let you . . . go now / get back to work / finish what you're doing / get back to normal" was the classic emergency-exit strategy. Evie knew because she'd employed that tactic herself with a few of the men she dated: the homely one who talked about how handsome he was; the one who was always looking around the room while he talked to her; the one who had dirty fingernails he cleaned with the tongs of his fork. She'd met nice guys too, but the worst encounters always made the best stories. Until now.

Evie put down the phone and waited for tears, but all she felt was a release of tension in her neck, looseness in her shoulders. It was better than checking something off the to-do list—it was deleting it. She would miss Scott. But did she want to be with someone who backed off at the first utterance of bad news—even if it was really bad news? Good riddance to bad rubbish, Bubbe would have said. Evie now had one less person to think about, worry about, plan for. With only a smidgen of regret, Evie smirked and shook her head at Laney, as if taking the breakup hit were an ordinary part of her day.

"What an asshat," Laney said.

Evie giggled thinking of Scott with a hat on his ass. Or wiggling his ass, a hat on his head. He did have a nice ass. And he looked good in hats. *Enough!*

"This is a lot for people to handle, Lane, I get it. I don't like it, but I get it." Evie opened the phone again and scrolled through the stored numbers. She deleted Scott in triplicate. Home, work, cell. "I can't worry about dating right now." The truth was, Evie didn't want to see his name every time she looked at her contact list.

Laney flipped her head and absentmindedly gathered her curls into a ponytail, even though Evie saw no rubber band or scrunchie or banana clip. "Okay, maybe Scott's not the right guy, but you can't stop trying."

Evie's stomach rumbled even though it was full. She wasn't hungry for food, just for simplicity. Maybe this would help more than it hurt. "I just did."

The phone rang. Did Scott change his mind? Evie had a moment of hope, but no, he did not. "Hey," Evie said in two syllables, her attempt at nonchalance.

"How about dinner?" Nicole said. "I made the macaroni salad the kids like."

Sam and Sophie liked macaroni salad? "Sure, five o'clock." Evie looked at Laney, who shook her head and waggled her finger.

"Should I bring Luca's food?" Nicole said.

Evie knew the answer without checking the fridge, but there was Laney sipping and listening and tapping her index fingernail on the counter. "I have some." Evie did because she bought Luca's favorites at the grocery store.

"You have some of what?" At least Laney waited until Evie had hung up the phone to ask.

"Food." No need to be specific.

"If you're not careful, that woman is going to eat you out of house and home. Or worse."

"Now you sound like my mother. And Lisa."

"Good, maybe you'll listen to one of us."

Evie was tired of listening. She was ready for doing. She scavenged the silverware drawer for the purple baby spoon and held it up to Laney. "Don't count on it."

The only things Evie counted on were transferring her savings account into her checking account on Friday, and the fact that Sam and Sophie would be going back to school on Monday.

Chapter 5

Evie paced, getting more exercise today than she had in the past week and a half. She skittered through the kitchen, then the living room, across the foyer and into the dining room, around the table and back again. Where were Beth and Alan? What was taking so long? They lived twenty seconds away if they cut across the front lawns or backyards, which they were apt to do, although not with two feet of snow on the ground.

Back in the dining room for another game of ring-around-the-table, Evie felt flushed and flummoxed. If there was a problem, Alan would have called, asked for clarification, told her he'd "run the numbers again." That's what money people do, and Alan was a money guy—a financial adviser, CPA, and a longtime instructor at the local community college. He and Beth were the couple with the answers, with words and solutions to live by—even for someone like Evie.

The clock on the sideboard ticked. The second hand hiccuped around the dial once, twice, three times. A knock at the door broke Evie's trance.

Alan arrived alone with one small envelope in his hand. It reminded Evie of how the doctor walked into the private waiting room of Lakewood Hospital after she'd been waiting there for word, for hope, for someone to say it had all been a mistake about

Richard. But it hadn't been a mistake, and this wasn't either. Alan was usually energetic, approaching with verve even a mundane task he could afford to pay someone else to do, like leaf-raking or snow-shoveling or car-washing. Today he stood straight and looked buttoned-up even though he wore a Northwestern sweat-shirt.

They sat in the dining room, usually cordoned off for holiday meals, gift-wrapping marathons, and homework sessions. The facts were indisputable.

"I'm sorry," Alan said. "I just never thought . . . we didn't plan . . ."

"You really mean I can't touch my own money?" Evie's voice rose, then drained to a raspy whisper. She drummed her fingers on the papers in front of her. Her knee bounced frenetically un-der the table.

"It's not that you can't, you just shouldn't. Really shouldn't. If there is any possible way to avoid it."

"There's no way around the taxes and penalties? Are you sure?"

"I'm sure."

The meticulous planning that had seemed so sensible now felt like a trap. With the massive hit Alan said she would take, her sav-ings seemed like a mirage.

No. This was a time for action. For navigating around the rules that already existed. For making her own rules. Maybe Alan would make an exception for Evie, his wife's best friend, and fig-ure out a way around the rules. What a joke. Alan was a rules guy. But there had to be a way she could get the money she had saved for herself. Maybe she shouldn't have made it about her. Maybe that money should always have been about the kids. No, that money was separate. Separate from savings bonds the kids were given at birth. Separate from the child support and the maintenance, meant to support them, the house, and their lives. The judge—and she and Richard—had agreed. She should put this money away for her fu-ture.

Except no one had imagined *this* future.

"I believe you," Evie said, deflated. It was no one's fault, although off-loading guilt sounded delightful at the moment. "I wanted the money away until I wasn't getting support anymore, wasn't even working part-time. That's what I asked you to do and that's what you did."

Evie hadn't considered the ramifications of paying taxes and penalties on her money if she needed or wanted it before she turned fifty-nine. *Why should she have?* Richard had been fit and healthy and arguably happy in his new life. Weren't happy people supposed to live longer? So much for that theory.

Nicole's suggestion that she and Luca move in with Evie and the twins poked at the back of her thoughts. The idea was ludicrous. Having her ex-husband's widow (was there a word for that?) living in her house . . . Who would do that? Why would she do that? Evie knew why. She'd do it so that she could pay the bills while she figured things out. Could she cope with Nicole as a long-term houseguest? A boarder? A tenant? And what about Luca? Babies meant diapers, toys, gates, locked cabinets, and covered outlets. It would be inconvenient, absurd, and disruptive. But at this point, what wasn't?

Alan had grown paler than usual. One sweat bead danced on his temple, and Evie wanted to offer him a napkin to sop it up, but instead she brought him iced tea and a plate of cookies. He touched neither. He hated bringing bad news, and Evie knew it. And that was also why Beth had stayed behind.

"I have to ask you, Evie, didn't Richard have a life insurance policy? Shouldn't that be enough to take care of the kids?"

"Yes, he did, but no, it's for college. After that, it'll help a little every month." Evie's jittering stopped and she slammed her hands on the table. "But Midwest Mutual is giving me the runaround. I have no idea why. I have no idea what's wrong. And I have no idea when it will be over. Do you know why they would do that?"

Alan grimaced and shook his head. "If there's a legal glitch—or any issues with the policy . . ."

"I know," Evie whispered. Her knee started bouncing again.

"We can loan you some money until you figure out what's going on," Alan said.

Evie took Alan's hands. She shook her head; her words crackled. "Thank you, but no."

"How about your folks?"

Evie shook her head.

"Your sister?"

Lisa would help if Evie asked, but she wouldn't ask. She shook her head again, out of words, out of ideas, almost out of hope—but that was not an option.

"I could move to a different house." That's what her parents and Lisa—and Laney and Beth—wanted anyway. "But I really don't want the kids to go through any more changes."

"In this housing market, I'm not sure it would do you any good to sell the house. And for what it's worth, I think you're right about the kids. They've had enough." Alan's unease dug lines around his eyes. He adored the twins and had stepped in many times after Richard had moved out, playing the role of "guy anxious to play catch with on a warm Monday evening" or "neighbor well versed in Thursday-night volcano construction."

"Sorry, it's none of my business." But it was his business because he cared. Alan walked to the kitchen and Evie followed. "You do what you think you have to do." He deposited his full plate on the counter and his glass in the sink, just as Beth would have. "Whatever you decide, your friends will support you, whether or not they like it."

Evie wondered if he meant Beth, his wife, who seemed to understand everyone and everything to a fault—or if he meant the blunt, beloved, and unsinkable Laney Brown.

Walking behind Alan to the front door, Evie stopped. "You

know, it's not just about the kids. Why should I have to give this up? I love this house!" *There, I said it.* Was it stupid or just selfish of Evie to think things were going to fall into place when their lives had been blown out of a cannon like pieces of confetti?

Alan turned to Evie with a resigned smile as Beth showed up at the door for *her* shift of Evie-care.

"You okay?" Beth asked. Evie didn't have to be okay around Beth, and that's what made her such a good friend. Beth had expectations of herself—like being president of the school board for the four years Cody was at Lakewood High and folding cloth napkins in swans or tulips for a Tuesday luncheon—but she didn't inflict those expectations on anyone else. Suggested, perhaps. Strongly suggested. But she always said *please*. "Please let me cook dinner for you and the kids tonight, please. I'll bring it over later."

Evie nodded. It would be nice to have something dropped off again, and it would be nice if it wasn't made of sugar.

"You'll figure it all out," Beth said.

Evie sat at the desk, one step closer to paying the bills. Beth, in perpetual motion, swept the table and countertop with her hand, dusting any crumbs into the sink and rinsing them away, and then she started opening the cabinets, the fridge, the freezer.

"There has to be a way for you to have more income while you look for a job, get the kids settled back into school, and sort through the mess. Maybe even a way for you to have help with the twins and give you a break. Everyone can use a break sometimes. You know, just a *temporary* solution." Beth was about as subtle as a rocket launch. Evie was silent. She had not mentioned Nicole's ludicrous proposal. She had thought about it, but she hadn't mentioned it. Somewhere in Lakewood, Laney's eyes were twitching, her best-friend radar picking up what Beth was suggesting. What Evie was considering.

"Oh, and I'm going to the grocery store, so I'll bring a few things by later. You said the kids are going back to school Monday, so I'll get special treats for their lunches." Beth reached into her pocket and pulled out her smartphone. "Let's make a list of everything you need."

Evie knew what she needed, and Beth wouldn't find her at the grocery store.

$$\text{---} \quad Chapter\ 6 \quad \text{---}$$

THE BASEMENT WAS DUSTED, VACUUMED, and rearranged. It looked as comfortable as any studio apartment, but was much better equipped than the one Evie had lived in with Richard during grad school. There was cable TV *and* a coffeemaker.

The bathroom sparkled. Evie had emptied the medicine cabinet. Towels were stacked on the vanity. They weren't new towels, they weren't matching towels, but they were hole-free, clean, and folded towels. The sheets and pillowcases Evie washed that morning did match, purchased for the sofa-bed guests who rarely visited. The linens filled one shelf in the narrow bathroom closet. Toilet paper and cleaning supplies took up space on another. A new plunger rested diagonally on the floor. Everyone deserved a new plunger.

Evie walked into the center of the large, windowless room for a final check. She picked up the sofa cushions, pounded them into fluffy rectangles, and repositioned them. She crouched, looked under her nineties, tufted, cabbage-rose, pullout couch and discovered one dog-hair tumbleweed that had escaped the vacuum's wrath. She grabbed the fuzz ball and surveyed the floor one more time. The solid-oak dresser, the one Evie had refinished before the twins were born, stood in one corner across from a white, up-to-code, wooden crib. Sam's and Sophie's DVDs and board games were stacked in another corner, half-hidden by a twenty-five-year-old minifridge. Evie had stocked it with soda and apple juice.

Beth had given her the names of baby-safe cleaning products and bought a few of the latest baby-proofing items. Laney said Evie was crazy, cleaning for Nicole, but helped her anyway. Evie wanted to present her home in the best light possible, even if that light was fluorescent tube bulbs in a drop ceiling. Evie succumbed to the ease and lure of looking frumpy, but she would never abandon her house to the same fate. This had been her home—in one familial configuration or another—for a dozen years. She knew that no matter who lived there, or didn't, this house was filled with vestiges of her past and dreams for her future.

Evie clung to both to save her own life.

Nicole held the banister and peeked down from the fourth step.

"Oh my God, it looks amazing." She looked around the basement, mouth open. "It doesn't look like the same room." She sank into the couch. "Reminds me of my first apartment back home. So cozy, so *lived in*."

Was it a compliment, or was Nicole expecting Ethan Allen to have made a delivery? Evie sat, leaving one cushion between them. She crossed her legs, leaned back, and admired her handiwork. "Thanks. I'm glad you like it. Amazing what packing up ten years of toys will do."

"What's the occasion?"

Evie smiled. "I have been thinking about your idea." *No turning back now.* "And if you'd like to move in here with Luca, just until we're both on our feet, I think that would be okay."

"Really?" Nicole's face expanded with a broad smile. "What made you change your mind?"

"I figure it's a win-win."

"I was right, wasn't I? You can't pay your bills." Nicole looked at her lap. "You don't want me to move in, do you? You *need* me to move in."

Evie noticed a smirk but decided to ignore it. "It's a combination." It was 99 percent need, but that 1 percent still constituted a combination.

"That's okay. I like being needed. And I like honesty."

The irony choked Evie.

Nicole smiled and put her hand on Evie's hand. It was an unfamiliar touch, somewhat unwelcome. Evie stopped herself from recoiling. *I can pay the bills, I can pay the bills, I can pay the bills, until I find a job or the insurance comes through, or both.* So, if Nicole wanted to play house, Evie would play house.

"What do you think Richard would say?" Nicole said, fingering her wedding band.

Evie had long stopped caring what Richard thought or said about anything she did. But for Sam's and Sophie's sakes, she pondered. "I guess he'd be glad his kids are together."

Nicole rocked in silence. Her mouth frowned, her eyelids drooped as if she were dozing, and she continued playing with the ring, drumming it, twirling it, feeling it. "It's good, isn't it?" she said, perking up, then reverting back to stoic. "Making the best of a bad situation is good, right?"

"I think it's practical. And practical is good. For now."

That night, with just the kids and herself upstairs in their bedrooms, Evie felt safe, at ease, content. The money from Nicole offered her a short respite from worrying.

"I don't feel good," Sophie said at Evie's bedroom door.

A short respite, indeed.

Evie hug-walked Sophie back to her room. Evie smoothed the curls out of Sophie's face and felt her daughter's forehead with her lips and a subsequent kiss. Cool. She drew back the blanket, and Sophie scampered beneath it.

"You're fine, sweetie. Probably just extra-tired. It was an exciting day." Change prompted sleeplessness and stomach pains in Sophie. As a baby, she needed her solid foods introduced at half the pace of Sam. Richard insisted they take Sophie to the pediatrician, convinced the cranky nights, baby belching, and explosive diapers were a result of trendy food allergies. The doctor said no, she was just sensitive to changes in her diet. When they heeded his word, Sophie ended up with a bigger repertoire of foods on her "will eat" list than Sam, only it took them months to find that out. The divorce did the same thing to Sophie—she couldn't sleep and walked around during the day complaining of stomachaches. The stomachaches were real, but never accompanied by a virus or fever. Postdivorce visits to a therapist gave her an outlet for her feelings, but didn't diminish the physical effects. Just as when Sophie was a baby, what she needed was time.

"Why do Nicole and Luca have to sleep in the basement?"

"You like having your own room, don't you?"

"But I don't always want to sleep there."

"I know. And that's okay. But Nicole's a grown-up and she needs her privacy. Plus, babies can make a lot of noise."

"Are they going to live here forever?"

"I don't think so."

"Will Luca go to Eden when he grows up?"

"I don't know, honey. But you like going to that school, don't you?"

Sophie nodded. "I like math."

"I know you like math! And you get to go back to school and do math in just a few days." Evie felt guilty counting down the minutes until the twins were gone six hours per day again. They'd be safe, they'd be cared for, they'd be with their friends and teachers. And they'd be two miles away from Evie. She could be there in three minutes if they needed her, and if they didn't, she could use the time to reconstruct the cornerstones of their lives.

Sophie, though, was still cornering her about Luca.

"What does Luca call you?"

Evie had no clue. "He doesn't talk."

"How about when he does talk?"

"He can call me whatever you want him to call me."

"Will they be here on our birthday?"

"I don't know, Soph. Go to sleep."

"How about on Luca's birthday? If he still lives here, can we have a party?"

"Of course."

"What kind of cake would we have?"

Exasperated, Evie tried to remember that Sophie was searching for order, just as she did. And Evie couldn't help but hear the lilt of excitement in her daughter's voice—now something to be cherished, not taken for granted. "Something yummy, okay? And we'll bake it."

"I don't like baking anymore," Sophie said, her body stiffening.

"Oh." Her daughter's reply was unexpected. "We'll go to Lakewood Bakery, then. Now you go to sleep and dream about that cake. From the bakery."

Sophie softened and shut her eyes. Her eyelashes were long and curved and dark. If she listened to Evie, one day teenage Sophie would forgo mascara, maybe just use an eyelash curler. Evie crossed her fingers and wished for the day that makeup and boys and even car keys and curfews were their biggest concerns.

Then she closed her eyes tight to make that wish really count.

Chapter 7

SOME PEOPLE WOKE UP EARLY to exercise. Some people woke up early to work. Evie woke up early to breathe. So, when morning sneaked through the slots of the miniblinds, Evie slid out of bed and Rex jumped in. The dog looked at Evie, wagged his tail, and put his head on the pillow. Evie couldn't remember the last time she washed the pillowcase or the dog, but she didn't care. A little dry drool never hurt anyone. Evie knew what Rex was thinking: *You're crazy, lady—even I don't get up at five-thirty.* But five-thirty was Evie's time—the put-her-head-in-the-sand-and-pretend-things-aren't-how-they-are time. It was the only time she could drink her coffee without gulping to a throat burn.

She tiptoed down the stairs and heard the soft whoosh of her newest infatuation—a programmable coffeemaker sent by her parents. "One less thing to do in the morning," her mother had said. Her dad admitted, "It's like having a maid. Okay, not quite," when Evie gushed over the gift. She smiled at her inanimate crush as boiling water dripped through the coffee—arabica breakfast blend mixed with a little cinnamon. After pouring the coffee into her mug, Evie retreated to the couch and tucked her feet under her favorite cotton throw. The weave had loosened from her wiggling her fingers and toes into it for the past eleven years, but like Sam's stuffed frog and Sophie's myriad of fuzzy, floppy dogs, Evie couldn't get rid of it. Washed a million times, it still smelled new and clean, like a promise. It was the same one she'd draped over her shoulders on cold mornings when she'd nursed the twins. That lap-size blanket was a constant, always waiting where she'd left it the night before.

Evie looked out the window to the snow-covered swing set and pictured two little kids swinging back and forth, high and low. She closed her eyes and waited for the silence to break. She savored the calm, and the warmth on her face from the steaming cup. After three weeks of mothering fatherless children, she stole moments from sleep to think and to speculate, to ponder and to pretend.

Evie opened her eyes and scanned the room, skipping over the photos of Richard that Sam and Sophie had dusted and placed on every shelf. Most were photos of the four of them, from the eight years they were a *regular* family, tethered, Evie believed, by their *ketubah,* a Jewish marriage license, and a common goal of raising kids in a family with *their* two parents. During the day Evie looked to the past with kind eyes, but she disinvited Richard from her personal sunrise. It was not disrespectful, it was necessary. She would suffocate if she couldn't get away, even if getting away was in the midst of the *mishegos,* the craziness. For the moment the craziness was quiet—and all hers. But Evie knew the memories and the rest of the morning were waiting at the bottom of the giant mug. She sipped extraslow, but not slow enough.

"Good morning," Nicole said, tiptoeing into the room.

"Good morning."

"Do you mind that I came upstairs? I can go back down, but Luca won't be up for another half hour or so. I thought I could help with whatever you're doing. I heard your footsteps."

"I'm sorry if I woke you." And Evie was. Because alone time wasn't alone when someone walked in.

"That's okay, I don't sleep much."

Evie sloughed off the feeling of being cornered. She had invited

Nicole to move in with Luca. There was no need to be annoyed except with herself. "Want some coffee? No, you want tea, right?" Evie said, heading toward the kitchen.

"I'll make it."

Nicole went to the right cabinet for the tea and the right cabinet for the sugar and the right cabinet for the mug. She programmed the microwave for a minute and thirty seconds, exactly the right time to bring the water to a boil. Nicole had been paying attention.

Settled across the table from Evie, Nicole sipped. The steam would have fogged up glasses if she wore them.

"Have you heard from your mother?" Evie asked.

"By e-mail. She still wants us to move back to Iowa. But I won't go back there. Ever."

"I'm sure once you settled in, reconnected with your old friends . . . I bet lots of them are having babies now or have little ones already."

Nicole rolled her eyes like a defiant teenager. Evie pushed away hard from the table and went back to the couch, reclaiming the morning. Peering into the living room, Nicole sipped her tea and stared.

"Yes?" Evie said.

"I'm sorry. I'm not going back home. Anyway, I thought you wanted us here."

"You know it's only temporary." Evie didn't know if *temporary* meant six weeks or six months, but she knew it meant not forever, and while that was daunting, it was also comforting. "So, your hometown . . . is it really that bad?"

Nicole nodded, and Evie imagined littered streets, trailer parks, cars on cement blocks, and crack houses where pinball arcades used to be.

"It's a dangerous area?"

"Oh, no, it's perfectly safe."

"Bad schools?"

"Great schools."

"No jobs?"

"Actually it's a great place to raise kids."

"Then why don't you want to live there?"

Nicole turned away. "It's not the right place for me and Luca."

"I don't understand. Why isn't it the right place?" Evie placed her cup on the end table hard enough to make a noise, but not hard enough to break it or spill the contents. Nicole whipped around.

"It's just not. You don't want to go back to where you're from, do you? I heard you say so. Why should I?"

Evie did not want to go back to Delaware, but she hadn't lived there since she was eighteen. Plus, she was woven into the fabric of Lakewood. Sam and Sophie were entrenched in school, sports, and friends. Nicole, on the other hand, was on the cusp of a life. She could plant her roots anywhere. Why choose Evie's basement?

"I can't go to school," Sam said.

"Sure you can." Evie patted Sam's back through the comforter. "You and Soph have already missed a week—you'll be okay. It's time."

Sam burrowed under his blanket as if in a long-ago game of blanket monsters with Richard. Although this time the monsters were in Sam's heart and Evie couldn't get rid of them by turning on the lights or tickling him. But it was time to go back to school. He'd get up. He'd get dressed. He'd muddle through today, and tomorrow would be better. She left his room and headed to Sophie's. *Seven-twenty.*

"Soph? You ready to get up?" Evie put her hand on Sophie's shoulder.

"School today?" Sophie squinted even though it was still dark in her room.

"Yep."

"I don't want to tell anyone what happened."

How long was Sophie thinking this that it was the first thing out of her mouth? Not "I'm cold" or "I'm hungry" or "I have to pee." A little girl should not have to protect her own heart until she's grown. Evie would do it for her.

"You don't want them to know about Dad?"

"No, I want them to know, I just don't want to tell them."

"You don't have to tell anyone anything, sweetie. They know. When the kids went back after winter break, Mrs. Thomas told them. Remember? They went back last week."

"What if I start crying in the middle of the day?"

"Then they'll call me and I'll come spend time with you or take you home. You'll be fine." *You have to be fine. Just from nine to three, then you can fall apart.*

"Okay." Sophie rose from her bed and headed to the bathroom. The door closed. One click closer to normal.

Seven-thirty. Back to Sam's room.

"It's time to get up, Sam. You'll be late."

Sam didn't move. Evie sat on the bed and put her hand on his back. The slow motion of his breathing was always a relief.

"I can't go," he mumbled. "I can't do math or listen to science. When I try to think about something else, I can't think about anything but Dad. I wish I could just spend every day with my friends."

His burden was more than that of missing Richard; it was that he knew his own mind and heart.

"But your friends are all in school."

"I want to be home. I want to be with you and Nicole and Luca and my friends and not go to school. I want to go, but I can't. I can't, I can't, I can't." He shook his head until Evie put her hands on his face to stop it.

"Kids have to go to school, Sam, it's the law." She looked into his blue eyes and he looked away. When she mentioned "the law," it was always the last resort. When the twins were little, it was "the law" to eat fruits and vegetables.

Evie's trick was past its prime.

What she didn't say was that she wanted—no, she needed—some time to herself. How would she have enough energy for the long nights if they weren't *both* at school all day? Evie needed to sort out the bills and call Midwest Mutual again. She had to look for a job or at least start to think about a job. She didn't expect them to be happy or fine or the same as before, but she did expect her kids to go to school. Was she delusional?

"I don't care. I'm not going."

Sam's tone was calm, not belligerent. He was matter-of-fact. Evie didn't know what she was going to do. It never occurred to her that after an extra week at home both Sophie and Sam wouldn't be itching to get out of there, back to building snowmen at recess and turning carnations blue during science. But if Sam had a meltdown in public, that would push him even further into misery.

She looked at Sam, shook her head no, but said, "Okay. But just today."

Sophie picked at her fingernails. "Where's Sam?"

"He's not going today." Evie picked up Sophie's lunch and placed it in her backpack, maneuvering it into the perfect spot so it wouldn't get squashed. "He *can't* go."

Sophie nodded. She understood in a way Evie did not.

The kids stored their grief on a shelf when they could. Sophie did that to go to school. The shelf was out of Sam's reach, at least today. That coping mechanism kicked in when needed. Evie read that online, or in a book, in the middle of the night. She didn't remember. And Sam needed it big-time. He would draw his legs into his shell at bedtime every night—the darkness would bring about the pain. He stared at the ceiling, he cried, he hyperventilated. In the light of day, the prospect of friends and video games and a potential snowball fight overrode any adult tendencies to mourn constantly. But now he was faced with school, not fun, and with teachers and classmates, not just friends. He would not be able to go into the bathroom or his bedroom at will to fall apart and re-group. He would not be able to emerge from a classroom and touch his only parent just to make sure she was still there.

"Stay home today," Evie said, back in Sam's room. "I have to take Sophie to school and walk her in. I'll be back in twenty min-utes. Nicole's in the basement if you need anything." She'd never left the twins alone for more than a few minutes, such as if she ran to Laney's to check out a new purse or Beth's to pick up a basket of whatever she'd grown in her garden. But Sam wouldn't be alone. The benefit of having a boarder. A tenant. *A widow.*

Evie spotted Rex in the hall and snapped her fingers. The dog padded over and Evie pointed to Sam. The furry lump jumped onto Sam's bed, and Evie sighed knowing Sam would have some company close by. "We'll figure this out when I get home," she said. Or not.

Sam nuzzled his face into Rex's neck and clicked on the TV he'd negotiated into his bedroom when Richard had moved out. Classic TV reruns had lulled him to sleep for the past three years, and Evie wished it were that simple now. Considering divorce simple, that was a switch. How she would love to hear that noise in the middle of the night and have her trip down the hallway result in just push-ing the OFF button. In those days, Sam was able to get up and go about his boyhood business because Richard showed up at the door every Wednesday at six and every other Friday at seven.

Missing someone who had moved across town was different from missing someone who had died.

Evie pulled back into the garage, turned off the car, but stayed in-side. She was alone. It was quiet. Sophie had gone into school as if it were any other day. Now Evie didn't want to go back into the house and deal with Sam, coax him out of bed, watch him watch TV all day, waiting as he had for the past week for his friends to come home from school. Those six hours seemed like twelve. She didn't want to yell at Sam or lecture him, but she didn't want to be complacent, as if his behavior didn't matter. It mattered that he wasn't in school. It mattered to Evie's sanity. It had only been three weeks since Richard died, and she hadn't even looked at a newspaper or a magazine or a book and barely been online. She knew the kids needed time to grieve, time to adapt. Lots of time. But to give Sam and Sophie the time *they* needed, Evie needed time of her own. She didn't know if that was reasonable or selfish.

She shivered at the thought of ignoring the kids' needs. That wasn't what she wanted. She just wanted a little bit of Evie time— even if she was just making insurance phone calls or filling out online job applications. She pushed away thoughts of how Nicole could help.

Out of the car and into the house, Evie developed a plan. Sam out of bed, into clothes, and helping with a few chores. A little sweeping and vacuuming never hurt anyone. Maybe he'd realize school was better than staying home if he spent more time with a broom in his hand than a remote. Then, after that, they'd review some old worksheets. Anything that would focus his attention away from himself and onto something else—anything else—would be a good thing.

Someone else had had the same idea.

"Hey," Evie said as she walked into the kitchen. She poured a cup of coffee, added the requisite stream of half-and-half.

Nicole smiled and raised her eyebrows. "Sam is reading to Luca." She pointed at the boys.

Sam held a chubby board book on Luca's high-chair tray and was turning the pages, reading the words and pointing to pictures. He didn't look at Evie, but he did smile.

"I figured that was better than more TV," Nicole whispered.

In twenty minutes Nicole had gotten Sam to do what Evie hadn't been able to get him to do in a week. Engage. Do something for someone else. Why hadn't she realized that someone else could be Luca? Why hadn't she realized that Nicole was good for more than a check?

Nicole followed Evie into the living room, leaving the boys in the kitchen. "Thanks," Evie said. "What did you do?"

"I just yelled up the stairs that Luca missed him and asked him to come down. He's not going to say no to me. I'm not his mom."

This was true, just the way the kids would eat broccoli at Laney's and drink orange juice at Beth's, but do neither in their own home. When Evie and Lisa were growing up, they always ate tomato soup with oyster crackers at Bubbe's, but when their mother made it—right from the can, with milk, just like Bubbe—they said it didn't taste the same because it didn't.

"So are you comfortable downstairs?" Evie didn't know what else to say.

"It's sort of lonely. But it's fine."

Evie would have loved a little lonely time right about now.

"Well, I never expected to raise Luca alone."

Silence dug a gorge in the living-room floor. Nicole looked far away and small, not size-two small, but Thumbelina small. Evie's nose itched but she stayed still. Did Evie need to remind Nicole that *her* life hadn't turned out as planned, not once but twice?

"I'm sorry," Nicole said. She picked up Luca's primary-color plastic doughnuts from the floor. She took her finger out of the hole in the dam. "I don't know what Richard told you about me, I don't. But I loved him, I truly loved him."

Evie was not buying a ticket to Nicole's Richard-fest. "What do you want me to say?"

Nicole shrugged.

"I appreciate that you're living here and helping out, I do. But I can't thank you twenty-four/seven, and I can't listen to you blabber about Richard. That's not my job. My job is to take care of my kids."

"I know." Nicole picked at her cuticles. "I just want you to understand."

Evie understood. Richard had a Ph.D. in math and was on the tenure track at Pinehurst College. Nicole worked in the campus salon cutting coeds' and professors' hair. Without an equation or theorem, Evie knew that Nicole's barber chair was Richard's pedestal. Evie understood better than Nicole would ever understand.

"Nicole, look at me." She did. "None of that matters. Let's just move on, okay?" *But don't push me.*

Nicole nodded and sniffed. The crying in Evie's presence would have to stop; Nicole needed a new mother figure and some new friends. Evie could get behind that, help her do it; Evie was good at making friends. Or, she used to be.

"You have a mom and extended family—and probably old friends back in Iowa. Why aren't you packing up Luca and heading west when there's nothing for you here?" Evie pictured a covered wagon bumping down the road, stopping in Nicole's driveway, her and Richard's matching luggage tossed through the opening in the tattered cover.

"I can't live with my mother, and Iowa has too many sad memories for me."

The entire state of Iowa was off-limits? Lakewood didn't have sad memories? "Why did you leave home in the first place?"

Nicole nuzzled Luca and whispered baby talk. She turned toward the window and pointed outside, still muttering. The sides of Evie's neck tingled and then itched. She rubbed her neck but the feeling remained.

"Are you going to answer me?" Evie said.

Nicole's hair flopped back and forth as she shook her head.

Beth's laptop lay on her family-room floor between Evie and Laney.

"This is wrong," Beth said, opening it. "We shouldn't snoop."

"That's what the Internet is *for*," Laney said, turning the laptop toward her and tapping the power button. In a convoluted tug-of-war, Beth turned the laptop back to herself. Then Laney turned it. Then Beth. Then Laney. Then Beth.

"Fine! If somebody is going to do it, I'll do it," Beth said, whisking the laptop off the floor and onto her outstretched legs. She huffed at Laney, admonishment usually left for someone who didn't do the dishes. "Unless you want to do it yourself," Beth added with raised eyebrows, looking at Evie.

Evie sank into the corner of the oversize love seat, faux-fur blanket around her covering everything but her face. She couldn't shake a chill. "I don't want to do it, but I have to know. Please?"

"You don't feel just *a little* bad that Nicole is home with Luca and Sam and you're over here digging into her past?"

"Why should she feel guilty?" Laney stood from the floor in one seamless motion without using her hands for leverage or balance. Upright, she was several feet taller than Beth. "If the widow is hiding something, Evie has a right to know. What if she shot a man in Iowa just to watch him die?" Beth looked up at Laney, then back at the laptop. She shrugged, then typed, the tap-tap-tap-tap-taps pounding in Evie's head like a jackhammer.

"Maybe it's a bad idea," Evie said. "No, go ahead, do it. No, wait, don't."

"She's making me crazy," Laney said to Beth.

Beth just stared at the monitor and typed. "Leave her alone, she can't help it."

"*She* is right here," Evie said, but she didn't care. They were talking about her in front of her, which she knew was better than when someone talked behind her back.

"Take a nap," Laney directed.

Evie closed her eyes. For once, she liked being told what to do, liked knowing someone else was taking care of business. Evie was tired. Tired of taking care of the kids without a break. Tired of having to have Nicole in the house. Tired of her neighbors not knowing what to say when they saw her in the grocery store. She was tired of wondering what would happen next. Keeping her eyes closed meant the next thing would be opening them. Sometimes, it was the little things. But closed eyes seemed to open a portal for her thoughts.

Why didn't she pressure Nicole to tell her about Iowa? Was she respecting Nicole's privacy? That did not seem prudent considering Nicole's privacy once included Evie's husband. It was just easier to invade Nicole's privacy online than in person.

"I'm going to look into the public court records in the county where she lived in Iowa. If you want me to stop, say so now," Beth said.

"Do it or don't, I don't care," Evie said, eyes open, portal closed.

"If you don't care, why are we doing this?" Beth said. "It's really not right anyway. If Nicole wanted you to know about her life in Iowa, she would have told you."

"You mean like with Richard? Look, I have to figure out how I'm going to live. *You* figure out what she's hiding."

"Our pleasure," Laney said as she sat back down next to Beth and took the computer for herself. Beth didn't argue. Beth didn't like doing this because Beth liked Nicole, and Evie knew it.

"Hey, what if Nicole is on the Internet looking up things about me?" Evie said.

"What's she going to find?" Laney said. "A bake-sale scandal?"

"Touché." Had Evie been that suburban? Yes. She was the volunteering, baking mom who brought a thermos of pink lemonade to the park with a stack of Dixie cups. *No one should be thirsty at the park.* She had only turned her back on the burbs on her weekends without the kids.

"Laney's right," Beth said. "Nicole doesn't need to look up anything about you. She knows everything she wants to know. Probably has since she met Richard."

"Right, I'm sure she had you all scoped out," Laney said.

Evie and Nicole's relationship—*Wait, they had a relationship?*—was like a one-way street, all roads leading to Evie. Now it was Evie's turn to see the world from Nicole's point of view. It wasn't a matter of trying to walk in Nicole's shoes as much as it was knowing just where those shoes had been and possibly what they'd stepped in.

"Just go home and ask her why she doesn't want to go back to Iowa," Beth said. "I think if you give her a chance—"

"She'll lie," Laney interrupted. "Once a liar always a liar."

Evie nodded. "Keep looking."

Maybe it was a mistake. Uncovering secrets didn't always solve problems, sometimes it was better not to know. If she didn't know for sure about Richard, maybe they would have stayed married. Instead of a Stepford wife, Evie could have become a *Lakeford* wife and just walked around in a daze, wearing pearls. Evie knew that the dissolution of her marriage became less about *what* Richard did than *how* he did it. Everyone thought he'd earned his Ph.D. in applied mathematics, when really his doctorate was in breaking promises. The half-built shed. The postponed vacations. The missed family dinners. The promises to stop breaking promises.

Unlike Richard to Evie, Evie had promised Nicole nothing.

"I'm hungry," Evie said. "And sweating."

"Should we get Sam, Nicole, and the baby and go out for lunch?" Beth said.

"No," Laney blurted. "I don't want to have lunch with her. Why can't the three of us go out for lunch?"

"I'm broke, remember?"

"I'll order Thai," Laney said. "My treat. Nicole can give Sam lunch."

"No, my treat," Beth said, looking at Evie. "I'm sorry that I made you feel like you shouldn't know whatever is going on with Nicole. You should. I know that. I don't want you to get hurt by her or anyone else. After pad thai and spring rolls, I'll keep searching."

"Might not need to. What was Nicole's name before she married Richard?" Laney said, drumming the sides of the laptop.

"Roberts," Evie said.

"And before that?"

"What do you mean *before that*?"

"Roberts was her *first* married name."

Evie paced. Then she sat. Then she stood, straightened throw pillows in the corners of the couch, moved framed photos around and then put them back. Then she paced some more.

Nicole was taking too long. Evie had asked her to come upstairs ten minutes ago. The kids were in bed. Awake, but in bed. If Nicole and Evie talked in the living room, with the TV on, the impending conflict would be muffled by the nightly news. Probably.

Nicole strolled in and sat on the couch. "What's up?"

"You were married before?" Evie blurted. So much for easing herself into it.

"Yeah?" Nicole said with the nonchalance of a teenager.

"What do you mean, *yeah*?"

"What do *you* mean? Of course I was married before."

Evie replayed Nicole's words in her head. What had she missed? *Of course she was married before?* With her mouth open, Evie jutted her head forward and stared at Nicole, waiting for more. Was the girl naive or taunting her? Or was she just plain stupid?

Evie threw her hands in the air. "Talk!"

"Wait a minute," Nicole said, even though Evie was clearly in no mood for waiting. "You didn't know about Peter?"

"Who's Peter and how am I supposed to know about him?" Evie raised and then lowered her voice. She sat at the far end of the sectional and tapped her foot as if she were listening to music with a fast beat.

"Peter was my husband. He was my high school sweetheart. You really didn't know?" Nicole scrunched her eyebrows together. She seemed to be concentrating, trying to figure out how this gaffe could be possible.

"I really didn't know."

"Well, now I know why you keep referring to Luca as my only child."

"Sam and Sophie are not your children." Evie was tiring of the word games, of drawing lines in the parenting sand.

"I'm talking about Lucy."

"Who's Lucy?" Evie's voice and intolerance rose.

"My daughter." Nicole rolled up her sleeve to reveal the rose tattoo. Evie leaned in and squinted. The tattoo said LUCY.

"You have a daughter?" A stifled scream scraped Evie's throat as she reversed into her spot on the couch.

"I'll be right back." Nicole jumped up and ran through the kitchen, the mudroom, and down the basement steps, then back up the steps and through the house louder than Evie would have liked with the kids upstairs trying to sleep. Nicole sat back on the couch before Evie had had a chance to review what she knew and didn't know.

Nicole reached into Luca's diaper bag and pulled out a pink, nylon wallet. She peeled open the Velcro and withdrew a stack of scissor-cut photos. Evie squeezed the cushion. The padding squashed in her grasp. Nicole handed the photos to Evie, who held them like live grenades, flipping them from one hand to the other and back again. Then she shuffled through pictures of a freckle-faced, blue-eyed, red-haired baby, then toddler, and a blond little girl, always with the same skinny, teenage boy, also red-haired and freckle-faced. Evie tucked the photos back into the wallet.

"Where are they now?" Evie's heart pounded. "Where are your *husband* and *daughter*?" she demanded.

Nicole lifted her clasped hands to her chest. "They were on their way to buy balloons. Lucy would've been two the next day."

"Would have been?" Dread filled Evie's belly and traveled to her throat. The leftover smell of a pizza lunch nauseated her, and she held her nose for just a second and then breathed through her mouth.

"They were killed by a drunk driver." Nicole rocked back and forth and cradled a pillow like a newborn, holding it like a crescent moon. "Lucy would be twelve now."

"Oh my God," Evie whispered. Peter and Lucy *died*. Evie's body was limp and heavy. She stifled an urge to put her arms around Nicole, which was easy because Evie was paralyzed. Nicole's voice sounded distant, as if she were speaking through a closed door, a door to which Evie had had no key before now.

"We named Luca after her."

They named Luca after two-year-old Lucy. Evie shuddered with shock. It was an unmitigated Jewish honor to name a baby after a deceased relative—but after a two-year-old who would have been his older sister? Although if there were still a Lucy, there would be no Luca.

"I was a good mom." Nicole sniffed and nodded. Her voice was deep, the words emerging from the bottom of her throat and memory. "I surprised everybody, even myself. We were just kids, but we did the right thing when I got pregnant. Peter had already graduated, so he got a full-time job as assistant manager at the Green Ferry Hy-Vee, and then we eloped. We thought it was perfect. My mother was livid." Nicole sighed. "She wanted me to have an abortion and go off to the University of Iowa like we'd planned my whole life, but I just couldn't. I wanted to have the baby. And I wanted to stay with Peter." Nicole's face brightened, as if, for one moment, she forgot the past and the present.

Then, her expression morphed into a deep frown. "I never thought I'd go through this again, losing the love of my life. But this time is different. I have Luca. I'll do anything for him." She straightened her stance and strengthened her voice. "So, I'm not running away from here the way I ran away before. I'm not leaving the place with the memories. I'm going to make a life with the memories. For Luca." Nicole pushed hair off her face. She picked up the wallet, kissed it lightly, and touched it to her chest.

The storm wall broke around Evie's heart. She stood and turned away as the lump in her throat dissolved into sobs. Evie rubbed her eyes and dragged her fists down her cheeks. For once she was glad to be on a makeup strike, as any mascara would have been lost in the flood. For four years, Evie had judged Nicole harshly. What would *Evie* have been capable of after losing a husband and a toddler? She blubbered and gasped for breath. Empathy overwhelmed her. It riveted her to the floor, yet her impulse was to lurch toward Nicole, to comfort and care for her. This was how Evie felt when her children hurt, not when Nicole hurt. The maternal pang was unwelcome, but not unwarranted because Evie was the unintentional matriarch of this absurd newfangled family. She hadn't been through half of what Nicole had been through. Thank God for that. *Losing Richard before I was really ready? Burying the twins?* A chill ran through her body and she shivered.

Evie flinched when Nicole's hand touched her left shoulder and then rubbed her back. Nicole was comforting *her.*

"I am so sorry," Evie said, hearing the same words she'd said and heard a thousand times in the past month. This time, she felt the simple, honest words lighten the air.

Chapter 8

A QUIET HOUSE IN THE late afternoon was glorious and magical and even self-indulgent. So why was Evie planted on the couch staring at the cushions? She patted the spot next to her, and Rex jumped up. Richard had never wanted the dog on the furniture, but Evie skirted that mandate every time he left for work. She'd overruled it entirely when he'd moved out.

"I wanted time alone and now I have it, Rexy. What should I do?"

She wanted to take advantage of the nothingness, to revel in being alone, but instead she petted the dog, stretched out her legs, and decided that an hour wasn't really long enough to do anything. She could soak in a bubble bath, polish her nails, or dig through her closet for something to wear to Laney and Herb's for dinner on Friday. She could close her eyes for a nap, finally try yoga, or bundle up and take Rex for a walk. Or, Evie could clean out the fridge, go through the bills again, talk to Millie, call her sister without hiding in the bathroom. She could call Midwest Mutual again. But nothing appealed to her.

Evie fidgeted, uncomfortable in her own house. She sat straight, slouched, crossed her legs, snuggled Rex. It didn't help. Maybe she was just uncomfortable that Sophie and Sam had gone back to "the house" with Nicole to pick up mail, more clothes, more baby supplies. Nicole's four o'clock mission made their living arrangement seem more permanent. The more stuff Nicole had in the basement, the more the basement was Nicole's. Evie knew that. But what could she do? She needed Nicole's "rent" to pay her mortgage, and she needed Nicole's presence to—to what? To give her an hour or two alone so she could spend the whole time deciding what to do?

Off the couch and into the kitchen, Evie dialed Lisa and wiggled in her earpiece so it wouldn't slip. Lisa had demanded a daily report after Nicole moved in, and this would be the first time Evie spoke above a whisper.

"There's no good food in this house," Evie said to herself, forgetting she was on the phone. She stared into a cabinet in an effort to conjure up a delicious dinner.

"What happened to all the food we left you?" Lisa said.

"We ate it. That was a month ago." Lisa sometimes forgot there was a world outside of Lisa.

"I hope Nicole is paying for her own food. It's bad enough you have to let her live there, she better pull her own weight."

"She is, don't worry." Evie hadn't figured it out down to the penny; with Nicole's check and the Social Security checks and her holiday bonus from Millie's, all the bills were paid. But next month was a different story.

But first, the cabinets. What *had* possessed Evie to stock up on Triscuits as if they could save the world, and who put them between the Tetley tea and cans of tuna? She accumulated bags of generic, unsweetened cereal that looked like Styrofoam peanuts, and the bags were stacked next to a jar of Cheeze Whiz. Someone had been messing in Evie's pantry.

Lisa interrupted Evie's inventorying. She turned away from the soldierlike cupboard contents. Her thoughts should only be as orderly.

"Has Sam gone back to school yet?"

"No. He will soon though, I can tell. He checks the clock starting at about ten in the morning to see when Sophie will be home."

"Well, when you have more time, I think you need a hobby. Not to mention, a job."

"I have a carton of that soy milk you like. And there are kumquats with the oranges. When did I get those?" Evie deflected. She noticed color-coded jars of baby food stacked behind organic, unsweetened applesauce.

"I don't drink soy milk, and I don't know a kumquat from a kiwi. You better throw them out. Don't ignore me. You need a job *and* a hobby."

"It must all be Nicole's," Evie said, sibling directives be damned. She shifted the pesticide-laden Delicious apples to the front of the fruit drawer.

"She's taking over your fridge. Your life is next. Wait and see."

"I thought this was sister-bonding time, not widow-bashing time."

"Same thing in my book. So, how *is* the job search?"

"I haven't really started," Evie said, inspecting the empty deli drawer.

"What are you waiting for? You taught for ten years before the twins were born. You have a teaching degree *and* a freaking master's degree in history. I told you not to become one of those stay-home moms. It melts your brain."

"I'm not having that fight with you right now, Lisa."

"Look, you have to be able to support yourself and the kids without a widow in the basement, which, frankly, sounds like the title for a scary movie. Have you gone back to Third Coast?"

"Not yet. But Millie said I could whenever I'm ready."

"Good. That's Plan B. Now, look for something that actually pays. Or at least has potential. Something challenging and out of your comfort zone."

"My life is challenging and out of my comfort zone."

They laughed, but it wasn't funny. Evie was weary of new and different; she wanted humdrum and monotonous.

"Like I said, you need a hobby—something just for you—even if you only do it once in a while. You know, like me and yoga."

"My hobby is figuring out how to make a life out of this mess Richard left, and with Nicole and Luca in the house. I haven't heard back on the insurance, and I'm hearing all over the place that people usually get life insurance payouts in a matter of days, not months. It's almost February."

"Call them every day. Twice a day if you have to."

"If I annoy them, it will only take longer." Evie didn't have the energy for more than one call to Midwest Mutual per day. It drained her. Not knowing exhausted her. The prospect of what might or might not happen terrified her more than the first time she was alone with both twins and they cried for three hours. And she felt just as alone even in a full house.

"I've got it. Call Scott!"

"For a job? Are you nuts?"

"No, for a date. You're bored, you're scared, you're lonely. Call Scott. You can knock out all three."

Lisa was man-crazy. She met men for drinks, she dated, she led a single Jewish lawyers' group in Georgetown that met once a week. Lisa claimed she never wanted to get married again, but she spent a lot of time scouting potential husbands. She claimed it was for sport.

"That's your idea of a hobby?"

"Consider it a necessary distraction. When I got divorced, that's all I wanted. Someone to take my mind off what's-his-name. Nothing takes your mind off reality like a handsome face, a good meal, a bottle of pinot, and a roll in the hay. You know that."

Evie did know that. She also knew that calling Scott would set her up for disappointment. He'd say no. But what if he said yes? What would she wear? How would she look? What would they talk about? A month ago she'd not have given any of it a second thought.

"Think of it as a fact-finding mission," Lisa added. "Maybe Scott has some insight into the whole insurance thing. You let Nicole move in, so make her do something useful and watch the kids at night when you can actually go out and have fun and not use the time to clean your kitchen and talk to me. When was the last time you heard from him?"

"Who?" Evie had tuned out her sister when she'd spotted the past week's leftover sandwiches next to two jars of spicy mustard and behind a supersize container of wheat germ that stood next to an unopened bottle of Kahlúa circa 2002.

"Scott. When was the last time you heard from Scott? Pay attention to me. The crap in your fridge can wait."

"I haven't heard from him since he asked me to call him when things were normal."

"Give him a call."

"But life *isn't* normal and I'm *not* ready."

"You know what I always say!"

"A girl's gotta eat." Evie giggled.

"Just leave out the bit about the widow and the baby."

"I can't, Leese."

"You have to. You never tell the bad stuff on the first date. You know that."

"This isn't a first date."

"See? You do want to go out with him."

Exasperated, Evie shook her head at the inadvertent confession. Lisa was skilled at getting Evie to say and do things. In high school Lisa spent four nights leafing through the prom issue of *Seventeen* magazine, dog-earing pages, saying, "Mrs. Lisa Feldman, Mrs. Lisa Feldman, Mrs. Lisa Feldman," even though Lisa was a sophomore and couldn't go to the prom. The next day Evie asked Howard Feldman to prom. He said no, but at least she asked.

"He'll say no," Evie said.

"He won't say no if you ask the right way. Tell him you need some advice and have been so busy that you'd really like to go out. Being busy makes you sound interesting."

"You mean I'm not interesting?" Evie snorted. This would have been a good time for her sister to lie. "I'm really fine at home, most of the time."

"Don't tell me that you like having them there?"

"It's okay."

"You better be careful."

"I don't think there's anything to worry about. So far the worst part is that the food in the pantry is alphabetical."

"Rearrange it."

Evie had already started. She couldn't hear it but she knew Lisa was tapping her fingers. Lisa tapped when she was nervous.

"There aren't a lot of women who'd become the willing landlord to their ex-husband's widow or let them organize the kitchen," Lisa added. "No matter how many catastrophes the bimbo racked up."

Evie squirmed. The name-calling reminded her of her history with Nicole, the reasons she hadn't wanted Sam and Sophie around her. Did any of that matter? Of course it did. Evie could take a loan from Beth and Alan and ask Nicole to leave. She'd given Nicole ample time to pack up her things, alphabetically and in size-order, of course. Evie wasn't heartless. Then that heart of hers thumped. It sounded and felt like Rex's running down the stairs complete with a thud at the bottom.

"I gotta go," Evie said.

"Me too. I have to go outside and find a wayward nymph to mother."

"Very funny."

"Call me when you talk to Scott."

Oh, right, Scott.

Evie studied the kitchen landscape, now lit by late-afternoon amber mixed with gray. Perhaps the only distraction she needed was Lisa, because one phone call, forty-five minutes, and two garbage bags later, the fridge and cabinets were dumped, scrubbed, and de-alphabetized.

Sam and Sophie were right. *There is nothing to eat.*

Maybe dinner with Scott *was* a good idea.

Chapter 9

EVIE AWOKE WITH NEWFOUND RESOLVE.

Sitting at the computer with a full pot of coffee by her side, she applied for jobs at all the school districts within twenty-five miles of Lakewood. She had a master's degree in U.S. history and an Illinois teaching certificate she'd never let lapse. Every high school kid in Illinois had to take U.S. history. Every high school kid in Illinois had to pass a U.S. Constitution test to graduate high school! Wasn't there a history teacher who was retiring or having a baby? Within the nearby McSuburbs wasn't there a school somewhere needing a teacher? If Nicole stayed in the house, Evie and the kids could make it until the fall. By September, Sam and Sophie would be at Lakewood Junior High. It was a longer day, and there were after-school sports and clubs. There was even a bus. Evie would have more time for whatever she needed more time for.

Evie stopped clicking Internet links and wiggled her bare toes in Rex's fur beneath her feet. She closed her eyes and pictured a warm and breezy September day, walking through metal doors big enough to swallow a tank—or an army of high school students. She saw herself striding through the crowd and standing at the front of a large room, eager faces staring at her. In this version of the future Evie's makeup was natural yet pristine like Beth's, her clothes were casual and elegant like Laney's, and her hair was shoulder length and cut back into the layers she loved. It even swayed when she talked the way Scott had always liked. But best of all, in this imaginary future, Evie was financially secure and her roots were done.

"Are you okay?" Nicole asked.

Evie opened her eyes wide as if she had been caught stealing a cookie when all she was doing was daydreaming. She hadn't even heard Nicole come into the room over the cheers of her adoring students. Evie almost giggled.

"Morning."

"Am I interrupting something?" Nicole asked.

"Not really. Well, sort of. I need to ask you for a favor."

"You're really okay with me going out?"

"Absolutely," Nicole said. "We'll have a great time here, won't we, kids?"

If being able to go out at night was one of the payoffs for having Nicole in the house, why did Evie feel that she should stay home? Dinner at Laney and Herb's was not the same as heading downtown in weekend traffic pretending she was urban chic instead of suburban shabby chic—but she was still going out. Going out without the kids.

"What's the big deal about going to Laney's for dinner?" Sam asked.

"No big deal," Evie said, patting her eggplant cotton sweater. It was nubby and thick and reminiscent of the ones she wore in high school, supposedly back in style. Last year. Or was that the year before?

"Then why are you dressed up?" Sophie said.

"I'm not dressed up, I'm just *dressed*."

Had it been so bad for the past six weeks that her kids marveled at their mother's manifestation as an actual dressed-to-go-out human being?

"What's on your forehead?" Sam said.

"Nothing." Evie brushed her bangs across her forehead and shook her hands through the hair to cover the dye stains at her hairline. Why did her kids have to notice everything? And why wasn't Nicole more careful when she helped Evie color her hair? Nicole was a hairdresser. Why didn't she own any of that dye-remover stuff? Nicole had said that toothpaste worked—but it didn't. The Nice 'n Easy #123 was there to stay for a while.

"Why can't we come?" Sophie said, her arms around Evie's waist.

"Just grown-ups," Evie said, looking to Nicole for a rescue.

"We always go to Laney's," Sam said. "We won't bother you."

The kids had grown accustomed to having Evie at home the past month and to her going nowhere and doing nothing without them. She did it to make them feel secure. Perhaps it had backfired.

Nicole stepped in. "Hey, can you guys go downstairs and bring up a few diapers and wipes, Luca's pj's, and some of Luca's toys? Then we can just stay up here until it's time for him to go to bed. And you'll help me, right?"

The twins shrugged but said, "Okay." They were not used to following Nicole's direction, at least not in Evie's presence. They disappeared behind the kitchen wall, and Evie waited until she heard them scamper down the basement steps.

"Thanks."

"No problem," Nicole said. "We'll be fine without you."

Evie was taken aback. She was only going next door. They better be fine, she thought, playing with the edge of her sweater. She felt a loose thread and pulled. And pulled. And pulled.

"I'll be right back," Evie said. "Tell the kids I didn't leave yet."

She ran back up the stairs into her room and traded the sweater for a black tunic turtleneck, a little faded but not unraveling. She double-wrapped a long strand of multicolored beads around her neck. Voilà. Her own version of style. She tugged at the seam of her stretchy, not-quite-but-sort-of- mom jeans to make sure they were still there and still stretchy.

For dinner at Laney's—without Scott or the kids—she filed and buffed, pushed back her cuticles, and painted a clear coat. Sam and Sophie might be alarmed at the transformation, but what was truly alarming was that Evie had forgotten the way she liked to look— what she wanted people to see when they looked at her. It was easy to fall prey to the vulture of grief, to not only allow herself to suc- cumb but to give up willingly. Did caring for her kids and figuring out a new normal preclude her from taking care of herself? A slump was only a slump if she emerged from it.

Otherwise it was a black hole.

The aroma of gourmet takeout wafted out of the warming drawer. Laney loved entertaining, but not cooking.

"Red or white?" Herb said. His mustache was neatly trimmed and it twitched. His eyes squinted behind his glasses as if he were waiting for the answer to a *Jeopardy!* question and the clock was ticking.

"White," Evie said.

"White?" Laney wiped her hands on her designer apron, but the action left no mark. "WWRS?"

Evie laughed. WWRS? *What Would Richard Say?* It was a long time since that was a relevant question, or it seemed like a long time. Wine was one of Richard's half-assed passions Evie enjoyed, unlike hydroponic gardening. Being told what kind of wine to drink at a certain time of year with different foods was one thing— harvesting tomatoes in the master bathroom was another.

Then, there was that laughter to contend with again. She felt guilty when she laughed. But it had been funny when he was alive. Did that mean it couldn't be funny now that he wasn't?

Beth and Alan walked in the front door, Beth carrying a Tupper-ware container by its handle. She was no poser. A cake made from scratch lurked beneath that plastic dome. Evie didn't even have to ask. She was glad Laney had insisted she bring only herself—and that this time Evie had done as she was told. At most gatherings Evie brought more than she was asked, always a plate piled high with cookies right out of the oven or some concoction out of a magazine or off the back of a cracker box. But today she let her friends pro-vide the sweet, savory, and emotional sustenance. So far, it felt right to indulge a little. She held out her glass and Herb replenished her sauvignon blanc.

Nestled into a customary seating arrangement around Laney and Herb's hearth, Evie closed her eyes. Her friends wouldn't mind. The background music and Italian aromas blended into a feeling of comfort. Evie leaned back her head, holding the wineglass at her side. Almost as good as a bubble bath. Hypnotized by the crackle of the fire and the tonal breadth of her friends' voices, Evie relaxed heavily—something she had not done since the night she got the call about Richard's accident.

That call came just as Evie had closed her eyes and sunk her head into her pillows, which she'd fluffed for the occasion of a night all to herself. It was her weekend without the kids, when she'd miss them but also when she would refill her internal well with patience. It was the time away that reminded her how much she enjoyed being defined by motherhood, being known as the twins' mom by the kids at Eden, being tapped for all things baking by the other Lakewood moms. She loved it all but reveled in her time alone, nights with Scott and outlet-mall shopping, and Food TV marathons. She was half-asleep when the phone rang, then she was wide-awake for the next two days.

But tonight when Evie opened her eyes, it wasn't the blaring bell of the telephone, but Beth clearing her throat, her hand on Al-an's knee. They were always touching each other. Petite in frame yet enormous in stature, Beth encompassed all that was right with the world: cupcakes, handsome husbands, and steadfast friendship. It was a smooth transition to waking up, a luxury Evie missed.

"Look who's back with us," Beth said.

"Nice nap?" Herb said. He gulped his red wine like a man content with life. Six weeks ago he was biting into conversations with sarcasm. Now he was teasing Evie and winking at Laney across the room. Next thing you know he'd be doing the dishes. And all thanks to Richard.

It didn't seem fair that her friends were able to sidestep Evie's reality. Their takeaway from tragedy, something harnessed in the lives they loved. Even Sam and Sophie put it aside, albeit briefly, to play, laugh, and cavort the way ten-year-olds should. Children grieved in batches. Evie had learned this from late-night research and from observing the twins latch onto random breaks in the waves of their sadness. She would gladly tuck her children's sorrow into her own pocket permanently if that were possible, but she wished someone could tend to her *tsouris* as well. Richard's death and its aftermath stuck to Evie like glue, and not the kind she had peeled off her palms in elementary school. But this short evening on the other side of the picket fence, where her friends commiserated not on the perils of dead ex-husbands, wayfarer widows, and unresponsive insurance companies, but on politics and economics and paint colors and the evils of skinny jeans for women over forty, served as a reprieve—and she'd take it.

"Beth says you're looking for a job," Alan said, leaning forward and pouring wine into Evie's glass.

"I am. For the fall." Evie smoothed her hair, in need of a cut and style. Could Nicole do that too?

"How about the summer? I know it's too soon right now, but by June? I know of something that's opening up at County." Evie had never considered teaching at a community college. Alan had taught accounting classes there for the past twenty years, in addition to owning his own financial-services firm.

"Really? What is it?"

"Something in the history department. I saved the e-mail. I'll forward it to you. And if you're interested, I can find out more. Put in a good word. Be a reference."

Evie wriggled in her seat, her pulse quickening. "Thank you."

Herb checked his watch and rose from the couch, waving the crowd into the dining room. Laney headed for the kitchen, and Evie followed.

"Can I help?"

"Sure." Laney motioned with her head. Her hands were full of salad bowls and a small cruet with faux-homemade vinaigrette. Laney didn't even bother hiding wrappers or containers at the bottom of the trash compactor. She was as transparent in cooking as in life. Evie carried the teak bowl filled to the rim with exotic tricolored baby greens and set it on the table. She sat between Laney and Alan, with Beth and Herb on the other side of the table. Without Scott—or Richard—the sixth chair was empty.

Later, when Evie returned from the bathroom, Alan and Herb were in the kitchen lovingly—or perhaps begrudgingly—doing the dishes.

"What is *up* with Herb?" Evie said. "I know things are better with you guys, but he's like a different man."

"Tell me about it," Laney said. "We just keep saying how it could have been . . . you know . . ."

Laney did not revel in the tragedy that had befallen her friend and neighbor, and Evie knew it. It was acceptable to feel happy and sad at the same time. It had to be.

"It's okay, Lane, I understand. If it can't be me, I'm glad it's you." Evie pointed to Beth. "This might be a weird question, but has this affected you and Alan at all? You're so ridiculously solid—does this make you think what-if like it did for Laney?"

"Absolutely," Beth said. "But honestly, Alan and I have always had that attitude, you know? Grateful for every day, not taking anything for granted. It's just how we are."

Laney nodded. A month ago she would have rolled her eyes.

"I know it's corny, but we don't make any assumptions," Beth said.

Evie always envied Beth and Alan's stalwart union. She imagined the two of them together could ward off evil if they tried; they probably communicated through mental telepathy.

"So what's shaking with the widow, babe?" Laney said, popping red-velvet cupcake crumbs into her mouth.

"Why do you have to call her the widow?" Beth said. "Why not just refer to her as Nicole?"

"Too much respect in that."

Beth shook her head.

"You don't really know her," Evie said. "I'm starting to, and, she's not so bad sometimes."

"Do not to the Dark Side go, Luke Skywalker," Laney said in her best Yoda voice.

"I have no choice, Lane. Not yet anyway."

Beth reached across the table, but Evie kept her hands to herself. "You're doing a great job welcoming Nicole into your life."

Is that was Evie was doing? Tolerating, putting up with, coping, yes. But *welcoming* was a rather strong word. Yes, they lived together in Evie's home, eating and talking and laughing. And despite Evie's best efforts not to like Nicole, she did. They cared about each other's children. Yes, Evie cared about Luca. And she felt sorry for Nicole. Sorrier than Evie's friends could ever have imagined.

"Just because you forgive someone doesn't mean you forget what happened," Beth said. "It's your right to remember."

"Damn straight you better remember!" Laney bellowed. "Now tell us what you've learned about *Nicole*."

Nicole had not asked Evie to keep a confidence, and even if she had, Evie owed her nothing. Secrets were a burden and one she was not willing to shoulder for Nicole. She told Beth and Laney everything.

"Holy crap," Laney said. "That's horrible to lose two husbands by the time you're thirty. And a little girl. It's awful. My heart goes out to her . . . but . . . it's all a bit fishy, don't you think?"

"How?" Evie asked.

"Maybe they never existed and she's just plying you for your sympathy."

"I'm not stupid," Evie said. "I saw pictures."

"You can get pictures of anything—and anyone—online."

"That would be dishonest," Beth added.

Evie and Laney cocked their heads and stared at Beth.

"Okay, okay, she doesn't have a history of honesty, but no one would do that." Beth crossed her arms for punctuation.

"Did you Google it?" Laney asked. "I'm sure it was in their local paper."

Evie shook her head. Was she so desperate to accept Nicole that she didn't think she might be manipulating her? She needed Nicole and Luca around. Nicole's making things easier was Evie's personal oxymoron.

Laney left the dining room and returned with Jocelyn's pink netbook. Head-to-head-to-head, the best friends found the information they sought.

"This sounds awful," Evie said. "But I'm glad she wasn't lying."

"Me too," Laney said. "It's still quite a coincidence though, don't you think? Two dead husbands? Two car accidents? You don't think she was responsible . . ."

Evie elbowed Laney and she gasped and rubbed her side, feigning injury to her body and her psyche.

Beth ignored Laney's comment.

Laney continued scrolling down the page. "There it is. The driver was charged with vehicular homicide and driving while intoxicated."

"I hate to say it, but that's a relief," Evie said.

"When is she moving out?" Laney asked.

"What do you mean? She just moved in," Beth said, sweeping crumbs into her hand.

"For now, it works. I don't know how she can afford to do it, although she does get Social Security for Luca."

"Who the hell cares?" Laney said. "Even in this market, if she sells the house, she'll have plenty."

"That house is mortgaged to the hilt, the cars are leased, even some of that furniture? Rent-to-own. That's why she's leasing the house to another professor," Beth said.

Evie gasped.

Beth's mouth twisted. "You didn't know?"

Evie shook her head, and she and Laney were silent, mouths agape as though they had stuffed noses and couldn't breathe.

"How do you know all this?" Evie asked.

"She asked me to recommend a Realtor, so I asked what was going on. She told me. Sometimes all you have to do is ask nicely."

"So where the hell will she go when Evie finally comes to her senses?" Laney snarled.

"My senses are just fine." But Laney was right.

"You're in financial turmoil and your savior is a young widow with a wad of cash and a bucket of secrets."

"Richard had life insurance that was part of your divorce, right?" Beth asked.

Evie nodded, even though she didn't remember ever mentioning it. "It'll pay for college—if it ever comes through. But even with Nicole helping, it's complicated. Paying COBRA eats a huge chunk of what I have, but after eighteen months, that's over. I can't add the kids to my health insurance because it's private, so if I don't find a job, I'm going to have to look into All Kids." Evie whispered the last two words. Considering state-sponsored health insurance for her children had never before been on her to-do list.

More silence. Evie knew her friends searched for words that weren't there. These things weren't usually discussed because they didn't need to be discussed. Health insurance, car insurance, employment, mortgage payments . . . they were all givens in Lakewood.

"So, you'll get a great job," Beth said. "And this living arrangement will really help when you interview. Nicole will watch the twins. She loves them."

"How about *Nicole* get a job?" Laney said.

"Right now her job is helping me make ends meet. If she moves out before I have all this figured out, I'm screwed," Evie said.

"Speaking of being screwed, have you called Scott?"

Evie shook her head, tipped back the last drop of her wine, and before she set the glass on the table, Beth had it refilled.

Chapter 10

EVIE PRAISED THE ANN TAYLOR gods for adding 10 percent Lycra to the fabric of her suit jacket. If she couldn't convince Sam to go to school without a meltdown, at least she could look polished and professional with nonpopped buttons when she went to see the principal. Evie had spent a week compiling all the relevant information and filling out all the officially required paperwork so that she could bring Sam's books and lessons home until he was ready— until he was able—to return to school. The blue suit added credibility, showed she meant business.

Her robe would not have been nearly as effective.

Sitting in the same wooden chair that had hosted a generation of students and parents, Evie looked down at her navy, stacked-heel pumps and leaned from the waist to wipe away the layer of closet dust visible under the fluorescent lights. The big, round, generic wall clock sounded like a heartbeat. The desk stretched from one wall to the other and appeared to have an intense wood grain. Evie feigned an itch on her calf and gave the desk a surreptitious pat, just in case someone was watching. Particleboard. Things were rarely as they seemed.

The bell rang. Evie heard feet scatter in the hallway, directions yelled in teacher voices, and a far-off recess whistle. She liked the sounds of children running and laughing; she missed those sounds.

She closed her eyes to hear it all more clearly, to insert her own children's voices into the mix.

The door opened and Evie opened her eyes. Mr. Mueller entered, looking more like a frazzled gym teacher than a principal, even though he wore a tucked-in, button-down shirt. Evie's mood was modern suburban *disheveled,* so his cockeyed tie put her at ease. But his broad shoulders underneath the oxford-cloth shirt, and arms that filled out the sleeves, did not. How had she never noticed that the kids' principal looked like a geeky Matthew McConaughey? Evie straightened a bit and scooched to the front of the chair. She glanced at his left hand. *No ring.* She ran her hand through her hair. What was she doing?

"I'm very sorry for your loss, Mrs. Glass," Mr. Mueller said. "But this is very unusual. We don't advocate you keeping Sam out of school, even if you are willing to *tutor* him."

The handsome-principal distraction vanished.

"Homeschool," she said. "Just until he's ready to come back."

"If he's ready."

Evie didn't want to think about Sam staying home with her until June, so she didn't. "He just needs more time to adjust."

"The school has requirements that must be met."

"Do you have children of your own, Mr. Mueller?"

"No, but I completely understand this type of situation."

"Did you grow up with two parents?" It was a risk, but everything was a risk these days.

"I did."

"Then you do not completely understand." Nor did Evie, but for the moment she was doing a good job at faking it. "To feel grounded, Sam needs to be at home, with me. If he's distracted at school, he won't be able to do any of his work. Which is why we're going to find a solution that meets his needs—not yours." *And not mine.*

"When we make allowances, sometimes children take advantage of us, Mrs. Glass."

She had considered that Sam was manipulating her, even just a little. But if it helped him feel as though he had some control, she didn't care. After this, he wasn't going to lie around playing video games for hours each day. A little nudging was going to be necessary; Evie just had to figure out how much was enough but not too much.

"You did a good job getting Sophie to come back to school. Maybe you could use the same incentive?"

Evie cringed at the word *incentive*. Was he suggesting she hadn't tried everything? That she didn't know her son? In this case the adage was true. Mother did know best. She placed her hands on the desk and leaned in. "Excuse me, Mr. Mueller." Evie looked at the diplomas on the wall. How could someone so well educated be so stupid? Maybe he should spend less time at the gym and more time with the students. "Don't compare Sam and Sophie. Different kids have different needs. But as an educator I'm sure I don't have to tell you that. Nor do I have to tell you that according to the Lakewood Schools Charter, I can keep my child home without your permission or input as long as I file the township paperwork. I just want Sam to be able to get right back into the swing of things here at Eden when he's ready, so I thought it would behoove us to work together on this. But if you don't want to help a little boy who just lost his father . . ."

Mr. Mueller twirled his pen like a baton and then nodded to a stack of folders on top of a filing cabinet. "Those are from Sam's teachers, full of the past month's lessons and assignments." His voice was soft. "Everything seems to be in order."

Not the words Evie would have chosen.

"What do you mean I have to do all my schoolwork at home?" Sam's blue eyes grew wide.

"It's just temporary, until you're ready to go back. If you don't keep up, I'll get in a lot of trouble. And if you don't keep up, *you* won't go to LJH next year." All the fifth graders looked at Lakewood Junior High with awe usually reserved for rock stars and professional athletes. If Evie's getting into trouble wasn't enough of a tug on Sam's heart and motivation, perhaps *not* being a Lakewood Lion would be. Sam looked at the floor and then up at Evie. "You're more than a month behind, sweetie, but we'll catch up." Evie double-pumped her fists and smirked. Sam rolled his eyes and smiled. He was too smart to fool and too sweet to tell her she was lame. Evie reveled in the flash of the Sam she remembered.

"I want to go to school at home too," Sophie piped up.

"You will because you'll do *all* your homework here with Sam," Evie said as she unzipped the sparkly Justin Bieber backpack. She slowed her pace to offset rising panic. Though Sophie sometimes slept with Evie, she got up every morning and went to school. A tidbit of normal. They were not going to move backward. She placed the books on the table in front of what would become Sophie's chair. Laying down the law was never hard for Evie, but now she tiptoed around *no* as though it were a disease.

"What's that?" Sophie pointed to the table.

"My stuff." Sam lined up worksheets edge to edge.

"I have math homework and spelling homework," Sophie said.

Sam looked at Evie, leaving his hand on his papers.

"Oh, right, you do too, Sam. I'll show you which ones." The twins were in sync but also competitive. Knowing that Sophie was moving ahead in her schoolwork might be the ticket to motivating Sam. And keeping Sam motivated would keep Evie motivated. She hoped.

Sophie sat in her chair, tucked one leg beneath her bottom, and slumped with her head on her hand, picking up a pencil and writing her name on the upper left-hand corner of the page on the designated line.

"Put your name on your paper, Sam," Evie said. He looked at her. "So when you go back to school, it's still a habit."

"Jessica doesn't have a dad," Sophie said without looking up.

"That's sad for Jessica." Evie mentally scanned the faces of familiar Jessicas but couldn't think of whom Sophie meant. "What happened?"

"He got killed in Iraq. He was a soldier."

Evie fumbled with a cup full of pens and pencils, flipping them all to be point down. "That's sad, Soph. When did you find out?"

"Jessica told me when I went back to school."

"Tyler never had a dad," Sam said.

"What do you mean?" Evie knew Tyler's mom from basketball and always assumed she was married to a workaholic. But if she was divorced, why didn't Evie know? She could have used the camaraderie.

"I don't know, I just know that one day at practice—Dad was there—and Tyler said he wished he had a dad."

Evie wished little boys asked more questions.

Lots of kids were without dads. Evie knew that. She also knew it didn't make anything easier or better or simpler. What it did was show Sam and Sophie they weren't the only ones. Just knowing built a bridge of sameness. Evie hoped her kids would hang on tight and cross that bridge, maybe one day offering a hand of hope to someone else.

Sam and Sophie were healthy, warm, fed, and loved. They had a roof over their heads, even if Evie didn't know for how long. They had TVs and telephones and a freezer full of rising-crust pizza. Evie swallowed hard and felt a tightening in her throat. She was fortunate simply because she was there.

"Mom? Mom!"

Evie snapped back to the dining room.

"I do want to go to school. But you'll still walk me in and pick me up, right?" Sophie begged.

"Of course. Not until you're ready for me to stop. Just like Sam can do his work at home until he's ready to go back. You guys need different things to make this hard time easier. Well, not easier, but less hard. You can both use this room for all your homework and projects, okay?"

The twins abandoned their books. Sam walked to the kitchen and Sophie toward the stairs, but when they nodded it was in unison, both heads tilted right.

Evie arranged books on the shelves where she'd stored family heirlooms. Now her legacy would be passing along a new normal. She lined up pens and pencils, calculators, maps, textbooks, and worksheets and stepped back to admire the order she'd just created. Neat and tidy wouldn't last long, but it sure looked good.

She ambled into the kitchen as the phone rang. When Evie saw the Midwest Mutual number on caller ID, she looked around for Nicole. She waved from the living-room floor, where she was camped out with Luca and a magazine.

"This is Evelyn Glass," Evie whispered, dispensing with the formality of hello. "Please hold on." Evie walked through the living room without looking at Nicole, took the steps two at a time, and locked herself in her master bathroom.

"I'm back," she said, hoping she didn't sound as though she was sitting on a closed toilet.

"Hello, Ms. Glass."

She recognized the nasal monotone of the agent assigned to her, Mr. Donald Baker from Midwest Mutual, but Evie did not want to seem comfortable or familiar or friendly. She was none of those, so it was easy. "Have you worked out the glitches with my ex-husband's policy?"

"Ms. Glass, we need a court-certified copy of your divorce decree along with the original marriage license for you and Mr. Glass."

A few years ago Evie would have corrected him. A Ph.D. made Richard *Dr.* Glass. She was no longer concerned with propriety or labels. "Are you kidding me? I sent you all that weeks ago."

"I wish I was kidding, Ms. Glass. We need certified and original documents. We also need the death certificate for your ex-husband."

A balloon swelled in Evie's throat, closing her airway; she gasped for breath. "What is the problem? He paid the premiums, didn't he? Oh my God, don't tell me he let the policy lapse."

"The policy was current at the time of death."

Momentary paralysis set into Evie's limbs. "What does that mean?"

"It means there were no problems before he passed. The problems with the policy are coming up postmortem, which is why we need the additional documentation. It's really just details, Ms. Glass. When the file is complete, we'll have resolution and disbursement of funds."

Evie shook her leg to stop it from falling asleep. "Doesn't anyone care that I have children to feed?" Silence. "How long will this take?"

"I can't say, ma'am."

"You can't say or you won't say, Mr. Baker?"

"I won't speculate. Every case is different."

Evie had started to hate the word *different*.

"I'll stay home with Nicole," Sam said without looking away from the computer monitor.

"No, you'll come with me. It's part of today's math lesson," Evie said.

Sam pushed away from the dining-room table. "The grocery store is math. *Right*."

"Right. Get your stuff on. Let's go."

"We'll come too if that's okay," Nicole said. She looked at Evie and winked.

"Sure," Evie said. "The more the merrier." The more the weirder is what she meant, but Nicole was trying to help and Evie knew it. *Be nice, be nice, be nice.* It was getting easier to be nice.

Walking through the grocery-store parking lot, Evie said, "Now remember, you're going to estimate the weight of the fruits and vegetables and cross things off the list as we put them in the cart. Maybe you'll even figure out the total bill before we get to the register."

"I thought you were joking," Sam said.

"Yep, I'm a comedian."

Sam huffed but followed her, and Nicole and Luca followed him. They were a freakish family parade going into Jewel. All they needed were some flags and batons.

"Hey, Evie, nice to see you," said Gwen Barton, who seemed camped out amid the organic produce. Gwen chaired Eden's PTO, had launched the neighborhood book club, and was president of their temple's sisterhood. She eyed the meager contents of Evie's cart. Evie knew Gwen had already snapped a mental picture of Evie's hoodie du jour and the banana clip in her hair.

"Nice to see you too, Gwen," Evie said. Gwen's cart almost toppled over with the green-stickered produce in her own reusable tote bags and three half gallons of soy milk.

"We miss you at Bunco," Gwen said, never taking her eyes off the nutrition label on organic soy cheese.

"Sorry I can't be there anymore."

"It's understandable. Karen had been waiting for a Wednesday-night opening, so it wasn't a problem. She was thrilled to take your place."

The story of Evie's life.

Gwen leaned over her cart handle and whispered, "How are the kids doing?" Her eyes were wide. She almost licked her lips. Evie knew Gwen anticipated an avalanche of information, which she could then disperse through an e-mail list or phone tree.

"They're both doing fine, thanks for asking." Evie stepped as far back from Gwen as she could get without landing in the arugula and risking a misting.

"I'm so glad. It must be so hard." Gwen's eyes shifted across the store, then back to Evie.

"The kids are doing fine. Thanks for asking." Evie felt like a doll whose string you pull and she says the same thing over and over and over. It was all she said to anyone about her kids. She was too tired to recount details that would evoke pity but no answers. Did Gwen want to know Sam was estimating the total so that they had enough cash? That COBRA ate half of the Social Security checks? Probably not.

Nicole pushed her cart, with Luca tethered into the seat, right up next to Evie. "Hi, I'm Nicole. And this is Luca."

"Oh, I'm sorry," Evie mumbled. "Nicole, Gwen. Gwen, Nicole—and Luca." Evie put out her finger and Luca grabbed it.

"So, I hear Evie took you in," Gwen said, lifting one eyebrow at Evie.

Evie gasped. "Where did you hear that?"

"Not much goes on without everyone knowing."

"Well, maybe everyone should mind their own business," Nicole said.

Naive Nicole. Gwen made everyone's business her own, so to her, she was doing just that.

Gwen looked Nicole up and down. "Sweetie, if you minded *your* own business, Evie wouldn't be in this mess."

"Knock it off, Gwen. Please," Evie whispered, and cocked her head to the right toward Sam. Then she remembered Nicole was listening too. "You don't know the whole story."

Gwen put up her hand like a crossing guard. "I don't want to know the whole story," she almost certainly lied. "I know quite enough."

"I'm happy to lend Evie a hand," Nicole said.

"I think Evie's had enough of your type of help."

"She's a big help with the twins," Evie said, touching Nicole's foot with her own. No one needed to know their living arrangement was because Evie needed Nicole in order to pay the mortgage. Let them all think it was Evie who was doing Nicole the favor, although Nicole could have used the good press.

Gwen looked at her watch. "Whatever works for you. Truly. *I don't judge.* But I do have to go. I'm meeting someone for lunch." She walked off pushing her cart without acknowledging Nicole.

"I'm sorry she was so rude," Evie said as Sam dumped bananas and apples and oranges and two cucumbers into the cart. "Get four potatoes," Evie said.

Sam sighed and Evie watched him scan the bins of yellow, white, red, purple, and sweet potatoes.

"She's rude?" Nicole said. "You didn't even try to tell her what's really going on."

"And what is really going on?"

"I can go back to my house, I could sell it and buy something else, I could go back to Iowa, I just don't want to. You *need me* to stay. You can't pay your mortgage or your bills without me."

Nicole had a firmer grasp of the situation than Evie had thought. "Beth told me you rented out the house, so don't threaten me with moving—because now you don't have anywhere to go."

"It's a month-to-month lease. I can go back anytime." Nicole turned away and then to Evie. "Beth told you?"

"I know Beth is nice to you. She's nice to everyone. But she's loyal to me."

Nicole shuffled her feet, as if trying to get away without moving. "So you think it's okay for that Gwen to think this arrangement is *charity* if the charity is *me*?"

"It's a little more complicated than that."

"Is it?"

"If I remember correctly, you so desperately wanted out of your house that you kept showing up at mine—uninvited."

"If I remember correctly, you offered to let me move in and said you'd accept my offer to pay. I didn't beg, I just suggested it would benefit both of us."

"Fine. You're right. Next time I see Gwen I'll make sure she understands."

"Thanks," Nicole said, her voice lifting.

"No problem." It was no problem because Evie would just make sure she didn't see Gwen Barton until the insurance money came through or she'd gotten a job, or both.

Chapter 11

LANEY STEPPED OUT OF HER car and trekked through the pristine foot of snow on the patch of grass that separated the friends' driveways, her boots disappearing under her knee-length coat. Evie knew what would follow.

"Why didn't you tell me you had a showdown with Gwen? I had to hear it from Beth, who heard it from Darcy, who heard it from Gwen! Don't leave me out of the loop like that!"

Evie clamped her lips to invoke Laney's silence.

"Hey, Sam!" Laney said, giving him a thumbs-up through her leather gloves. "He didn't hear me," she whispered.

Sam stood his shovel in a pile of snow and waved.

"Finish the bottom step and then you can be done," Evie said to him. "I'll make hot chocolate when I come inside."

Sam scooped the final bit of snow, stomped into the house, and slammed the door before Evie could tell him not to. Evie wondered if he took off the boots or if she'd slip on the wet floor when she removed her own boots. Time would tell.

"So why didn't you call me?" Laney said again. "If you're going to bite someone's head off, give *me* a heads-up next time."

"It wasn't a showdown. And believe it or not, this isn't about you." Evie turned her back and shoveled imaginary snow.

Laney grabbed the broom that was leaning against a bush and

swept away the snow dust left on the walkway. "She said you were rude. I said you were exhausted. I have a feeling it was both." Evie felt pushed into a corner with each swoosh of the broom. Laney cared. Laney meant well. Laney pushed more than snow.

"Really? She said just 'rude'? She was a pain in the ass. It's over." Evie surveyed her blanketed front lawn, then walked down the clean driveway to look at the house from the street. Alan had used his snowblower on the driveway, but Evie insisted he leave the path and steps for Sam. Sam needed to know that being home meant pitching in, not watching TV. Standing at the curb, Evie thought the new snow on her roof made her house look like an iced cupcake; the icicles hanging off the edge of the roof were like candy decorations ready to be plucked and eaten, except that one was big enough, and looked sharp enough, to spear a fish.

Laney, chic even when bundled up, shooshed her way to Evie and stood shoulder to shoulder, speaking without looking at her. "It looks perfect. Your house always looks pretty in the snow." Evie knew it did. She and Richard had bought it in winter, snow-covered. It looked like the front of the Christmas card she'd never send.

"On the outside," Evie said. "The inside is a freaking mess." Although with Nicole's housework OCD, it was tidier than ever.

Laney looped her arm through Evie's. "I know." Laney tugged, and Evie let her friend lead her up the driveway and to the front door. "I won't tell you what to do, but maybe it's time for a little housecleaning."

"What do you mean you won't tell me what to do? You *always* tell me what to do." Evie's voice was louder than she intended.

"No. I tell you what I *think* you should do. What *I* would do. Obviously you do what you want." Laney rolled her eyes and smirked. Evie knew Laney expected her to laugh, but it wasn't funny.

"Well, now I want you to come inside and . . ." She wanted to ask Laney to scavenge in Evie's closet for interview clothes. She wanted to ask Laney to keep her company while she scoured more websites for jobs. She wanted to sit in the kitchen and sip a lukewarm cup of coffee and solve the world's—or at least Lakewood's—problems. Evie wanted help, and asking for it was harder than shoveling snow.

"And what?"

"Never mind."

Evie turned the doorknob. She was relieved she hadn't been locked out. Banging on her own front door, Rex barking, Nicole and Sam running to the door to let her in was more action and attention than she wanted at the moment. She wanted to slip inside unnoticed. She wanted to slip inside unneeded. Just for a few minutes. Help from Laney came with effervescence and energy. Evie was too tired for help from Laney.

"Don't do that to me. I'll come in, just tell me what you want me to do. You want me to tell Nicole to leave? I'm all over it like wasabi on sushi." Laney grabbed Evie's arms and Evie pulled away hard.

"Don't do that," Evie yelled, her affection for Laney sidelined. "You can't do this to me anymore. She's not going anywhere. It's working for me."

"It's fucked up."

"Nobody asked you!" Evie pushed open the door and stepped, slamming the door shut behind her.

Laney stood on the other side yelling, "Hey, don't shut the door on me!"

She didn't have to be part of the solution, but she couldn't be another of Evie's problems. Evie couldn't deal with Laney and then come in and check the floor for slush, look for a job, chat with Nicole, dole out Sam's schoolwork, and call Midwest Mutual. Not to mention make hot chocolate.

Heart pounding from exasperation as well as exertion, Evie slid off her boots and put them on the vent. Sam's boots were neatly off to the side. Coat and hat in the closet, Evie considered her attire. Just like her house, she was appropriately dressed on the outside but a mess underneath. Evie had traded in her robe for a faded White Sox T-shirt, stretchy pants, and a hair clip. She was one sensible-shoe step away from embroidered kitten sweatshirts. She was glad Laney wasn't there to see the latest outfit; although Evie was surprised Laney didn't follow her into the house demanding something or other. Evie stayed on the rug in front of the door and looked at the floor in front of her. It was dry, no footprints. She tentatively walked through the living room to the kitchen without slipping.

Then through her thawing nose, Evie smelled hot chocolate.

"Sam? Did you make hot chocolate?" The kids had just started using the microwave on their own, but almost-boiling water was tricky. Two seconds too short, it's not hot enough; two seconds too long, it's scalding. Evie wondered if he was gulping clumps of powder or scorching his throat. Or both.

"Nicole made it," he said as Evie walked in.

Sam was sitting at the kitchen counter, Nicole on the stool next to him. They were slurping. Steam was rising from the cups. Evie looked at the pot on the stove. Nicole had made hot chocolate from scratch. Evie knew it was easy, but her hot chocolate came with tiny, cute marshmallows and out of a paper envelope. Her secret was adding a drop of vanilla and orange zest. Her concoction always smelled like winter—a potpourri of warmth and sweetness. She hated to admit that what had simmered on the stove smelled even better.

"Oh," Evie said. Yummy as it seemed, *she* had wanted to make hot chocolate for Sam, to sit and have a mom moment with him before she opened up the textbooks again and became the taskmaster and teacher. She wanted time for just the two of them that wasn't in the middle of the night when they played with Sam's demons. Evie fumbled for words. She did not want hot chocolate that Nicole had made, but it was nice of Nicole to do it. Nicole had probably wiped the water from the floor and stood Sam's boots in the corner. Was this what it was like to have an au pair or a nanny? Those were two things Evie had never wanted—and still didn't. She wanted help with the bills. But help with the twins was something she wasn't used to—and didn't want to get used to. There had to be rules to follow in this new arrangement. Was Nicole a tenant or family? Could someone be both? Did Evie want either?

"There's plenty left," Nicole said. "I'll get it for you." She slipped from her seat and wiped her mouth with the back of her hand and grabbed a mug.

"I don't want any, but thanks," Evie said. "It was nice of you to make it for Sam."

"I was glad to have a little one-on-one time with him while Luca is napping."

Nicole's having one-on-one time with Evie's kids wasn't what she had in mind. Problem was, Evie didn't know what she had in mind. Thoughts fired like little pops of light going this way and that. Job, kids, house, Nicole, Scott, Lisa, Beth, insurance, Laney.

Laney. She'd opened the door for Nicole, but shut it on Laney.

That was wrong. But wrong was working just fine.

The house was night-quiet. Evie sat on the couch, water glass on the table next to her, bowl of popcorn nestled in her lap. She closed her eyes, just for a second, and listened to nothing. Then, Rex jumped next to her, and she opened her eyes in time to catch spilling popcorn and push it back into the bowl. She leaned on the big dog for comfort, and he nuzzled into her thigh.

Nicole appeared at the doorway in her robe and slippers. "I just wanted to say good night."

"Good night." It was time for movie and popcorn for one.

Nicole leaned against the wall with her shoulder, as though she had wiggled into a nook. "What are you going to watch?"

"Just a chick flick."

"I love chick flicks, which one?"

"Not sure," Evie said, lying. She always popped in her DVD of *My Big Fat Greek Wedding* when she needed a laugh. This was her second copy, and she was betting she'd need a third before summer.

"Enjoy your movie." Nicole stepped backward slowly, navigating the short ridge between the living room and the kitchen without looking. "See you in the morning." Her feet padded so slowly, Evie knew she wasn't going anywhere fast. "Good night."

"Good night."

"Do you mind if I make some popcorn? I'll take it downstairs. I'm not really very tired."

Evie sighed. "Get a bowl. There's too much here for one person." Although she knew she could have downed the whole thing, Evie was willing to share the popcorn, but not the movie.

Kumbaya moment complete, Evie assumed she'd cuddle up to Rex, hit PLAY, and giggle into a happy, sleepy stupor. Instead, she hit PAUSE when she heard water flowing, and swishing and scraping noises coming from the kitchen.

"What are you doing?" she said to Nicole, who was up to her elbows in yellow rubber gloves.

"It's just a little Ajax."

Evie knew what it was, she just didn't know why Nicole was doing it. "Why are you cleaning the sink at eleven o'clock?" Anyway, the sink was clean.

"Look, thanks for, um, rearranging the pantry," Evie said, putting the cleanser under the sink. "You don't have to do this kind of thing." Evie had switched back the cabinets, and once Nicole left the kitchen, she'd drip something into the sink. "And thanks for folding Sophie and Sam's laundry and for feeding Rex, but those are the kids' chores."

"I'm just trying to help." Nicole backed away and into the counter. She pulled off the gloves, stared at the surface of the counter, grabbed a sponge, and rubbed off dried mustard.

"Must be from Sophie's lunch," Evie said. She'd have noticed it by tomorrow's lunch. Probably.

"I clean when I'm tense," Nicole said, scrubbing harder and longer than it took to remove a raindrop-size bit of dried mustard from the granite. Then her arm stretched across the counter as she wiped stripes of damp sponge in neat rows. Top to bottom, lift, top to bottom, again and again. And then, Nicole started to cry.

It was too late for more than just a scrap of sympathy. Evie rubbed her hands on her thighs to stop herself from reaching out, touching Nicole, offering comfort. Evie had to reserve her energy and her touch for her children. But she could spare kind words. "You can put the pantry back in alphabetical order in the morning."

"That's not it. I'm sorry." Evie slid a box of Kleenex across the counter, crisscrossing the neat, damp rows. Nicole moved closer to Evie. "I talked to my mom today."

Evie plucked a bunch of tissues, handed them to Nicole, and said nothing. She only thought of what waited for her at the top of the stairs. More crying? Or, as on some nights, would the kids sleep until morning, allowing Evie only her own disruptive sleep to contend with?

"She just doesn't get it," Nicole said. "She didn't get why I left and she doesn't get why I want to stay. She wants us to move back and live with her."

Not until I get a job. Please don't leave until I get a job. "What did you say?"

"I said you needed me here. And she freaked."

Evie grimaced even though it was true.

Nicole grabbed Evie's hands. Nicole's hands felt small, like a child's, but her grip was more like a vise. "My mother rehashes *everything.* She says if I hadn't had Lucy, none of this would have happened. She wanted me to have an abortion."

"You told me."

"She makes me feel like I set this whole thing in motion."

She had. They all had. If Nicole's mother hadn't had Nicole, it wouldn't have happened either. If Richard had been a barista instead of a grad student, they wouldn't have met in the library that day. If Lucy and Pete hadn't died; if the road wasn't icy; if Nicole had stayed in Iowa; if Richard was faithful; if Evie had not given him one more chance more than once.

If, if, if.

"Maybe you should go to therapy. I think it might help for you to have someone to talk to."

"I have been going." Nicole pulled her hair into a ponytail. Evie had seen Laney do the same thing a hundred times. Evie felt a pang but wasn't sure if the surprise or the familiar instigated it.

"Really? When?"

"On Tuesday afternoons. I take Luca with me."

When Nicole left to run errands, Evie didn't ask where she was going, ever. Where else did Nicole go? What else did Nicole do? "Oh, good for you." Evie stopped herself from giving a thumbs-up with her response that sounded like the perfunctory "Good job" that parents were taught to say no matter what their kids did, as long as they tried. But in this case, it got her off the comment hook. Maybe that's how all parents used it, as something to pull out of their back pocket when there was nothing else to say. But she wasn't Nicole's parent. Evie had two grieving children and did not want a third. And she no longer wanted to watch a movie.

Upstairs, the peaceful-sleep theory was also being challenged. In Evie's bed, Sophie was asleep with the blanket up to her neck, stuffed animals on her right, peeking out at Evie. Evie turned on

the night-light and took her place next to a floppy tiger and thread-
bare hippo. Sophie opened her eyes.

"How long are Nicole and Luca going to live with us?"

All Evie wanted was to go to sleep. "I don't know yet, Soph. It's
too late to talk about it now. Plus, there's a lot for me to think
about."

"Like what?" She closed her eyes. Instant sleep would have
served Evie well, but Sophie's eyelids fluttered. She was awake and
waiting. Had Sophie slept at all?

"Like the fact that everything is new again for our little family."
Not *incomplete*, not *broken*, not *unfinished*. *Little*. It sounded cute, or it
did when Richard was alive and Evie had settled on that label. "Every day we're figuring out something new about what it's like for
you to not have Daddy around anymore. I just don't know if I want
someone else to be part of that."

"Luca is our brother."

Why did everyone keep reminding her when all she had to do
was look at Luca and see bits of both of her kids in his dimples and
curls? "I know he is, sweetie, which is why you'll always be part of
his life. I'm just not sure that has to mean he's living here forever,
that's all. But I won't make any decisions without telling you,
okay?" Evie cursed Richard for leaving a legacy of strangeness.
She kissed Sophie on the lips. "I'm going to check on Sam. Go to
sleep."

It might have been after eleven, but Sam was sitting up in bed
and the TV was on.

"Not tired, Sam?"

"Not really."

Evie sat on his quilt. Sam wiggled his legs so she had more space.

"How long is Luca staying?"

"Sophie just asked me that. Is this a plan to gang up on me?"
Evie squinted in faux dismay and crossed her arms in a make-believe
huff. She remembered well the times the twins had concocted

schemes to stay up later, eat more dessert, score a new video game. It had been a while; she'd have welcomed being undermined.

"No, I'm just wondering. I like having them here but . . ."

"But what?" Did Evie have a ten-year-old ally in her not-knowing-what-to-do quandary?

"Why is someone else living in Dad's house?"

"Yeah, why?" Sophie stood at the door, curls a mess, nightgown twisted. She climbed onto Sam's bed and stared at Evie with pining eyes.

"How do you two know this?"

"Nicole told us the last time we were there that we wouldn't be going back," Sophie said.

Parenting Evie's kids without her permission was worse than rearranging the soups and pastas. "Houses cost a lot of money. So that family is paying Nicole to live there, and Nicole is helping out here by giving me some money for living here." Evie fast-forwarded her thoughts. It seemed like too much information, but she wanted always to be honest with them. Within reason.

"If someone else is living in Dad's house, then Nicole and Luca can't leave. They won't have anywhere to go," Sophie said.

"Don't worry about it. No one is going anywhere." Not yet.

"I hate that someone else is living in Dad's house," Sam said.

"Me too," Sophie said, wiggling closer to her brother.

Strangers were sitting in their chairs, sleeping in their beds, doing everything but eating their porridge. Interlopers peppered all their lives.

"Will we have to move and let other people live here?" Sophie gasped.

"No! We're staying right here." Evie couldn't undo the divorce or bring Richard back, but she could keep her kids in their home feeling safe and comfortable.

"How do you *know*?" Sam challenged her, always.

"Because I said so, that's why," Evie snapped. That old-fashioned answer would have to suffice. The better answer was *Because I'm going to get a job and because that insurance money is going to cover some expenses and pay for college. That's how.* The thoughts bounced around in her brain as if they were in a pinball machine, but she still wasn't convinced.

That had to change.

Chapter 12

JOB, JOB, JOB, JOB, JOB. Evie pushed the power button on the computer, then crossed her fingers. Ever since Alan had told her about the job at County, she was stuck on it—and for once she liked being stuck. It didn't matter that she imagined herself in a graduation gown with a mortarboard on her head, as if that were Casual Friday attire for a suburban pseudo-academic. She thought of the body and hair flaws it would hide, then shook her head to release the image and got back to the reality of being unemployed in her pajamas.

The first sip of coffee was always the best, and Evie downed the cup and scanned the list of e-mails that had arrived since the night before. Eden Elementary News, Lakewood Library Newsletter, coupons for pizza, Scott, junk mail from foreign countries, soccer registration.

Scott?

Evie had never e-mailed Scott. She'd placed him to the side of her thoughts. It had been almost two months since they were a couple if she counted the first night of shiva as their last date. Evie could just delete the e-mail without reading it. That would simplify things—but that was rude. Evie closed one eye, which for some reason always made reading something unpleasant a little less so. She read the first line: *I miss you.* Then she opened her other eye.

"Laney is better at this than me," Beth said, shaking her head as if disapproving of the rift between her friends, not the outfit of choice. "Here, try this." Beth unclasped her everyday pearls, held them up to Evie's neck, then put them back on herself. "If I dress you, you'll look like me," she said. "Laney has a knack."

"Laney has a knack all right," Evie said, ignoring Beth's nudge and draping a scarf around her shoulders, which she then fashioned into a stylish noose. "I could do worse than to look like you." Evie untwisted the scarf and stuffed it back into the drawer. Evie checked her fading roots in the mirror, grateful for poor lighting. Nicole had done a good job on the touch-up, but the cheap stuff from the box just didn't last as long as the expensive stuff from the salon. "I'm wasting my time."

"It's not a waste of time to look nice tonight." Beth rummaged through Evie's closet, pulled out a cardigan, and put it back. "Are you sure I can't call Laney? You can't stay mad at each other forever."

"She has to stop telling me what to do."

"Nobody's perfect."

"You're pretty close."

Beth placed her hands on Evie's shoulders and squeezed with gentle, Beth-like pressure, then let go and backed away. "Nobody's perfect, Ev. Not Laney, not you, and certainly not me. Let me call her."

"No." Evie had missed Laney since she'd slammed the door in her face. She'd driven past Laney at least once a day and given a perfunctory nod. Other times she'd noticed Laney outside, so Evie stayed inside. She had not ignored someone since eleventh grade when Hannah Brooks betrayed her by joining the cheerleading squad instead of the pom-poms as they'd planned, but that exercise in silence and snubbing only lasted from lunch until seventh period. Evie hadn't spoken to Laney in six days. She had almost called her countless times. But almost didn't count.

"I'll probably have to turn around when I'm halfway there because the kids are upset."

"You're underestimating Sam and Sophie—and Nicole. And me for that matter."

"What are you talking about?"

"Your kids need to see you going out and coming back. It's the normal stuff that's going to ground them. Besides, Nicole adores them and they adore her."

"Don't remind me." Evie traded her gray blouse for a black knit tee and then back again. "What does that have to do with you?"

"I told Nicole I'd hang out here, keep her and the kids company."

"You have a playdate with Nicole?" These shifting allegiances were making Evie dizzy.

"I'm helping out."

"By spending the evening with Nicole."

"Yes. You want us to be nice to her, right?"

"Right."

"I'm being nice."

Too nice, Evie thought.

Downstairs, with Beth as her escort, Evie spun around, wishing her long, black skirt were wide enough to twirl.

"Why are you all dressed up?" Sam said.

"I have a meeting."

Sam stared at her.

"A dinner meeting with some businesspeople and . . ."

That was TMBI—too much boring information—for a ten-year-old. Sam went back to his video game, head near the screen, knees tucked to his chest.

"What do you think, Soph?"

Sophie shrugged and rolled the ball with Luca.

"Well, you look great," Nicole said.

"It's amazing what a little makeup and a flat iron can do."

"Important meeting, huh? Just a meeting? Are you sure?" Nicole smiled without showing her teeth, an all-knowing smile, and Beth winked at her.

As soon as Evie was out of her driveway, the cell phone rang. *Please let it not be Sam or Sophie or Nicole or even Midwest Mutual.*

"Where are you going?" Laney said.

"That's what you say after a week?" This was obviously how the friend fence-mending was going to happen. On the phone. While driving. On Laney's terms. As always.

"Chill. I just happened to see you pull away, and I noticed there were no kids in your car. And you look—well—you look *dressed.* I'm not mad at you anymore for slamming the door in my face."

"Then I'm not mad at you anymore for being a pain in the ass." That part was the truth, and it surprised Evie, but the reconnection soothed her.

"So Nicole is watching the kids?"

"Very good, Lane, you used her name. Yes, Nicole is watching the kids. She does live with us, remember? And Beth is there."

"Beth is with Nicole?"

"That's what I said."

"Does that bother you?"

"Should it?" Evie turned up the volume on her earpiece. This conversation might get her most of the way downtown.

"Well, I don't want to spend time with her."

"You don't like her. Beth does."

"And that concerns me."

It concerned Evie too, but she didn't concede that to Laney. She was willing to share her house, but not her best friends. "She's doing it for me, not for Nicole."

"If you say so. As long as Beth doesn't think the widow is hanging out with us when we have coffee."

"It's no big deal, Lane. It's just a few hours."

"Whatever. Where did you say you were going?"

"I didn't, but I'm going to meet with—with—with my lawyer."

"On a Friday night?"

"Yes."

"Right. Well, it doesn't matter why you're out, I'm just glad you're out of the house with lipstick on."

"Thanks." Evie laughed. "I'll talk to you tomorrow, okay? Come for coffee. I'll hold the door wide-open."

"Sounds perfect," Laney said with a chuckle. "Just one more thing."

Evie merged into Friday traffic where the express lanes were clogged but the local lanes flowed. "Fine. One more thing."

"Tell Scott I said hello."

Evie parked the minivan and checked her hair and lip gloss in the rearview mirror. Only then did she dare look at her watch. Twenty minutes early. Out of the car, she slid her debit card into a parking meter and picked the maximum amount of time—three hours.

She walked up Taylor Street toward Café Rosa. Streetlamps, trash cans, and newspaper boxes lined the curb in Little Italy, which was not so trendy when she used to go there with Richard. Evie strode slowly, with purpose. Her intention was not to be too early and to look as though she belonged. Only a few months back, driving into the city to have dinner with Scott was commonplace yet exciting. She'd have spent the evening, then the night, then the weekend, at his Lincoln Park condo. They'd have brunch at Nookies, meander through the zoo, or walk along North Avenue Beach. They'd often concoct a late-day feast from findings at Green City Market. Evie shivered, and the memories fell away. Navigating Chicago for six months had earned Evie her grown-up city stripes—but in the past two months she'd been demoted to full-time suburbanite. Now every step reminded her that heels hurt, she sweated when she was nervous, and the city was colder than Lakewood.

The aromas taunted her. The drama of strangers' conversations baited her. And the hum of the motors and the pop and slam of car doors, the whistle of buses and swish of their brakes, all begged to replace her current life in Lakewood.

Disappointments overwhelmed her lately, and there had been enough of them to last a lifetime. She focused on Café Rosa, two corners ahead. One step at a time would get her there; even with baby steps she'd arrive on cue. The temperature was still cold enough to keep the snow atop the awnings looking fresh and her breath like puffs of white smoke, but not so cold that she would arrive at the restaurant with teary eyes. She was grateful for the small things, or tried to be.

The windows showed her reflection. The transparent image revealed grown-out layers: full hair where she wished it were flat, and flat hair where she wished it were full. Her trench coat was no longer fully double-breasted. The mirror at home was much more forgiving. Or maybe she was ambivalent when she looked into that mirror. When she was there, it didn't matter who looked back.

People scurried along the street, toward buses and idling cars. Some people sauntered and window-shopped. They were seeking the perfect apology bouquet, the right dessert for their weekend dinner party, or the latest edition of the newspaper. Evie searched through the glass for her newest identity.

Café Rosa had a wooden façade with an oversize revolving door that turned automatically. With her first step Evie knew, had she just kept going, she could have left the restaurant the same moment she entered it. Instead, she landed at the foot of the wine bar.

She positioned herself on one of the black leather barstools and folded her coat over its back. She crossed her ankles.

"What can I get you tonight?" the bartender asked.

"Shiraz," she said with assurance.

The wine was in front of her in an instant. Evie slid a few bills across the bar, sipped, examined her claret lipstick stain on the wineglass, and looked around for an inconspicuous way to detect Scott's entrance behind her, perhaps in a reflection from a wine bottle or a wall mirror. She counted the decorative bottles lining the wall to her left and lost count at eighty bottles. Using her thumb, she twirled her delicate divorce-ring around her finger. Someone touched Evie's shoulder.

She spun around, disarmed, for just a moment.

"Scott!"

They eased into a hello hug. He kissed her cheek and grabbed both of her hands.

"You look great," he said.

Scott, in a knit turtleneck and sport coat, with his receding hairline unapologetically gelled to one side, was such a cute liar.

He motioned for her to walk ahead of him to their table, pulled out her chair, put his hand on her back as she sank into the tufted seat as if to make sure she didn't drown in the white tablecloth. Evie smoothed the napkin on her lap for something to do, tucking it just under the hem of her gray silk blouse. At five foot four, her legs never made a ninety-degree angle when she sat at attention, so cloth napkins had an annoying way of sliding to the floor.

"I'm glad you wanted to see me. I'm sorry it couldn't be last weekend," Scott said, folding his hands on his closed menu. He leaned forward just a few inches, an attentive gesture Evie had forgotten. She swatted her hair from her shoulder, and the dos and don'ts of dating resurfaced as if they'd been waiting on the bench to be called into the game. Smile. Keep it light. *Keep it light. Focus on the positive.*

"You got called away, I understand." It didn't matter where he was or what he was doing, he had wanted to see her, and now she was on a date.

"Good! Now tell me what's going on with you."

"I applied for a job at County College," she said, genuine excitement resonating in her words. "To teach history."

"That would be perfect for you."

He was right. And he knew Evie well enough to *be* right.

"I hope you get it," he added. "I've been known to have crushes on my teachers." Scott reached across the table, tapped Evie's hand, and slid his hand into it. With the other hand he then opened his menu, his eyes zigzagging across the page too fast to be reading it. Evie's heart thumped in her ears. The back of her neck perspired. "How are your kids?" he said without looking up but with a little squeeze.

A hollow dread replaced the fluttering in Evie's chest. She dropped her gaze to the list of appetizers. He didn't want to hear about the nights she'd lain awake waiting for Sam to throw up or the mornings she pored over scores of websites hoping to find an extra dollar coupon or the job of the century. It wasn't easy to explain the strange connection with Nicole or how she had begun noticing nuances about Luca. Scott might have insight into Midwest Mutual's runaround, but did he really need to know her finances were a mess? Like her reflection in the shop window, Evie's thoughts revealed what people feared most.

The truth.

Scott's and Evie's knees touched beneath the table. She didn't know if it was an accident or a nudge but didn't take it as a push to purge.

"Things are getting a little better every day," she said. That wasn't a lie. It was enough. And it was what people wanted to hear.

"I'm glad."

"So," Evie said, invoking one of the most important rules of dating, the one she wished more men adhered to. *Turn it around.* "Tell me what's going on with *you*."

Scott's flair for storytelling rivaled his knack for listening. Evie laughed through her salad course. Their linked fingers stayed attached atop a few scattered bread crumbs until the waiter arrived with their entrées. Evie's cheeks ached with evidence of happiness, her long-lost friend. It was good to be out with Scott; Lisa was right. Belly full of laughs and dinner, she could admit that. Maybe they would pick up where they'd left off with the rugelach, and maybe dates would always be as easy as a cheap dye job and two willing babysitters.

Then her phone buzzed in her purse.

Evie deflated. "Excuse me," she said, glancing at the phone. Home. She didn't ignore it but pretended to.

"You should answer it. I don't mind." Scott tore a piece of bread and searched the table landscape for the pats of butter, which were right in front of him. She and Scott had never experienced kid intrusions on their weekends before because the kids were with Richard. Scott didn't know Evie the mom, only Evie the woman. And she knew more than ever before the two Evies were not always the same person.

"I do mind. We're having a nice dinner and I don't want to change that." She smiled and poked her fork into something beige, then pushed it off the fork. Interruptions were not good for the appetite. She felt as though she'd disappointed him—and didn't like that feeling. It was hard to date men without children. They didn't get it. Or that was what Evie told herself so she could blame someone besides her kids.

The phone buzzed seven more times. "I'm sorry. I need to call home."

Standing in the ladies' room, Evie dialed Beth's cell phone.

"What's going on there?" Evie said without saying hello.

"Nothing," Beth said. "We're doing great. Why did you call? Go back to Scott and have fun."

"My phone keeps ringing."

"Hold on a sec."

As if holding on while standing in the bathroom of Café Rosa were better than actually talking on the phone in the bathroom.

"Nicole said she didn't call you. It must be your kids calling from the basement phone. They keep going down to bring up new toys for Luca to play with. Hold on."

Evie felt her whole life was like this phone call.

"Yep, it's your kids. They want to say good night. I'll hold out the phone and they can do it at the same time."

Evie pictured Beth giving the twins a one-two-three signal, then heard, "Good night, Mom!"

"Did you hear them?"

"The whole bathroom heard them."

"You're in the bathroom? Get back to dinner! I'll be here with Nic when you get home—we're going to get the kids all into bed then have a glass of wine."

Nic? Wine? Maybe Evie should go home.

"Ev?"

"Yes?"

"I'm sorry the kids called. They're fine, really. You go have fun and don't think about any of us."

Beth had surely lost her mind.

Scott stood when Evie returned to the table. Impeccable manners. Tailored clothes. Straight teeth and an Ultra Brite smile. Evie sat and hoped the noise from scooting in her chair masked her audible sigh of delight mixed with fear.

"Everything okay?"

"The kids just aren't used to me going out. They wanted to say good night."

"That's nice." Scott looked left, then right, then right at Evie. "They could *get* used to it, right?" he said, eyes stretched wide with childlike anticipation.

Evie almost agreed, but the truth cut in line. Anyone she dated would have to acclimate to the way things were—just like her parents and Lisa and Laney. Two kids, no dad. A widow and a baby.

Everyone stubborn enough to stick around was figuring it out along the way—just like her. Evie shrugged.

Scott smiled not out of happiness, but understanding. "Your life isn't getting back to normal anytime soon, is it?" He reached across the table and cradled her cheek the way she'd seen in the movies, but this was not going to end with happily ever after. His fingers trailed away but left an indelible mark.

"No," Evie said.

Scott looked away, then right at her. "It's so complicated."

"I know."

"Too complicated."

"I know."

"I can't—"

"I know," she interrupted, and lifted both her eyebrows so high her temples tightened. Then, once she released, Evie's neck muscles loosened. Her arms and legs softened. Evie looked at Scott. He had an inherent ease about him, even now. He looked the way she felt. Without the weight of more wondering about what-ifs and maybes, perhaps she'd stop thinking and just enjoy the evening out—and Scott.

"Are you okay?" he whispered.

Evie shimmied up her seat. "You know what? I am." She took his hand and squeezed to prove she meant it.

Scott held on. "Do you have a curfew?" He signed the credit-card slip with his free hand and closed the black folder.

"Nope." Evie quipped, "The troops said I could stay out as late as I want. I guess I'm being rewarded for good behavior."

Scott chuckled as he stood, pulling Evie with him in a dance move. "Well now, *that* works for me."

"Me too," she said, allowing herself to be kissed tableside.

"We'll put more time on the meter and come back for your car later, okay?" It wasn't a question.

Evie nodded and leaned in for another kiss.

A girl had a right to some dessert.

Evie walked into the house at two A.M. She assumed Nicole would be asleep on the sofa. She did not expect to find Beth and Laney sitting on the couch playing gin rummy.

"Welcome home," Beth said, laying down a hand of fours. "Gin." She looked at Evie.

"What are you doing?"

"This one came to her senses around eleven," Laney said, stacking and shuffling the deck. "She told Nicole to go downstairs and she called me."

"In Nic's defense, she wanted to stay up and wait, but I convinced her she needed her sleep."

"Plus I was coming over. I think I scare her."

"You think?" Evie sat on the arm of the sofa. "Why are you here?"

"To keep Beth company while you're out gallivanting around Chicago," Laney said with a wink.

"I am so sorry! I thought Beth would go home and Nicole would fall asleep out here until I got home. I didn't think you'd wait up for me like you were my parents or something." Evie was touched. And mortified.

"She's kidding! Do not apologize," Beth said. "The kids were fine and we were fine."

"And from the looks of it, Scott was fine too," Laney said.

Beth swatted Laney. "Did you have fun?"

"Did she have fun? Look at her."

Evie ran her hands through her hair. She hadn't considered trying to tuck in her blouse or even make sure it was correctly buttoned. She'd assumed she would slip into the house and into bed unnoticed. She had assumed wrong.

Good thing *wrong* felt very right.

"When are you going to see him again?" Beth said while clapping without making a sound. "Want to triple-date?"

"I'm not dating him."

"What do you mean you're not dating him?"

"What do you mean, what do I mean? I'm not dating him. He's a great guy, but it doesn't work. Not now anyway."

"But you did sleep with him, right?" Laney said. "Because if you didn't, you should know, *disheveled* is not a good look for you."

"Yes, I did," Evie said, less embarrassed, more empowered than moments before. She shifted her skirt to the right position with the zipper in the back.

Laney presented her palm to Beth, who shook her head and handed over a dollar.

Chapter 13

EVIE WAITED FOR NICOLE AND Luca at the front door of the Lakewood Sports Center. Evie had brought the twins early—Sophie to practice with her team and Sam to hang out with his friends, like regular kids. Evie liked when it was *just three*. The instantly larger family of five had its benefits beyond the financial, but sometimes she wanted the twins to herself, even if they were nowhere nearby.

The ecofriendly building housed four gyms, and at nine A.M. the place buzzed with a five P.M. vibe, including parents in designer combat gear vying for the best seats on the bleachers.

Evie watched Nicole as she approached the building. She bounced as she walked, her head bobbing in a sea of parents and kids and strollers.

"Want me to push?" Evie asked.

Nicole stepped aside and Evie marched behind the stroller.

"Did you have fun last night?" Nicole asked.

"I did." Evie was getting comfortable sharing her house, but not her personal life.

"Beth told me you saw that guy. The one I met at shiva? I'm glad for you."

Evie would talk to Beth about discretion. "It was just dinner, we're not dating."

"Oh." Nicole clamped her mouth shut.

"Let's go find Sophie's team."

They walked down a long, glossy hallway past gymnasiums and bathrooms and down another long hallway past classrooms and the beloved concession stand to the Blue Gym. Sophie's team was playing in a fifth-grade-girls, double-elimination tournament. The screech of basketball shoes on the highly polished, paid-for-with-your-tax-dollars floors along with the jumbled conversations of parents escaped the open door. Evie knew many parents silently prayed for a loss so they could go home and get on with their day. Evie also knew many more prayed for a win. It didn't matter that all kids under twelve walked away with a "real" medal and coupons for free pizza and pop; or that Lakewood's version of March Madness was intended as a respite from the harsh Chicago winter. The daylong extravaganza was more about community spirit than the number of basketballs dunked. Evie hoped everyone remembered that as she stepped into the gym, Nicole by her side, Luca as their point guard.

Sam sat alone on one end of the first row of bleachers, a big T-shirt draped over his shoulders like a tallis, a Jewish prayer shawl.

"Why are you sitting here?" Evie said.

This was not what she had planned. She looked around the gym and saw familiar faces, but not the fifth-grade-boy faces she expected. "Where are your friends?"

Sam shrugged and whipped the shirt off his neck and pushed it into Evie's hands. She shifted the stroller back to Nicole and scooted next to her son. As Sam reached out his hand and touched hers, Evie's arms tingled as the blood drained. *Richard's shirt.*

"This is *Dad's* shirt," Sam said.

Evie remembered Richard had signed up to coach Sophie's team for this event. Which insensitive ass had given Sam the shirt?

"I remembered he was supposed to coach so I asked Soph to get it for me."

Evie put her arm around Sam and he leaned on her hard. She

glanced at the bench—girls in blue and yellow, lined up in front of two familiar Lakewood dads wearing shirts identical to Sam's. The coach-dads were bent forward, hands on their knees, mouths moving in pep-talk fashion as they primed their weekend, ponytailed athletes.

"Do you want me to keep it for you?" Evie asked.

"For a second." Sam twisted his arms, removed his hoodie, and thrust it at Evie inside out. He snatched the T-shirt with solemnity and pulled it over his head, further mussing his hair. The shirt reached to Sam's knees like a dress.

"Go find your friends, sweetie." Evie's shoulder tickled as she felt Nicole watching them, taking notes perhaps, and filing them away for future use.

Sam walked away without enthusiasm, but at least he walked away. She settled onto the first row of bleachers, leaving the end for Nicole and the stroller. With the bustle of the parent-fans around her, she closed her eyes to rest them—just for a second. Or so she thought.

"Sleeping on the job, Evie?"

Evie flinched, opened her eyes, and was face-to-face with Darcy Levin, Lakewood yenta extraordinaire. By noon everyone would know Evie was snoozing before the game. Conjecture would be she'd had trouble sleeping, which wasn't true. She just had trouble waking up. The inside of Evie's mouth was woolly and dry, but her lips and chin were wet. She was *drooling*.

"Hi, Darcy," she said, surreptitiously wiping her chin on her shirt before lifting her head.

Darcy eyed Luca.

Evie sat straighter and noticed the gym was more full than when she'd entered. She had actually dozed off. And drooled. Had she snored? Whimpered? *Talked?* Evie looked around. No one was even looking in her direction. She tapped Nicole's arm. "How long have I been asleep?"

"Five minutes. I figured you needed the nap, but don't worry, I wasn't going to let you sleep through the game."

Maybe Nicole should have jostled her so Evie could appear to be like the rest of the parents—ones who didn't fall asleep at basketball tournaments because they weren't out until 2:00 A.M. having good-bye sex with their now-ex-nonboyfriend.

Maybe Nicole *wanted* Evie to look like a slacker.

"Oh, here," Nicole said, digging into her diaper bag. "I brought you a bottle of water."

Darcy cleared her throat, unaccustomed to serving as an unwelcome third wheel. "This must be *the baby*."

"This is Luca, and this is Nicole," Evie said. "But you know that."

"Oh, forgive me for being rude," Darcy said. "We met at shiva. Your house is lovely by the way, if I didn't mention it then. I heard you rented your house to another professor from Pinehurst. When are you leaving Lakewood?"

"Thank you, it is a nice house," Nicole said, unfazed. "We're not leaving."

Darcy looked around the gym as if searching for words Evie knew were in her back pocket.

"Lakewood is a great place to raise children," Evie said, nodding.

"It's just strange that she, uh, Nicole, wouldn't want to be near her family at a time like this," Darcy said, staring wide-eyed at Evie, trying to interject subtext that Evie ignored.

"*She*—is right here. And what's strange about wanting to raise your child in a nice town near Chicago—*at a time like this*?"

"Nothing, I guess." Darcy raised her eyebrows at Evie.

Evie wiped the back of her finger across her eyebrows as if Darcy were telling her she had something on her face.

The yenta sighed.

"What's wrong, Darcy?" Evie asked.

"I heard a rumor. And you know how I hate it when rumors litter our little community."

Nicole swiveled away. Evie put her hand on Nicole's shoulder and turned her toward them. "You don't have to turn away. Anything Darcy has to tell me is fine for you to hear, especially if it's something she wants to tell me in the middle of a loud, noisy gym during a *family* event."

"Oh, sure. I just don't want people saying things that aren't true—especially when they're so *outlandish*."

"Well, if it's that good, *please* don't keep it to yourself."

Darcy leaned in for the gossip kill. "People are saying that she's staying with you. Permanently." Darcy stood straight and held her hands out in front of her. "I know, it's a funny thing to say, but I heard it. Twice. Such a pity when people concoct things for their own amusement."

"Such a pity when people dig for information," Evie said.

"I just thought it was a shame that tales are being passed around." Darcy put her hands in the air, surrendering. "Far be it from me to judge, but if it were me, I wouldn't want someone thinking the wrong thing."

"And what would that wrong thing be? That we're trying to make the bad situation a little better by helping each other out? Yes. Nicole is helping me by staying with me and the twins."

"*Oy, oy, oy.*" Darcy's eyes shifted to a group of women across the gym who were all looking at them. Darcy nodded and took a giant step back.

"Don't worry, Darcy." Evie rested her hand on Nicole's shoulder, just skimming the fabric. "We're not contagious."

"You were amazing with that Darcy woman." Nicole spit out the words as she and Evie waited in line for halftime coffee and Krispy Kremes.

"She pissed me off. Nobody messes with . . . with . . ."

"With what?" Nicole asked.

"With my family." *There. I said it.*

Nicole smiled. "Remind me not to get on your bad side. I mean, again."

"That would probably be your best bet."

"Hi, Evie, hi, Nicole."

More unwelcomed, long-unheard-from neighbors. At least Tina and Belinda had the moxie to address them by name.

"How are your kids, Evie?" Tina said.

"It's been really, really hard on all of us," Evie said, putting her arm around Nicole. No time like waiting in line.

Belinda knelt and put her hand out to Luca. "Babies are a good thing. No matter what."

Evie and Nicole both smiled. They knew it was true.

Tina said, "I'm sure it is hard. But one day at a time, right?"

"Right," Evie and Nicole said. Oversimplified to say the least, but still right in many ways.

"So is Sam coming back to school soon? Tyler misses him."

Tyler played with Sam twice a week after school, and they were on the same soccer team.

"I'll tell Sam that Tyler says hi."

"We're going to get to the back of the line," Belinda said, sliding her hand away from Luca. "Good to see you."

"That was an easy one," Evie said to Nicole, who nodded. "I guess not all hope is lost."

The line moved quickly, and between ordering and juggling Nicole's Pop-Tarts and her own burning coffee cup, Evie avoided any further questions until they were back in the gym, their seats occupied by a gaggle of library moms. Had she forgotten to return books?

"Hey, Evie," Lynn Rosenberg said. She was benign. It would be another easy nonconfrontation.

"Hi, Lynn." Evie nodded toward Nicole. "I'm not sure you've met Nicole."

Lynn shifted in place. "We met at, we met at, we met at . . ."

"I remember you," Nicole said. "Nice to see you."

"Same here," Lynn said. "So, Ev, how *are* the kids doing?"

"It depends on the day." *It depends on the minute.*

"Well, that's great. I'm glad to hear it. Let me know if you want to start volunteering at the library again. We could use your help— and a donation of course if you're feeling generous. Or if Nicole is feeling generous."

Oh my God, Lynn didn't even want to know about the kids. She was hitting Evie up for money. Darcy's news of their living arrangement had obviously not reached this do-gooder. A loud whistle blasted. For one second when Evie turned toward the court, she expected to see Richard. The memory lapse brought the glazed doughnut into her throat.

"If you don't mind, we'd like to sit and watch Sophie play the second half," Evie said. "We'll let you know when we can help you, though, thanks for asking."

Someone tapped Evie on the shoulder. The entire town seemed ready to pounce, to infringe on her personal space as a way to osmose information. She guessed it was more fun to do it in person than on Facebook, Twitter, or through text messages.

"Hi, Penny," Evie said.

"I don't want to bother you, but I wanted to ask how your kids are doing."

Evie turned to Penny, huffed, and then looked at the court. Pressure built on the top of Evie's head, as if it were going to implode. She ignored the rage. Sophie had the ball and was dribbling, dribbling, dribbling. All Evie wanted to do was cheer, but yelling echoed inside her. When Sophie passed the ball, Evie relaxed. She could squander a moment—just a moment—on regaining calm. Then, Evie turned to find Penny looking at her, eyebrows raised. Evie wondered, if Penny stayed that way through the whole first quarter of the game, would her eyebrows freeze halfway up her forehead? The thought made her smile. Perhaps she could get Penny to cross her eyes too.

"Evie, I said, how are your kids doing?" She put her hand on Evie's back and looked deep into her eyes. *Foiled.* Penny always wore too much eyeliner, and it flowed like brown creeks into the fine lines beneath her eyes. Evie wanted to watch basketball, drink her now cold coffee, and suck the sugar off her fingers. She wanted everyone to make space and keep quiet.

"It's terrible for them."

"Oh." Penny sat up and leaned back. Again, fear of contamination permeated the air. "But Belinda said that Gwen said that you said they were coming along fine."

"Then why did you ask?"

Penny blinked fast, rummaging through her mental list of answers. She didn't find one.

"They're not fine. Their father died. How would your kids be if Stephen dropped dead two months ago?"

Penny's eyes widened. "I just wanted to know how your kids are doing. You don't have to get defensive. But I realize it's not the real you talking. You're under a lot of undue stress." Penny glanced at Nicole and back at Evie.

"The undue stress came from your question." Evie stood. "I know you're interested . . ." She was going to say, *I know you care,* but that wasn't what she meant. The people who cared called, stopped by, and put in useful two cents when it was welcomed and even when it wasn't. "I am really just tired, Penny." Evie didn't want the Lakewood ladies as enemies, but they weren't her friends and she was tired of pretending otherwise. "I'm sure I'll see you around."

"I'm sure." Penny turned to walk away and turned back. "I do hope you and the kids are okay."

Evie forced a smile. "Thanks." She knew that exchange would make an excellent Bunco snack.

Nicole pulled on Evie's shoulder. Evie was sweating, her pulse racing and her throat dry. Without a word Nicole handed Evie her bottle of water.

"I want to say something," Nicole said.

With the hum of the spectators behind them, the bouncing ball, and the referee's whistles, it was easy for Evie to pretend she didn't hear. "Excuse me, what did you say? It's hard to hear you." Evie didn't want another confession or inappropriate remark or heart-felt admission. She just wanted to watch the basketball game.

Nicole made a megaphone with her hands and leaned toward Evie. Thank God for peripheral vision. Evie grabbed Nicole's hands and pressed them to the bench between her and Nicole and held them there.

"I've always loved watching the kids' games. I didn't know if it would make me happy or sad today—and it made me happy."

That was too much information for Evie.

"No matter what happens from here on out, I just wanted to tell you how much Luca and I appreciate being part of your family. I know it will work out. I know it will always work out for us."

Evie gulped Nicole's water as the ref's whistle blew.

Sam nudged himself between Nicole and Evie, his sweaty head gleaming under the bright lights. "Jacob called me a baby. Then they were *all* calling me a baby. All they want to know is when I'm coming back to school. I told them to shut up, that I didn't have to go back to school, ever, if I didn't want."

Evie blanked. "Well, saying 'shut up' wasn't very nice. Plus, it's the law, you have to go school eventually." *There was that law cop-out again.* She took his hand and he pulled it away. He was too old for public comfort, something she didn't like but knew was right. "Oh, here come the boys!" Sam winced. "Oh, I mean *guys*. Here come the guys. I bet they want to apologize for teasing you." She knew boys at that age didn't apologize without prodding from their parents, and Evie was comforted by the unexpected, invisible hug.

The four boys walked over to the bleachers, passing Nicole without a nod or notice.

Jacob gave a rehearsed, three-cough, throat-clearing "Mrs. Glass?"

Nicole's head popped up. "Yes?"

"He means me," Evie said.

Nicole tipped down her head and nodded.

"Sam punched me and my mom says he has to apologize," Jacob said, staring at Evie, taking a stance like Superman. He *had* been well rehearsed.

Evie flinched. Sam punched Jacob? Sam didn't say he punched Jacob.

"I saw the whole thing." Gwen skittered over to Evie. Where did she come from? Gwen "Miss America" waved to Nicole and stood with her shoulder touching Evie's. Evie took one baby step to the left. "They were teasing him, yes, but Sam really overreacted."

"If you saw the whole thing, why didn't you stop it?"

Gwen raised her eyebrows in a meager attempt at self-defense.

And wait, was there no free pass for a kid with a dead parent?

Sam twiddled with the bottom of his T-shirt, not making eye contact with anyone. Evie turned her back to Gwen. "Sam? You punched Jacob?"

She wanted to blame Jacob for bothering Sam, taunting him, teasing him for staying out of school. But Sam hit him. Neither she nor Richard spanked or hit the kids—ever. They had considered it old-fashioned, ineffective, and barbaric. And now their son was swinging his fists. Was he simply defending himself?

Sam looked up, eyes red in anger not sadness. He talked through a tight jaw. "He was bugging me about going back to school. *I told you.*"

"You didn't tell me you *punched* him!"

The boys stared at Sam. Two had their arms crossed and stood in a slouched hip-hop pose, and one shifted from foot to foot as if he had to pee. Jacob now had his hands in his pockets. The left side of his mouth twitched, and his eyelids had an inherited droop. The posse would have been intimidating—if Evie were ten. She could feel the almost-tweens trying to ooze testosterone.

She yanked Sam next to her. "Say you're sorry for hitting Jacob."

Sam raised his head but turned away from Evie with a smug air of defiance. He had not been reprimanded in months.

"Say you're sorry, Sam. Now. I'm not joking."

He looked in Jacob's direction. "Sorry."

Now, the real order of mother-business. Evie knew she was using her outside voice, but the acoustics in the gym sucked. There was no whispering in basketball or in boyhood scrapes. Evie crouched to nose height with the boys and put her hands on her knees for stability. The boys stared at her, expecting another apology, maybe a lollipop.

"Now, *you* apologize," she said with maternal authority.

A jumble of *We didn't do anything*s and *He hit Jacob*s and *My mom said*s came at her.

"Did you tease him for not being in school?"

Silence.

She glared at Jacob, bitterness rising in her throat. "Did you call him a baby?"

Jacob looked at his shoes.

Velcro. Someone should teach the kid how to tie a bow.

"His dad died," Evie said, almost spitting. "Look at me."

She looked deep into each boy's eyes, her pupils searing theirs. These boys were free of pain, verging on arrogant, but tinted with fear.

"*His. Dad. Died.*" She hated being blunt with Sam next to her. She hated playing the dead-father card, but it was time for the boys and the bleachers to know that everything had changed. No more whispering. No more *everything's fine*. No more *thank you for your concern*. She would acknowledge Richard's death out loud.

And while Sam didn't need a reminder, it worked. The other boys' lips quivered. Feet shuffled. Shoulders sagged.

"Say you're sorry."

A quartet of mumbled apologies followed.

Evie nudged Sam toward the boys. "Be nice to each other. All of you. You've known each other since you were two. Now get out of here and get doughnuts or something."

The boys skulked away in a line, Sam included. He looked back at her, and Evie pointed toward the door, although she wanted to open her arms for one more hug, give a thumbs-up, or blow a kiss across the air that would land on the soft summit of his cheek. But that wouldn't help with name-calling or punching. It all reminded Evie of when the twins were three and she scolded a five-year-old on the playground for cutting in line for the *little-kid* slide. Five-year-olds looked gigantic when Sam and Sophie were three. Almost as big as ten-year-olds.

Gazing into the well-coiffed bleacher crowd, Evie realized no one was looking, but she knew they saw her wrangle the boys. She turned and looked at Nicole, knowing *she* would not look away.

"Sorry you had to see that," Evie said. "Sorry I had to do it," she muttered to herself.

"You did the right thing. I would have done the same thing for Luca. We have to stick up for our kids. No one else will."

"I'm so tired of this."

"Of basketball?"

"No, I'm tired of acting like everything's okay, and I guess Sam just pummeled me out of that. My kid who is being teased for not going to school clobbers one of his best buddies—that's not okay. But every time someone asks, I say we're just fine. That the kids are 'coming along.' I don't want to tell anyone our business, but the truth is, it's exhausting trying to pretend that nothing has changed when every single thing has changed. And I can't believe that people don't know that, so I don't know why they ask."

"They're trying to be nice."

"Now you sound like Beth."

"Thanks!"

Evie had not meant it as a compliment.

Nicole handed a plastic, chunky cell-phone toy to Luca, who stuck the thick, blue antenna into his mouth.

Evie reached into the basket under the stroller and pulled out a bib and a zwieback. "Try this," she said, handing it to Nicole as she realized Nicole had already dealt with teething, and more.

Nicole took the offerings and smiled but held them in her lap. The whistle blew and both women woo-hooed and clapped in unison.

God, they reeked of family. And that was another thing; Evie was tired—no, exhausted—from defending her decision to let Nicole and Luca move in. Everyone but Beth made it seem as though the new living arrangement were the end of the world when it was really just the beginning.

"Great game, Sophie-Trophy," Nicole said as Sophie bounded over during a break in the game.

Evie's stomach lurched. Just when she was feeling all family-ish, Nicole invaded Evie's personal mama-space. *Sophie-Trophy* was a term of parental pride or a brotherly whine when Sophie's team won more games than Sam's. Not another *Sophie-Trophy*! *Sophie-Trophy* was off-limits.

"Yep, you're doing great! What's next?" Evie handed Sophie a baby wipe for her hands and a towel for her face.

"I'm going back in for the last quarter," Sophie said, handing the sweaty stuff back to Evie.

"I'll be watching."

The game clock ticked and the score was tied. Sam ran toward Evie, swung his arms, and jumped the last few feet, landing with a thud. His hair was slick, pushed back off his forehead. He smelled like sweat and cotton candy, his cheeks puffed like a chipmunk's.

"They're tied!" he said.

"I know! Here, sit down. Watch Sophie."

Evie made space between herself and Nicole. Then, Sophie had the ball. With three, two, one second to go, she threw a long shot. It swooshed through the lowered hoop. The buzzer blared. Evie, Sam, and Nicole sprang to their feet, arms waving above their heads, jumping, cheering. Sophie whipped around, errant curls unfurling around her face as her eyes locked with Evie's. Smiling broader than she had in months, Sophie revealed unfiltered joy, and the dimple just like her dad's.

"Oh, yeah," Sam yelled, still facing the court. "I want to go to school Monday."

An hour ago he was never going back.

"Okay." Evie swallowed her hesitation. Through Sam's heavy breaths and reddened face, she glimpsed the boy from before. She swelled with the pride of recognition, even though it was tinged with the ache of things unknown.

Chapter 14

THE MINIVAN GLIDED TO A stop outside the school. The twins scooted from their seats and stepped out, arranging their backpacks, zipping their coats halfway. Evie buzzed down the window on the passenger side, and Sam and Sophie leaned in, next to one another.

"Love you, Sam."

"Love you, Mom."

"Love you, Soph."

"Love you, Mom."

Together Sam and Sophie walked toward the mass of "big kids" on the playground. And then they were gone.

Evie sat in the car until all the kids and the teachers had filed inside. Then she still sat, car idling, radio on. It had been three months since she had been alone for more than the time it took to use the bathroom. What would she do with a whole six-hour day?

But she wouldn't be alone. Nicole and Luca would be there. And Beth and Laney were coming for coffee and cookies. Evie should have left the morning open to climb back into bed with a book—or to pound the Internet pavement for a job.

Only no-thank-you's from her application madness. And no word from County. Maybe Alan's recommendation wasn't worth much after all. Regret crept into Evie's thoughts, but she pushed it aside. There was no room for regrets.

At home Evie cleared the kitchen counter. She stacked her disheveled to-do lists and grocery lists on the desk next to the computer. She smiled at the thought of spending her first morning "off" with Beth and Laney, and how it was pointing her internal compass toward normal. But pushing aside the business of death and job-hunting made her feel as if she were halfway to the grocery store and had realized she'd left the iron on. Her conscience tugged at her, so she appeased it. With Nicole and Luca at the beach taking advantage of the early-spring temperatures that would probably disappear for one more frost, Evie could spend just one or maybe two more minutes searching websites before putting on the second pot of coffee, pulling out the container of frozen cookies, and brushing her hair so Laney didn't collapse into an I-have-an-ungroomed-friend frenzy.

When Evie looked up from the monitor, thirty minutes had passed. Beth and Laney wouldn't care that the coffee wasn't made or that the cookies weren't thawed, but Evie cared. She looked at a folded piece of paper on her desk. The e-mail address Alan had given her for the job at County College. Maybe she'd typed it in wrong. She double-checked. How long did it take someone at a community college to send a form rejection or a simple thanks-but-no-thanks e-mail? It was rude. Yes, that was it. They were rude. She did not want to work for a rude institution, absolutely not, but she wanted to make sure they'd received the application they were going to deny. As she landed on the County College website—just another few seconds—her monitor winked at her; a few more swipes and clicks and *under review* popped up next to her name. She bookmarked the page and closed the website. Evie opened the freezer as Beth knocked on the door.

"Come on in," Evie said, waving her arm. She slid a container of unidentifiable cookies across the counter. Laney entered, talking on her phone. She grumbled, "Whatever," then laid it on the table.

This was all followed by the kerplunk of a stroller and Nicole's walking into the kitchen with Luca on her hip.

Laney commandeered her spot next to Beth. They stirred half cups of coffee—a new pot was brewing—and rooted through the defrosting Tupperware contents.

"Did you have fun at the beach?" Evie asked, reaching for Luca, who stretched out his arms. She took him from Nicole, then handed him back, realizing that without Luca in her arms, Nicole seemed aimless and empty.

"It's perfect weather to let Luca sit in the sand for the first time," Nicole said. "I can tell you about it later." She pulled out a piece of lined paper from Luca's diaper bag and handed it to Evie. "She called while you were driving the twins to school. Gerry somebody or other from County College. She said their server has been down since Friday."

Evie took the paper from Nicole and held it up to Beth and Laney like a six-year-old's first lost tooth.

"Did she say anything else?"

"She apologized for taking a few weeks to respond."

"Oh," Evie said. "I mean, thanks."

"No problem. That's the job you want, isn't it?"

"It is."

Nicole looked away from Evie, blinking hard. "I know you ladies like your coffee time and I am not going to interrupt. I'm going to take Luca downstairs for a nap. I have some paperwork to do anyway."

Laney waved and crinkled her nose at Luca.

"You can join us for a cup if you want," Beth said.

Evie glared at boundary-defying Beth.

"Thank you, that's sweet, but I'm going to go downstairs. I'm sure I'll see you both soon." Nicole disappeared into the basement stairwell.

"You're going to get that job at County. I just know it!" Beth said. She leaned her chin in her hands.

"We don't know what this woman wants," Evie said, flicking the paper, but she had a good feeling. Actually, she didn't have a bad feeling, which was as close as she'd gotten in a while.

"What are you waiting for? Call that woman back," Laney said. "We'll be quiet." She put one hand over her mouth and crossed her heart.

"In a minute." Evie looked at Beth. "Do me a favor?"

"Anything!"

"Don't invite Nicole to have coffee with the three of us."

"I was just trying to be nice."

"Don't."

Beth shrugged and bit into a chocolate-chip cookie. "I don't get it. You want us to be nice, but you don't want us to be nice?"

"Exactly. She is part of my life, but she's not part of this." Evie drew an air-triangle connecting herself to Beth and Laney, and Beth and Laney to each other. "Some things are off-limits."

"Like husbands?" Laney said.

"Oh my God, Lane, knock it off already," Beth said through a grimace.

"I'm just sayin' . . ."

"Can you call County or can we change the subject?" Beth said to Evie. "Or I'm going home. I was just trying to be nice to Nicole. I wasn't trying to add her to our trio. I only asked her if she wanted a cup of coffee."

"Look," Evie said. "I feel bad I don't want her up here with us, but I don't. I don't know if that makes me a bad person, but for right now at this moment with this pot of coffee on this day, I just want it to be the three of us."

"Amen to that," Laney said a little too emphatically.

"You know," Evie said, "I'm getting tired of this good-cop/bad-cop routine with Nicole. She's not perfect. This isn't perfect. But no matter where I go from here, this is where I am now, okay?"

Beth attempted a smile. Laney fiddled with the wooden buttons on her stubbly cardigan. Even in her one-of-a-kind knit, insolence did not become her.

"What's up with you?" Evie asked, pointing her chin in Laney's direction.

"She had a fight with Herb." Beth bit her lip.

Laney shoved a cookie into her mouth. "We're falling back into old, crappy patterns."

"Even though Richard is still dead?" Evie hoped humor would ease Laney's tension.

"Ha ha, very funny, Ev. Yes. But this time we're working on it."

"Good for you guys," Beth said.

"Yeah, I guess so. It's just . . ." Laney said.

"It's just what?" Beth prompted.

"Oh, say it." Evie had a low tolerance for woe-is-me marriage stories. When the kvetching revolved around husbands, Evie usually tuned it out—but this was Laney.

"I was just going to say that I knew that good marriages took work—but I didn't realize how much work. And that it's not always fun or easy or fast. Those things that got on my nerves about Herb before Richard died? They're still there. And frankly, that pisses me off."

Laney's phone buzzed. They all knew it was Herb—and snorted short bursts of laughter.

"Just go," Evie said. She opened the door against the March wind. Laney backed out the door and saluted her friends before running across the yard. Evie might even have seen her skip.

Beth held out her hands as if to inspect her nails, but her eyes fixed on the eternity band on her left ring finger. Beth's sense of humor did not extend to marriage. "It's worth it to make a marriage work."

"Well, tell me something that I don't know. Of course marriage is worth the work. And I did the work, you know? It's just that . . . God, Beth, sometimes you do everything you can and it still doesn't work out."

Beth shrugged. "Guess so."

Evie shrugged back. What did Beth know of the thousand little compromises that made up Evie's marriage? What did Beth know of the compromises that made up Evie's day? Her friend's life was so regimented, so calm. Beth and Alan ate meat loaf every Tuesday. Bunco was Wednesday. Tennis on Thursday. They went on a date every Friday night. When Cody, their son, was little, they spent Saturdays at all his games. Now they Skyped while he was in Paris for a semester.

Of course Evie knew better than to judge things by appearances. Well, by appearances only. But Beth was rock solid. Beth and Alan were rock solid.

The two women sat in a growing silence. Beth folded her hands and twirled her thumbs.

Evie had never seen Beth fidget. "What's wrong?"

"I need to be honest with you about something. Something I did."

"Something *you* did? You're like a Jewish Mother Teresa in pearls and pink argyle. What on earth did you do? Put the salad fork next to the soupspoon?"

Beth twirled her thumbs again.

"Oh my God! Stop with the thumb-twirling and tell me what's wrong."

"I had an affair."

"Oh my God!" Evie grabbed Beth's hands to stop the jumble of movements and words. "You cheated on Alan?"

"No!"

"So it was like a zillion years ago." Evie let go of Beth and fanned herself.

"Right. And it doesn't matter now."

"It must matter if you want to tell me about it after all this time. So, what's the story? You cheated on a boyfriend and now he found you online?"

"No."

"Then what?"

"I was like Nicole."

"What do you mean you were *like Nicole*?"

"I had an affair with a married man."

Evie's face contorted and she sat on her hands. "You did not. I know you."

"You're right, you *do* know me. But you're wrong because *I did*. That's the point."

Evie's mouth dropped open. Her throat was dry. She walked to the sink in rapid, little steps, turned on the faucet, cupped her hands under the water, and sipped. She stared into the stainless-steel basin and watched her moral certainty wash down the drain.

Beth slept with someone else's husband? Beth was like Nicole— but Beth was nothing like Nicole. Beth was a community matriarch, a beloved wife and mother, Evie's confidante. She fussed over seating arrangements for dinner parties, changed her curtains with each season, and was the closest a grown woman could come to being a Boy Scout. Evie's limbs ran cold. Did this mean Nicole could be *like Beth*?

Evie wanted to be alone. No, she wanted the kids home. No, she wanted to be back at Laney's house for dinner so she could drink more wine, come home without Beth and Laney, and fall right to sleep. The insides of Evie's sleeves itched as if the fabric had turned from cotton to wool. She rubbed her arms, turned back to the sink, her cheeks burning. Evie cupped her hands again and filled them with cold water. This time she splashed it on her face. To hell with mascara and with Beth.

"When *exactly* was this?"

"I was twenty-six." Beth stood, walked around the counter, and ended up behind Evie. Evie grabbed the spigot, afraid she was going to lose her balance.

"I'm not who I was twenty-five years ago. You're not who you were two months ago or four years ago. We all change."

Evie let the quiet hang between them until she burst. "Does Alan know that you had an affair?"

Beth inhaled deeply. "Alan knows because it *was* Alan."

Evie tipped her head to the side, repeating the words to herself. *It was Alan.* She paused and swallowed each word separately.

It was Alan.

Alan was married before, and Beth was his mistress. How could Evie not have known? She felt middle-of-the-night nauseous and the room seemed to sway. Alan was Richard. Beth was Nicole. Then who the hell was Evie? She looked at the floor to stop the rocking and blocked the echo of Beth's words by counting indentations in the tiles.

"Look at me," Beth said.

Evie looked up and past Beth at the wall behind her.

"Can we sit down?"

"I can sit. *You* can leave."

"Scream at me or something, please." Beth's voice was the same as always, yet completely unfamiliar to Evie.

"I don't have the energy to scream at you. I'm not your mother. Oh, yes, you must have made your mother so proud!" That was mean. Beth's mother had died years before.

"Stop it."

Evie stepped backward away from Beth and ended pinned against her own counter with nowhere to go. Beth walked to the other side. The counter had always served as a gathering place. Now it was a gulf between them.

Beth reached across toward Evie, who laid her hands on her thighs.

"Does Laney know?" Evie sniggered. "There is no way Laney knows."

"No one knows." Beth spoke slowly, deliberately.

She faded right in front of Evie's eyes. "You're full of it, Beth. How can no one know? Alan was married and had an affair. *With you*. His wife knew, and how about his family and his friends? Oh my God, does he have other kids? Is Cody *yours* or did you steal someone's husband *and* child?"

"Cody is nineteen, and Alan and I have been married over twenty years. Don't be ridiculous."

"You're a slut and I'm ridiculous. We're quite a pair."

Beth's face drained from springtime peach to pale ash, but Evie didn't care. She'd been duped by someone she loved and trusted. Again. There were secrets. Big secrets. Again.

"I know it sounds cliché, but they weren't happy. He asked for the divorce because of me, but the marriage wasn't bad because of me. They got married after college, and this happened within a few years."

"You didn't care that he was married, did you?" Evie whispered.

Beth gulped and looked down. "It just happened."

Evie guffawed.

"I know its cliché, but it's true. We were friends and then . . ."

"And then you were naked. That's a logical progression for this cliché of yours."

"It was so long ago, it was a different lifetime. It doesn't matter how it happened. Alan was married for four years, and a year later he was married to me. In a synagogue, by a rabbi. You've seen the photos a million times."

"I don't get it. How could you not have cared that he was married?" Evie said, her throat stretching, almost cramping. "How could you not have ever told me with everything you knew? We were best friends. I told you everything."

"I did care, Ev. But I loved him. And I didn't tell you because I love you too. And I was scared you would hate me."

"God, no wonder you were always so understanding of Richard. And now Nicole. It all makes sense. It's like a little club. Do you have a secret handshake? A password?" Evie handed Beth her coat. "You see yourself in Nicole, don't you? It's why you make excuses for her, why you whisper to her, why you want her to have coffee with us."

"I feel bad for her. I know that just because she did something hurtful doesn't mean she's a bad person."

"In case you missed it, I didn't say she was a bad person. I asked her to move in here. I'm the one eating dinner with her every night. I'm the one who acknowledged her as part of this convoluted family. Frankly, at this point, I'm fine with Nicole. You seem to be the problem. At least with her I know what I'm getting."

"I just thought if I told you . . ."

"What?"

"I don't know what I thought. I just wanted you to know."

"It was eating away at you, and now that you got it off your chest, your betrayal can eat away at me. Great, thanks, because I don't have enough to worry about."

"I didn't betray you by having an affair with Alan."

"No, you betrayed me by lying. By breaking a promise to be straight with me, and to having insight that might help me when I was going through everything."

Evie slumped in a chair and glowered at the stranger-friend standing in her kitchen. Beth's aura was tarnished, which made Evie sad when she wasn't seething. It was never fun to watch someone change before your eyes when you needed her to stay who she was. Who Evie thought she was.

"I can't defend what we did, but I'm not going to apologize for having a solid twenty-four-year marriage with Alan."

Evie leaned back. "So, are you going to tell him you told me?"

"Of course."

"How do you know he hasn't cheated on you? He did it once . . . he could do it again."

"I trust him."

Evie sneered. "How does he know you haven't cheated?"

"You know me better than that."

"Do I?"

"Yes, you do. Circumstances *do* come into play in life. And people can learn and make choices that point them in different directions than in the past. If Alan and I ever had problems, we wouldn't look to someone else, we'd look to each other."

Evie looked at the clock on the microwave. "You need to go. Unless you just want to go downstairs and hang out with your protégé." The words shot out of Evie's mouth. She was glad to see them go. Better out than in.

"I'm not leaving until you tell me you don't hate me."

"I can't do this."

"You can't do what?"

"I can't have you in my house."

"I'm so sorry, Evie." Beth reached for her and Evie recoiled.

"Just go."

Evie pointed toward the door and Beth winced. She left in silence without putting on her coat, pushing in her chair, or closing the door.

Chapter 15

EVIE JIGGLED THE STATIC OUT of her pant leg and surveyed Lakewood County Community College. It was late March. The trees were still bare, but large planters overflowed with pansies and daffodils. Men and women of all ages, sizes, and colors sauntered past, some with backpacks slung over a shoulder and others with briefcases swinging from one hand. There weren't a lot of low-riding sweats with phrases across the tush, and there weren't many logo hoodies. Evie sensed no preppy vibe at all, quite the switch from her memories of Northwestern, which consisted of late-eighties big hair, stand-up collars, and shoulder pads.

County geared its courses to adult students, most of whom worked full-time. These students would be mature and motivated, and thankfully, they were not slaves to college fashion trends, no matter the decade. They'd enroll to start a degree or learn something new or finish what they'd started when life got in the way, and not because their starched and pressed parents packed the car, set them up with a laundry service, and dropped them off with a credit card. Not that any of those things had happened to Evie. The students at County were here to change direction or find one. Evie could relate. Maybe she'd suggest that Nicole go back to school. Or maybe Beth had already suggested that during one of their secret meetings. Evie pushed Beth out of her head the way she'd pushed the flowers Beth had left on the doorstep to the bottom of the kitchen trash can, the same way she'd banished her from the kitchen four days ago—with force, and a modicum of regret.

"Think about yourself," Evie said aloud. She rubbed her lips together. The hint of gloss felt dry, almost chapped. She headed toward the entrance and imagined discussing Abraham Lincoln and the emancipation during a cross-campus walk. She imagined herself advising a student during office hours, and providing valued input in faculty meetings. Above all, Evie imagined the self she wanted others to see, and that was not a divorced mom, a retired dater, or someone who lived with her ex-husband's widow. To the naked County College eye, she would be nothing more—or less—than normal.

Sam had been in school for over a week. Sophie no longer appeared at Evie's door in the middle of the night. Nicole had stopped trying to re-reorganize the cabinets. And now Evie was interviewing for a job she wanted. A job that could offer her a new identity and a chance to move forward.

Hopefulness felt sweet and familiar.

"Good morning, I'm Olivia Talbot." The chair of the History Department was a dark-skinned African-American woman with little, yet impeccable, makeup. She was tall, even in flat shoes, wearing slim, black trousers and a long, white tunic. She wore large gold hoop earrings that swung when she moved her head, which she did not do often.

"It's a pleasure to meet you. Thank you for meeting with me."

"Have a seat, let's get down to business." Dr. Talbot sat and drew a multicolored scarf over one shoulder, creating a look of academic elegance. She glanced at a legal pad on her desk. "You haven't taught at the college level before, but your credentials are excellent. Northwestern and U of C." It was as though Evie were eavesdropping as

Dr. Talbot talked to herself. "I understand taking time off to raise a family."

Evie nodded but said nothing. She wasn't giving anyone ammunition.

"I did the same thing years ago, started back part-time as well, and eventually earned my Ph.D. at DePaul. About fifteen years ago, I came here."

Maybe she was older than Evie thought. She couldn't imagine getting a Ph.D. while the kids were at home.

Dr. Talbot motioned to the window, which overlooked a green expanse. Outside that window it looked like a college: picnic benches and trees in a big square outlined by buildings. "County is very academic, Mrs. Glass. For a community college. Do you go by Mrs. or Ms?"

"Ms."

Dr. Talbot picked up her pen and made a note on the top page. Being a Ms. was a good thing to Evie. Was it a good thing to Olivia Talbot?

"As I was saying, though this is a serious institution of higher learning, you'll find County more laid-back than what you're used to academically." She glanced down at her paper again.

What Evie was used to academically were fifth-grade dioramas and Pokémon pencil toppers.

"It sounds like there's a good balance." Evie hoped it would rub off.

"That's true. As you know, we need someone to teach Early American History two nights a week for the summer session. Would that be manageable for you if we offered you the position?"

"It would be." Nicole's face appeared before Evie's eyes. "Absolutely."

"I'm glad to hear that. After the summer the position is still part-time, but the class is during the day, not at night." Dr. Talbot looked at her computer screen, her watch, and at Evie. "Now then,

I have a division meeting to attend, so I asked one of our more senior professors to give you a tour and answer any questions you may have. Sandy teaches European History as well as History Ed Theory. I'm sure you'll get along."

Was this a second opinion, or was Evie being pawned off to a department peon? The brush-off would be easier if it was quick.

"We've worked together now for almost ten years, and I trust Sandy's opinion," Dr. Talbot continued. "The class you're being considered for will be in the lecture hall Sandy uses during the day. You'd share office space as well."

"I understand." Professor Sandy had tenure. She was probably a displaced academic snob—all prep school and penny loafer, a Brown reject with attitude—the yin to Dr. Talbot's yang.

Someone tapped on the door and opened it before Dr. Talbot said another word. A man in his fifties grasped the door as if ready to pull it shut again. He had a salt-and-pepper crew cut—more pepper than salt—and wore a pale pink oxford tucked into belted, olive chinos. When Evie had imagined her potential adult students, she'd pictured women. Of course there would be men too. Handsome men.

"Oh, I'm sorry, I thought you were finished," he said.

Evie looked at the doorjamb. Salt and pepper was six feet or six-one. She'd learned how to gauge height during a women's safety course as an undergrad. She didn't feel unsafe with the man at the door, more like unsettled.

"Good timing," Dr. Talbot said, standing. Evie followed. "Ms. Evelyn Glass, this is Dr. Alexander Perlman. Ms. Glass is applying for the summer adjunct position."

Dr. Perlman extended his right hand to Evie. It dwarfed hers, and heat transferred from his palm. Evie's acute physical awareness released unanticipated memories. And hormones.

"It's nice to meet you, Dr. Perlman. Please, call me Evie." She pulled back both her hands and slid them into her jacket pockets.

She was thinking about flirting with a colleague. Better than with a student, but probably not a good idea. If Evie got the job, would she see Dr. Perlman on campus?

He looked at Evie straight on with his bright blue eyes. A brief smile softened his square jaw. He jerked his eyebrows. They were not yet gray. "Please, call me Sandy."

Evie gulped, then coughed to cover her shock.

After leaving Dr. Talbot's office, Sandy unfolded a campus map and handed it to Evie. "At first, these halls and atriums and paths all look the same. It's kind of the same way with the students."

"Thank you." Evie tucked the map into her purse. His stride was twice as long as Evie's, and she scampered to keep up, glad she wore kitten heels and not the three-inch pumps Laney had suggested.

Sandy smiled at her and slowed his pace. "We'll start here." He stopped in front of an office with a door that matched every other door she'd so far seen.

He slid a keycard through the slotted black box, and just like in hotel rooms from Evie's other life, a little light flashed red, then green. Inside, the room was dark and small, with a 1970s teacher's-style oak desk in one corner. Not old—*vintage*. Sandy flipped the wall switch and the fluorescent ceiling panels flickered. The book-shelves were filled with textbooks. The desk, cluttered with papers and stacks of folders and more books, sat kitty-corner to the metal shelves with the windows to the left. Framed railroad travel posters adorned the walls, along with a couple of framed college degrees with print too small to read. The room smelled like a college professor's office—a mix of must, antiseptic wipes, and stale coffee.

"We'll put a desk on the other wall. And add a bookshelf, I guess." Sandy scrunched his face, as if he'd never considered the ramifications of sharing his office. "It'll be tight, but, whatever. No budget, no choice." He thrust his hands into the air. "Sometimes we just have to make things work."

He has no idea.

Sandy patted the back of a wooden swivel chair. "Have a seat." It was less of a suggestion, more of a command.

Evie sat. Sandy leaned on the desk next to her. Now he was two feet taller—effective for negotiating—she'd remember that.

"I can tell Olivia likes you. She goes with her gut as much as someone's CV when she hires."

Evie wouldn't be lured into saying something inappropriate. "Thank you." With Sandy as a conduit, she could ensure Dr. Talbot knew she was interested, in case her inadvertent emotional drooling hadn't been obvious. "The position seems perfect."

Until her divorce Evie was only academic by marriage. Even with her master's degree, she was a subset of Richard's Ph.D., relegated to the role of late-night coffee pourer, early-morning alarm clock, proofreader, cheerleader. Evie's forays into the world of Pinehurst College had faded. The faculty-spouse soirées were stored in her Before Divorce mental filing cabinet. Her personal history was not unlike any other kind of history, bruised—and healed—by the slap of hindsight's wisdom. But hindsight wouldn't help her today. Teaching college, even at a county college, was all about her. She wasn't the wife, the girlfriend, the date, the mother, or the friend. It was all Evie all the time, for the first time in a long time. Maybe for the first time since she'd met Richard.

She wished she had the formula for doing and saying everything right. That was where Richard excelled. Following directions (but not rules), solving problems (but not those of his own making). Surprises weren't boding well for her lately. She wished she had the foresight to know what was next. But only fools rely on wishes, Bubbe had said. She'd said it when Evie and Lisa wished for Hanukkah ponies, for better grades, for bigger boobs and smaller hips, or to win the lottery. Evie was no fool.

"What's your best advice that will help me get this job?"

"Just be yourself. Olivia can see right through a poser."

Be yourself. The advice of mothers everywhere.

"How long have you been teaching here?"

"Ten years."

Ten years ago Evie had infant twins, a house with a newly sodded lawn, budding best friendships, and a husband. Ten years ago Sandy Perlman was probably as old as she was now. When she was fifteen, he was twenty-five. When she was twenty, he was thirty. But it didn't matter. This was an interview, not a date, which probably meant that running her fingers through her hair and shimmying her shoulders would be unseemly.

So instead, she just nodded and said, "Wow."

It covered everything.

Chapter 16

Rex wagged his tail, well aware the best scraps came from a baby in a high chair. Sam and Sophie deposited their dishes in the sink and sauntered off to do homework. Nicole rinsed and loaded while Evie grabbed a baby wipe and cleaned Luca's hands and face.

"I'll finish the kitchen if you want to get Luca in his pajamas," Nicole said.

"Sure. C'mon, Luca, Auntie Evie will take you downstairs." Nicole smiled. Evie kissed Luca's head and tasted essence of smooshed peas. Some things never changed.

Evie rarely entered Nicole's basement domain, just as Nicole rarely visited the second floor of the house. They occupied group space on the first floor, sharing the kitchen, living room, and dining room as if it were the common space of a dormitory. In a way, it was.

The boxes of toys Evie had stacked in the corner were now arranged in a square, covered with a vinyl tablecloth and some of Luca's plastic trucks. It was the perfect height for him to pull himself up on for a round of cruise, play, cruise, play.

Luca banged on the makeshift play top and Evie turned. Easy, breezy baby play. If only adults could emulate the joy and innocence.

She looked at a photograph lying on the table that captured a moment that did not belong to Evie. Nicole looked like a bride out of a magazine in a traditional ball gown with extra sparkle, an updo, and a cascading bouquet of calla lilies. Two bridesmaids had donned mauve taffeta dresses they'd never wear again.

Evie would not do the fancy-white-dress and updo thing if she ever remarried, although that probably wasn't going to be a problem since she wasn't dating. She twisted the back of her hair off her neck absentmindedly and sucked in her stomach, just to see if she could.

"Where do you put the wet diapers?" Evie yelled after removing herself from the imaginary aisle. Nicole appeared at the top of the steps.

"The diaper pail is outside the bathroom, thanks."

With a cotton-footie-pajamaed Luca on her hip, Evie walked to the bathroom. Out of the corner of her eye she saw a pile of mail. It was still delivered to the other house; the family that had moved in didn't mind, Nicole told her.

Stepping on the pedal of the white plastic can, Evie spotted an envelope with a familiar green label. She would never go through Nicole's mail, but what if Nicole had brought Evie's mail downstairs by mistake? The letter from Midwest Mutual was addressed to Nicole. She must be dealing with them too. Maybe getting the same runaround? Financial details were something they didn't discuss, except Nicole's weekly contribution for room and board, which she always paid on time and in cash.

Evie scanned the room for more of Nicole's personal effects. No photos of Peter or Lucy. Nicole carried those photos with her. No pictures of her mother or brother. Nicole's life before Richard existed only in her head and heart.

Evie didn't know what she would do without Lisa or her parents. They were far away, but close at heart, their photos lining the shelves. They descended for holidays, called all the time (sometimes too much), and met her and the kids for annual vacations in

Rehoboth Beach. Nicole had set one life aside to start a new one. Evie had just blended hers.

Upstairs in the kitchen, the twins bickered. Although it was music to her ears, this sign of normalcy, Evie was inclined to stop it.

"What's going on in here?" she asked, standing under the arch that separated the dining room from the kitchen.

"I'm trying to figure out this math problem and Sam keeps telling me to be quiet."

"I can't think when she taps her pencil."

"Okay," Evie said. "Soph, don't tap your pencil. Sam, be patient."

"Fine," he said. "When I'm done, I'm going to ask Alan to help us with our science project."

"Not today."

"Why not?" the twins whined in unison.

"Because he's busy."

Sam rolled his eyes and scooted his chair closer to Sophie. They held their pencils the same way, the way Richard did, resting it on their right ring finger instead of their middle finger. They also stuck out their tongues to the left when deep in thought. Fragments of Richard were embedded in their beings.

"You carry this number over here," Sam said. "Keep it under this number and you won't get mixed up."

"I know," Sophie said with a smile.

"Good job, guys. You guys are good students *and* good teachers," Evie said. "Just like your daddy."

Sam and Sophie lifted and tilted their heads in unison. Their eyes blinked hard, but shone. Evie relished the glimmer of gladness. Her heart ached for more, and then the twins released wide, toothy smiles.

Just like Richard's.

Laney appeared in Evie's back-door window. She waved her in, filled their mugs with hazelnut blend, and pointed to the two oblong, plastic containers on the counter.

"You *are* still going all *Barefoot Contessa*," Laney said. "Thank goodness."

Laney reached for just-baked lemon cookies. Evie went right for box-mix chocolate chip, but stopped, remembering the snug waistline of the blue suit.

"I hope you don't flake out on the baking with your new, fancy job!"

"I didn't get it yet," Evie said. "But you know what?"

"What?"

"I think I will."

They high-fived as if they were toasting with champagne.

"I guess if you're not going to get laid, the next best thing is getting paid," Laney said.

Only Laney could make that kind of connection.

Evie sipped the cooling coffee and reached back into the container of cookies, took one, but just put it in front of her.

"I'll be so disappointed if I don't get it, but it's at night, twice a week. I can still work at Third Coast part-time while the kids are in school and camp."

"You'll get the job. They'd be fools not to hire you," Laney said.

"I'll be sure to give them your recommendation."

"You do that."

The two friends laughed. If only they could fix things for one another with just a phone call.

"Did you tell Alan?" Laney asked.

"I got the interview because of Alan." Evie looked away from Laney and into the cookies. "I want to get the job on my own." *I don't want to tell Alan anything.*

"When will you know?"

"They said a week or two, so I guess I'll find out any day." Evie's stomach flipped.

"And you don't have to remind me, with Nicole here, you won't worry about the kids." Laney grimaced.

"That's the point."

"Where is she anyway?"

"She's out running errands and Luca is sleeping. I don't know what her plans are. For now I don't have to move or find a sitter." Evie looked at her best friend and took a deep breath. She thought of Sandy Perlman and jutted her hands over her head in a faux hallelujah. "Sometimes we just have to make things work. And that's what I want to talk to you about."

"Uh-oh."

"No uh-oh, Lane. I'm just thinking that things are finally getting back on track. A little bit at a time." Evie left out being off track with Beth. It would come out soon enough. "The kids miss Richard. Some nights are really hard." The words caught in her throat. "But slowly, really slowly, I feel like one day we'll all be okay. Really okay, not pretend okay. So—I want to go back to Bunco. I want to let Nicole have coffee with us—sometimes. I want people to know that she lives here for now and that it's for both of us. I don't care if people know that Midwest Mutual is being a pain in the ass and that I needed money to pay the mortgage. That's my real life. And once I have the money for the kids and some bills, I might still want Nicole to stay because she helps with the twins. And I do love little Luca."

"Lord, it's like *The Brady Bunch* but without Mike Brady."

"No, it's like *Kate and Allie,* without the ex." Evie clamped her hand over her mouth as if she'd said a dirty word. "My life is private, but there are no secrets. I cannot handle any more secrets."

"Got it. And since we're being nonsecretive, tell me what the hell is going on with you and Beth."

"We had an argument."

"So?"

"A big one. And don't ask me, because I'm not telling you. If you want to know, ask Beth." It wasn't Evie's story to tell.

"Well, whatever happened, remember, sometimes the friendship is more important than the hurt feelings."

The next afternoon Evie pulled into the driveway after dropping off Sam and Sophie at indoor soccer and basketball practices. Beth was standing in the rain, tending goal at the garage door. *Beth.* A liar in Lilly Pulitzer. A fraud with a French manicure. A con with a Coach purse. A home wrecker with a flair for home décor. *Oh, I could go on and on.*

Beth came to her window. "Please talk to me."

Evie stared straight ahead, the lump in her throat the size of a marble, but as Beth put her hands on the car, her voice trembling a litany of *please*s, the lump grew to the size of an apple and sprouted quills. Evie popped the locks, gripped the steering wheel, and stared at the water cascading down the windshield.

Beth climbed into the backseat and scooted over to the passenger side. "Ev, you have to talk to me. We've been friends for too long to let this come between us."

Evie adjusted the rearview mirror.

"I'm sorry that I hurt you. You know that, right?" Beth pleaded.

"Do you have any idea what this did to me?" Evie's voice rose higher than she intended, and she hoped the volume would drown out her despair. This was how she felt during periods of her marriage. The suspicion and insecurity devils were back on her shoulders, not obliterated as she'd thought, simply lying in wait. *Whom can I trust? Whom else have I misjudged?* Death brings out the worst and the best in the living. Evie had witnessed both. She'd felt both.

After all, Evie had never fought with Beth or Laney before Richard died, but since, she'd fought hard with each of them.

"I thought you wanted me to be honest. I wanted you to know where I was coming from when it came to Nicole. Why I get her."

"Hearing about your affair with Alan brought back a lot of memories. Awful, godforsaken memories, Beth."

Evie glared into the small mirror, daring Beth to look back. Evie didn't need to rehash anything aloud. Beth had been there from the onset of each of Evie's frenetic inklings. They'd waited up for Richard to come home later than he should have, sat by the phone waiting for Richard to call. Beth helped her ransack pockets, drawers, financial records, phone records. Together they counted the broken promises and tried to piece them back together. Beth had maneuvered Evie like a masterful puppeteer on days she didn't have the wherewithal to function on her own. Unrelenting, both Beth and Laney reminded Evie of what she most often forgot. *That I deserved better.* The best, they'd said. And they helped Evie find the courage to believe it. And now, when her life was starting to look, once again, like something she could settle into for the next forty years, Beth unleashed poisonous reminders. They pulsed through Evie, and she tasted the bile of past betrayals along with this new one. *How dare Beth do this to me!*

"Your happiness came as a result of her pain—you know that, right?" Evie's throat ached from squelching her sobs.

Beth was crying. "I shouldn't have told you."

"Maybe you shouldn't have slept with someone else's husband."

"I shouldn't have," Beth whispered. "I've never said that before." She leaned her head against the window and gazed out into the same gray that had seeped inside the van. "I saw how Richard hurt you. I felt it," she said with her hand on her heart. "How you'd been . . ." She stopped, her voice breathy and low, as though she were talking to herself. "Abandoned. I couldn't believe I helped Alan do that to Maeve."

Maeve. Evie was glad to know her name. She deserved a name.

"I hope one day you'll forgive me. Forgive me for what I did and for not telling you when I should have. Or for telling you at all. I'm not sure what's worse."

Neither was Evie.

Beth continued, "I would never trade a moment of our friendship for anything. Even now. I know that sounds weird, but it's true. I'm a better person because of it. Because of you."

Sometimes it was tiresome being the teacher. Evie just wanted to exist alongside everyone and not stand at the front of life's classroom. Momentarily, the women's eyes met in the mirror. Evie looked away, the barren landscape of their friendship too new. If she looked at Beth, it would be hard to be mad, easy to forget this betrayal.

"I'm so proud of you," Beth said. "For who you are and for who I know you're going to be. And one thing's for sure—you will be fine. No, better than fine. *The best*." Beth touched Evie's shoulder and whispered into her ear with zeal, "Don't you dare doubt that or let anyone convince you of anything else."

Beth stepped out of the car and walked through the rain without putting up her hood.

Evie sat perfectly still and cried away an old friendship.

Tossing and turning when all she wanted to do was sleep, Evie kept thinking about Beth. She couldn't erase the friendship's facts. The winter they all went to Snowmass, Beth stayed with her on the bunny hill when Beth could have skied a Black Diamond. Cody stayed with Evie, Richard, and the twins for a week when Beth and Alan went to Bermuda for their fifteenth anniversary. Evie shared Bubbe's cookie recipes; Beth taught Evie to tack a hem. They attempted découpage and birdhouse building and failed; they attempted a book club and Bunco and succeeded. Beth held Evie's hand for an hour the first time Armando at Superior Salon covered her gray; and Beth reliably invited Evie for dinner every other Friday when the kids were with Richard. Beth called Evie first when Beth's mother passed away five years before, and Evie called Beth first with the news about Richard.

While Laney was Evie's blustery confidence, Beth was Evie's quiet strength. Evie was *their juste-milieu.* Or she used to be.

Evie eased her misgivings with a midnight snack even though it was only eleven. She rummaged in the back of the freezer for emergency cookies wrapped in aluminum foil. Darkness amplified Evie's thoughts. She was living with Nicole but had written off Beth. It wasn't logical—it was just a head-heart continuum that had yet to find its constant. So, with each frozen snap between her teeth, Evie tried keeping Beth at bay, except the only cookies left were cranberry oatmeal. Beth's favorite.

With Nicole gone for therapy and errands, Tuesday afternoons had become Evie's alone time. Today she decided to try yoga. She pulled on the organic-cotton stretch pants and special socks—at least she thought they were socks—unrolled the mat, and slid in the DVD, all sent by Lisa weeks before. "You have nothing to lose by relaxing," she'd said. Rex agreed and nestled into a corner of the living room that had trapped an errant sunbeam.

During her first modified cobra, the phone rang. For a slow count to three she considered letting it go to voice mail, but not with the kids in school. She'd at least have to check caller ID. *Midwest Mutual.* Evie started flitting around the living room like a four-year-old on Pixy Stix. Don Baker said he'd have news the next time he called. The kids' college funds would get their share, and then, if she landed the job at County and used a little of the insurance money, she would be able to afford soccer cleats, groceries, and the mortgage. Evie's personal trifecta of modest suburban solvency.

"Hello?" She paused the DVD as the instructor shifted into a low warrior.

"Hi, Evie. It's Don Baker. I hate to do this to you, but I have to fill out another report."

Evie sat on the mat with a thud and channeled Lisa by tapping her fingers on the floor. "Are you kidding me?"

"I wish I was. I need documentation of your official capacity as defendant."

"I'm not defending anything. I'm the mother of Richard's children. His *ex*-wife. C'mon, Don, you have two notarized copies of the divorce decree." She'd also sent the *get,* the Jewish divorce papers, as backup.

"I need to put you on hold."

"I'll be here when you get back." That's what Evie always said when he put her on hold. She crossed her eyes at no one. "I cannot believe this," she said aloud. She'd sent them all this information in triplicate in January and again a few weeks ago. Evie walked to the dining room and paced.

When Don was back on the line, his voice was grainy but loud. "What I was starting to tell you was that a second claim has been made on the policy with the two minor children as beneficiaries."

"What? Is that what this holdup is? A clerical error? There *is* no one else." Evie's arms and hands were cold even though she'd warmed up during yoga.

"Like I said, a second claim has been made—"

"Don, what does that mean?"

"It means that a third party is trying to be renamed as a beneficiary of that policy."

Something tugged at Evie's memory like a toddler who wanted attention. "You mean someone *else* wants the money Richard left my kids?"

"Precisely, Evie. I'm so sorry. It's out of my hands. Now the case goes to interpleader."

"To what?"

"Interpleader. The insurance funds have been handed over by Midwest Mutual to the federal courts, and a judge will rule on the outcome."

"Are you kidding me? My kids are the beneficiaries." Evie was shaking. This had to be a joke, a wake-up-from-a-nightmare kind of joke. When they'd headed for divorce, Evie wouldn't sign the papers until Richard had enough life insurance to make sure the kids would be able to finish college if anything happened to him. They never thought anything would happen, but isn't that why you buy insurance, so you don't need it? "I don't understand."

"The policy is titled so that funds are to be used by you, for the benefit of your and Richard's children in the case of his death. But now the *intent* of that policy at the time of the owner's death—Richard's death—has been challenged. Between you and me, you should get a lawyer. The other party has secured representation."

"Intent? The intent was that Richard's *children* be taken care of."

"That's the plaintiff's case as well."

"If you can't tell me who it is, how am I supposed to fight this?"

"How many children did Dr. Glass have?"

Evie groaned. She knew the speech by heart. "Don, I had fraternal twins with Richard in 2001, at Lakewood Hospital in Lakewood, Illinois. Samuel Alexander and Sophie Elizabeth. Their social security numbers are—"

"How many children did *Dr. Glass* have, Evie? Not you. Your ex-husband."

"Three." *Were there more?*

Then the Midwest Mutual envelope addressed to Nicole flashed into Evie's head. Her blood turned to ice, the skin on her torso prickled, and then her limbs stung as if she'd been pelted with hailstones from inside.

"Oh my God, it's Nicole."

"I'm sorry, Evie . . . I can't confirm."

"You don't have to."

She clicked the END button and held the receiver to her chest, swallowed hard, speed-dialed Laney, and left a message. But when the kitchen door swung open two minutes later, there was Beth.

"You don't have to forgive me, but you have to let me help you." Beth tucked her foot against the door so Evie couldn't slam it.

"Did you know she was doing this?" Though Evie's gut told her no, she wasn't so keen on her gut lately.

"No!" Beth sounded insulted. "Please let me in. Really, I'm not asking you to forgive me. I'm asking you to let me help."

Evie stepped aside. She felt as if her life had defeated her, that no matter what she said or did or wanted, nothing would ever be good again. So she relinquished her make-believe control. Beth walked into the kitchen and sat at the table, not the counter.

"Will you let me help you?"

Evie just shrugged and sat one chair away from Beth. "Promise me you didn't know she was doing this. Swear on Cody's life." Beth hated any kind of swearing and Evie knew it.

"I swear." Beth made an X on her chest. "If I'd known, I would have told her to come to you, to be honest about what she was thinking. Or I would have told you."

Evie believed Beth. "Things with us can't be the same, you know."

"I know, but we're on the same side. That's a start."

"Maybe."

Laney barreled through the door and threw herself onto the chair between Evie and Beth. "Catch me up."

"I don't have more details. All I know is what I told you." Evie sneered. "What you told her." She looked at Beth's face and tried not to see the empathy.

"Now, will you stop making excuses for her?" Laney turned to

Beth. "Your best friend is sitting here, and the woman she took into her home is now after the money she needs to raise her kids. Did you kick her out yet?"

Evie shook her head.

"What are you waiting for?"

"She's not here. Plus, I need to be prepared when I ask her about this. I have to know the facts and I have to know my rights. I need a lawyer."

Evie was shaking. Shit happens. She knew this better than anyone, yet was continually surprised when things didn't follow a straight and narrow path. Richard would have said she was naive. Evie felt plain stupid.

"You need to kick her ass out of this house is what you need to do," Laney said.

"Oh my God, the kids. What am I going to tell Sam and Sophie?"

"You're going to tell them it didn't work out, that Nicole and Luca needed their own trailer. I mean house. They'll get over it."

Laney was so resolute Evie almost believed her.

"I'll talk to Nicole," Beth said. "Something's got to be up."

"Yeah, her gig is up, that's what," Laney said. "She can't be trusted. Once a cheat always a cheat."

Beth crossed her arms, opened her mouth, but closed it without a word.

"I'm going to have to sell the house. Can I even sell a house in this market?" Evie said. "I'm going to have to move."

"No, you're going to get that job and you're going to be fine, this is just a setback," Beth said.

"I think I'm going to throw up." Evie dashed to the bathroom, sat on the floor, and waited for the nausea to subside. She followed the advice she gave Sophie during the three-month string of morning bellyaches and took slow, deep breaths. She pressed her cheek against the cold wall and closed her eyes. When she opened her eyes, she fixed her gaze on one spot, rose from the floor, patted cold water from the spigot on her forehead, and went back to the living room, ignoring the lump of lunch at the base of her throat.

Evie lay on the couch with her head propped on two pillows. Beth put a cold washcloth on her head. Images of Sam, Sophie, Nicole, Luca, and even Richard collided. She was wide-awake, the nausea was gone, but her thoughts were hazy.

"That bitch," she said. "It was all about money. Wiggling into my family and my town and my life—and now my kids' college funds."

"There ya go," Laney said.

"How dare she play the sad double-widow card with me. And I fell for it. What else do you think she has going on in that trailer-park brain of hers? Oh my God, what if she won't leave? What if I tell her she has to go and I have to call the police." Rage and fear fought for supremacy in Evie's thoughts.

"I think you need to wait. Try to understand where Nicole is coming from." Beth was on the losing end of this argument but Evie knew if anyone could find out more information, it was Beth.

"Stop defending her. Tragedy is not an all-purpose excuse for bad choices and reprehensible behavior," Laney said.

"She adores your kids, Evie. She wouldn't want to hurt them, but she's looking out for herself. She couldn't protect her little girl, and now she's doing whatever she can think of to protect Luca."

"You're pissing me off," Laney said. "She wasn't protecting Luca or thinking of Evie's kids when she shampooed her way into Evie's marriage."

"Shh, please. I need to think," Evie said, knowing that no one cheated who didn't want to cheat and that there were many kinds of cheating.

"Sam and Soph can sleep at my house if you want them to," Laney said.

Evie knew Laney was sincere, but also knew that would never work. "Just let them hang out with you guys for a while after school?"

Laney nodded and pulled out her cell phone. "I'm just going to give Herb a heads-up. Maybe he can take Sam to the park for some soccer practice. And the girls will keep Sophie occupied."

Beth gathered her jacket and purse. "Look, there's got to be more to the story. I know it's hard, but we shouldn't jump to conclusions."

"I didn't jump," Evie said. "I was pushed."

Nicole walked into the kitchen holding Luca in one arm and a bag from Jewel in the other.

"Where are the kids? Soccer practice? I didn't see that on the schedule."

"They're at Laney's."

Nicole laughed. "That's why it's so quiet in here!"

Evie nodded but said nothing.

"What's wrong?"

"Have a seat."

Nicole pulled out a chair and sat with Luca facing her. He only wanted to stand, so close to walking at nine months. They all took turns holding both his hands and walking him from room to room to room. Evie loved his slobbery smile and baby words. For Luca, and for her own sense of propriety, she vowed to remain calm. Another excursion on the high road for Evie. Her emotional energy would no longer be used for Nicole's benefit. "I know about Midwest Mutual."

Nicole jumped from the seat. Luca gasped from the jolt and cried.

"I can explain—"

"Don't."

Luca wailed an I'm-scared-and-I-need-a-nap wail.

"I want to put Luca in for his nap. Then we can talk. I'll be right back."

This was no time for napping, for Nicole to gain composure or for Evie to lose her mojo. Her heart pounded against her chest and she reminded herself no one could hear it or feel it but her.

"This won't take long. Just sit." Evie pulled out a chair and pointed, but instead of anger bursting out, she was bereft. She'd been emptied, instead of filled, by an insatiable quest to restart their lives. It was Evie's choice to let in Nicole that night in December. Evie chose to make over the basement and to accept Nicole's help. What was she thinking? She'd let a predator into their home, and hearts. *What kind of woman am I? What kind of mother am I?*

"I said I'll be right back." Nicole's words were articulated slowly and deliberately. She walked out of the kitchen and down the basement stairs.

She came right back and sat even though Luca was still crying.

Evie scraped her fingers through her hair hard, grabbed her scalp, and rubbed, like acupressure. She moved her hands to her ears to muffle the noise and exhaled more air than she thought she could hold. She grabbed a box of tissues from the counter and dropped it on the table. This wasn't Luca's fault. But she still wasn't letting Nicole leave until she finished.

"You moved in here to get the inside scoop on what was going on. To trick me. To take advantage of my children. To make them—to make us—want you here."

"Oh my God, I love your kids. You don't understand!"

"I do understand." Evie's voice was quiet and sounded as if it were someone else's voice. That was probably because although Evie was right there in the kitchen, gripping the chair, feet flat on the floor, she was becoming someone new all over again. "I understand that once again you want what does not belong to you. The difference, though, between Richard and this life insurance? Would you like me to tell you?"

Nicole nodded.

"You're not getting the life insurance."

"I don't want to fight with you, I just want to share."

"Sharing time is over."

Nicole pushed back her shoulders. "You're going to be sorry."

Evie bristled at the threat. "I'm already sorry. I'm sorry I trusted you. You tricked me—and it's my fault that I fell for it. But it won't happen again. And this time you won't get what you want."

"I want us to be a family! And I didn't trick you. I love being here. Luca loves it. And I don't want all the money." Nicole's voice cracked. "Richard wanted all of his children to be taken care of. It's rightfully ours too."

Evie grabbed the table edge. "What's rightfully yours is that big house across town and all the bills that go with it." She felt an edge to her voice that both stung and soothed her.

"You can't afford to stay here without me." Nicole stood and put her hands on her hips. "Are you so selfish you'd make your kids move just so you don't have to help me? I've been helping *you* for three months by living here! Where would you be without me? In your parents' condo in Florida, that's where!"

"Wow," Evie breathed. "And for the record, I'm not leaving this house. Ever. But you are leaving. Today."

Evie was resolute only on the outside. Inside, she was hollow, as though everything she had to give had been given.

"I love all of you." Nicole had gathered her shirt over her heart into her fist and tugged. "I loved you enough to help you."

"Then your idea of love and family sucks. Love is behavior, not just a feeling." Evie didn't believe that Nicole felt love. What Nicole felt was entitlement. Evie held up the Midwest Mutual envelope she'd taken from the basement and slapped it on the table. "This isn't love. This isn't family. This is betrayal. So, no thanks. I've had enough of that for one lifetime." Conscious of her slow words, mellow heartbeat, and warm skin, Evie wondered if she was going into shock. She also wondered if she was losing her mind, or if it was already long gone.

"You're going to separate the kids? Nice. How are you going to explain that to Sam and Sophie?" Nicole sputtered, and twisted her mouth. She was nervous, surprised, maybe she was the one in shock.

"Don't worry about my kids. Go back to your house or go to Iowa and move in with your mother. I don't care."

"We have an agreement. And I've paid you through the end of March. You can't make me leave."

That broke the spell. Evie hated being told what she could and couldn't do. Which is what got her into trouble when she'd let Nicole move in. She slapped cash on the table and stood.

"You need to leave my house. Now."

"Are you kidding me?"

"What did you expect?!"

Nicole grunted and stomped around the kitchen. "I expected you to be reasonable."

"If that means risking my children's future, well, you were dead wrong."

"Richard would have wanted us to work this out!"

"I stopped caring what Richard would have wanted a long time ago."

Nicole's eyes grew so wide Evie thought they might fall out of their sockets. "You're so mean!"

Nicole had no idea how mean Evie could be. She considered her options and then flung her words. "You do know you weren't the first?"

Nicole collapsed back into her chair. "I *know* you were his first wife, Evie," she snapped. "You really don't have to keep reminding me."

"That's not what I mean, Nicole," Evie said with a bite. "You weren't *the first*."

"What are you talking about?"

"You weren't his first dalliance, his first affair, his first girlfriend on the side. I dealt with that crap for years."

Nicole face turned red. "That's not true," she bellowed, and the words pierced Evie. The gash of finding out hurt like hell and Evie knew it.

"I don't care if you believe it. I found out that Richard broke his promise again—to not let it happen, again—and I kicked him out. Which is the night he moved in with you. Want me to tell you the date?"

Nicole stood again, fists clenched. Her face reddened and tightened and looked sunburned. "You're lying to hurt me."

"No. You're wrong. I'm telling the *truth* to hurt you."

Chapter 17

EVIE HAD ALWAYS BEEN THE one to deliver bad news. *No dessert tonight. We're not getting a rabbit. Your game's rained out. We're getting divorced. Your dad died.* And now *this*. There was no right way to explain *this* to the kids, simply because it was so difficult to even describe what *this* was. But there was no getting around it. Just before their dinner—the conciliatory blue box of macaroni and cheese—Evie announced the change in living arrangements.

"They need their own space," she had said, trying to sound oh-so-matter-of-fact. "It was too cramped down there anyway. And musty." Neither of which was true. "And our basement doesn't have any windows." That was true. "But I printed out your basketball and soccer schedules so they can come to the games." True again.

"What if Nicole doesn't know where the fields are?" Sam asked.

"She knows where the fields are," Evie said, trying not to sound dismissive.

Sophie batted her eyes, holding back tears. "What if she forgets? Who will remind her?"

"She won't forget."

"But—"

"No buts, she won't forget."

"Where did they go?" Sam asked.

Damn. Evie hadn't a clue. "To a friend's."

"Which one?"

"Sam! I don't know. I do know they're fine. Nicole is an adult and she can take care of herself and Luca. She can remember your games and she can find the fields, okay?"

"What if—"

"Stop! It's enough already." Evie thought her remarks might fluster the kids, but the mandate seemed to settle them.

"I'm hungry," Sam said.

"I'm not," Sophie said.

"Fine. Macaroni for you. No macaroni for you." Evie filled one bowl and gave it to Sam with a snack-pack of peaches. The meal was at least three food groups if the orange powder she'd whisked into sauce counted as cheese. And today, it did.

Sam ate in silence. Sophie sat in silence. Even now, that wasn't the norm. And since it was Evie's job to emit a normal vibe, she'd bake cookies. It would be a distraction as well as a form of simple bribery, and no, she wasn't above it. Without a word, Evie rose from her chair. The kids watched as she gathered the mixer, bowls, flour, and sugar and set them on the counter.

Sam started eating heaping spoonfuls. Apparently the "finish your dinner before you get dessert" mantra had penetrated. Evie hoped Sophie would help her bake as she always had before.

"What should we make, Soph? Chocolate chunk? Peanut-butter kisses? Sugar cookies? You decide."

But instead of deciding, she ran out of the room.

"Sam, finish your dinner, put the bowls in the sink, and then go out back with Rex."

"What about the cookies?"

"Sam!"

"Okay, okay. But I have to finish my homework." Evie knew he just wanted to find out what was going on with Sophie. So did Evie.

"Sam, please don't argue with me and we'll make the cookies

later. Or we'll go out for ice cream." Or fly to the moon—which now seemed more likely than baking any cookies.

When Evie found Sophie, she was sprawled facedown on her bedroom floor. Evie stared at her daughter, not even an official tween for another few months, but already taking after her aunt Lisa in the teenage-drama-queen department. Evie eased herself down on the floor and flung her arm over her daughter.

"You can't make me bake with you!"

"I thought you liked baking. But if you don't like it anymore, we'll find something else fun to do together. Something special, okay?"

Sophie nodded.

It didn't make sense. Baking resulted in licking the bowl and the spoon and eating cookies right out of the oven, sometimes before they were fully cooked, which was Richard's favorite. Richard.

"Soph? Did you have a baking date planned with Daddy?"

She nodded her head, then buried it in her arms.

"But you didn't get to do it, did you?"

She shook her head.

"So baking makes you sad because it makes you think about your dad."

Sophie, with her curls matted against her forehead, looked at Evie and nodded. "He went out to his meeting and was going to get more flour on his way home." *Sophie means the other home she used to have.* "If I didn't want to bake with him, he wouldn't have been driving and he wouldn't have had The Accident."

"Oh my God, Sophie!" Evie clutched her daughter. "It's not your fault that your daddy died in that accident. It was because the weather was terrible and icy on that road."

"But if I didn't want to bake—"

"Sophie, listen to me." Evie stayed on the floor, nose to nose, cradling the sides of her daughter's face in her palms. "Your dad was happy thinking about baking those cookies with you, I'm sure of it. You did not cause the accident. The snow and wind and the ice and the road did. It was not your fault." Evie's chest tightened and then expanded as if to bring Sophie inside.

"Promise?"

"With all of my heart," Evie said with authority, because she felt every piece of it.

"Plucking is not adequate when you have a second interview," Laney said. She pressed the cotton strip over Evie's eyebrows and smoothed it. *Rip.* "So you really told her about Richard?"

Evie felt her eyebrows. Dry. No blood. "Yes. Don't gloat. Just do the other one."

"I'm not gloating, I just want to hear it again. Slowly."

"I told her Richard had other girlfriends." Evie sat straight, cotton stuck to her brow. "I don't get a thrill out of admitting that I knew my husband was cheating on me for years, Lane. I hated spitting out those words. Makes me look like an idiot."

"No, it makes you look like someone who loved her husband and believed in her marriage. I know you didn't like doing it, but you told her for the right reason. To hurt her because she hurt you. And I don't mean when she was with Richard."

Revenge was not Evie's MO. She shrugged. Weren't right reasons supposed to uplift you and not make you feel as though you were being buried in the sand and couldn't get out? "It was just a reaction. I didn't plan it."

"It's okay if you had."

"I didn't."

"Do you think if you forgave him *again,* he'd have stopped?"

"No. But it stopped mattering because I stopped loving him. I couldn't love someone who disregarded me. I did for a long time . . .

but then I just stopped. The same way one day a person looks at another and thinks, 'God, I love you so much,' one day I looked at Richard and thought, 'God, I do not love you at all.'"

"I can't imagine not loving Herb. That asshole." Laney put her arms around Evie and patted her back. "You did your best, Ev."

"Did I?" She pondered this as she pulled away. Should she have just accepted Richard the way he was, allowed his string of indiscretions, and continued to accept his apologies and promises? Could she have tried harder to be compliant and to exist within the frenzy of their lives? She knew the answer was no. "Do my other eyebrow."

"Lie back and hold still."

Evie lay on the edge of her bed and Laney stood. She ripped the hot wax off the second eyebrow. It didn't hurt as much as Evie had expected.

"So, do you think he was cheating on Nicole?"

"Honest?" Evie said, checking her groomed brows in the hand mirror.

"Of course honest."

"I think he was happy with her."

"I didn't ask you if he was happy. I asked you if you thought he was cheating."

"Well, I don't know. But he came on to me once." Evie shifted to her side and leaned on her elbow.

"You had ex-sex!"

"I did not!"

"You did!"

"I did not . . . We kissed, though," Evie whispered. "It was no big deal. Actually, it was kind of gross."

"Shut up!" Laney fell back onto Evie's bed holding her head with both hands. "When?"

"Well, technically we were still married because it was before our divorce was final." Evie shuddered at the memory.

"You've got that right," Laney said, bouncing to shake the queen-size bed. "You should've slept with him. Just to fuck with him. And *her*." She kept bouncing.

Evie was stunned into silence. Laney was *giddy*. Laney, who had a zero-tolerance policy for aberrant marital behavior thought Evie should have slept with Richard out of spite. The people she knew best seemed to surprise her the most.

"Okay," Laney said, breaking the quiet. "Enough about Richard and his child bride. Right now we're going to focus on this second interview, okay? You're not going to get the job if you look like a beleaguered hausfrau."

Laney was right, of course, but Evie reached back, grabbed a throw pillow, and hit Laney in the stomach. They belly-laughed until Evie was gasping for breath. She stood and walked to the closet, resolute. She slid the closet door open wide. How had there ever been space for Richard's wardrobe? She saw at least twenty black T-shirts hanging in a row—short sleeved, long sleeved, no sleeve, three-quarters. There were half as many black bottoms—jeans in several sizes, out-of-style stretchy pants, and even a pair of worn-out corduroys, not to mention dressy slacks. Did anyone say *slacks* anymore? Evie skimmed a row of black dresses with her fingers, feeling each fabric and trying not to notice the dancing dust.

Laney folded and hung up every item her friend discarded. Then, Laney reached into the abyss, pulling out wrinkled, camel-color pants. "Wear these pants with a white blouse and a cardigan. Unbuttoned. The cardigan, that is, not the blouse. Although that might help get you the job." Laney chortled and slapped her hip. She was her own biggest fan. "It's academic, it's classy, and it's functional. It's an outfit that multitasks. It can take you to court and the classroom."

Evie held up a long, navy cardigan and smoothed her hair. She closed her eyes to picture the outfit, but it didn't come together in her head the way it obviously had in Laney's.

"And no pearls, June Cleaver, I'll lend you a funky scarf. You can be cool and sophisticated. Oh, and wear your diamond-stud earrings. That's classic without being showy."

"Are you sure this is okay?"

Laney cocked a sideways smile. "You know it is."

"But . . ."

"But nothing. If you look confident, you'll act confident and eventually you'll feel confident. Plus, this is more *you* than any blue suit from 2002. There is nothing wrong with looking like *you* again, Evie. It's time."

"You're going out *again*?" Sam said.

"Another interview," Evie said while looking in the mirror, checking her teeth for runaway lipstick. Laney was right. Evie looked maternal and professional. She looked the part, now she had to get the part.

"Who's going to stay with us?"

"Jordyn," Sophie said from the living room. "Right, Mom?"

Evie looked at Sam. "I won't be long. This is important stuff, remember? I could get a job teaching at County."

Sam rolled his eyes. "It would be more fun if Luca and Nicole still lived here," he said without looking at his mother.

"You like Jordyn!" she said, but Sam was right. Did he have to remind her?

"What if I get sick while you're gone?"

Evie took Sam's hand and led him to the couch. She pulled him onto her lap even though he was too big for that. He didn't resist. She pushed the hair off his forehead, but it fell back into its genetically predisposed position. "You're going to be fine. I'll be gone a few hours. Sophie is here."

Sophie stared at the TV but put both hands in the air.

"You're without me all day in school."

"Yeah, but then I know you're at home."

Evie patted his back. "You'll be fine."

"What if *I* don't feel good when you're gone?" Sophie asked.

Sam shuffled to his feet and Evie stood. "Everyone is going to be fine," Evie barked. She pointed to Sophie. "You're going to be fine." Evie pointed to Sam. "And you're going to be fine." Evie pointed to herself. "And *I'm* going to be fine."

The last part was the hardest to believe—and that's the one they all depended on.

Driving the twenty minutes to County College, Evie replaced thoughts of the twins with thoughts of Sandy Perlman and how his blue eyes brightened when he talked about his students. Evie had noticed the naked ring finger, but asked if he had children—a lesson of divorce. Sandy lit like a neon sign when he mentioned a daughter and snarled with a smirk when he mentioned his ex-wife. He was smart, funny, and *very* handsome. Her heart pounded and she flushed. Evie had given up dating—but she wasn't blind. Apparently she still wasn't dead either.

The students would be easy to relate to, but Evie wasn't sure about relating to Sandy Perlman, and not just because he smelled like Aramis and apple pie. She'd been part of Lakewood's suburban milieu—in various configurations—for a dozen years. Wouldn't even mild academia smell her coming from a mile away?

She pulled into a visitors' parking spot, imagining herself in the staff lot around the back, closer to the main building. She smoothed her hair and turned her chin, peeking back at her profile in the rearview mirror. She tapped twice under her chin with the back of her hand. Minimal jiggle. Evie stretched her neck forward for an instant—and revocable—necklift.

This time as Evie walked to Dr. Talbot's office, she strode secure, not looking at the map in her hand. The hallways were narrower, the ceilings lower, the distance shorter.

Evie opened the door, saw Dr. Talbot, and said, "Good afternoon."

Evie had hoped for the smiley buffer of the secretary, which could have served as her hot tip as to what was next.

"Good afternoon, Ms. Glass." The chairwoman stood straight, clutching a stack of folders.

Dr. Talbot didn't keep her waiting. "Please, sit."

A second interview conducted in a waiting room? At a secretary's desk? If County didn't want her, they could've called, e-mailed, or even texted.

"Obviously I asked you back because I'd like to offer you the summer teaching position."

Obviously. *Not*. Evie's people-reading skills lacked finesse. She'd work on that in her spare time.

"Thank you." Evie did not say, "Thank you thank you thank you thank you," though it stuck in the back of her throat.

"These are contracts and HR papers and lessons and procedures, but I guess you'd like to know how much the position pays before you accept."

Since it was more than zero, Evie ached to stretch out her hand and say, "I'll take it," followed by jumping up and down on the desk. Instead, she stayed seated, nodded once, and said, "Yes, thank you, I would."

Evie knew the pay wouldn't be much, but that it would be enough. For now. What Evie didn't know was that she'd be taking another walk with Sandy Perlman.

"Sandy will show you his—and your—office space again. He'll give you a schedule of faculty meetings. You should start attending now, if you can, so when you start in June, you'll be familiar with everyone and everything."

"Absolutely." Evie prayed the meetings were during her kids' school day.

Dr. Talbot directed Evie to Sandy's office. "He's expecting you."

Standing in front of the office she'd share with Sandy, Evie knocked. No one answered. She knocked again. *So much for being expected.*

Evie slipped her new ID card through the reader, turned the knob, and opened the door as if someone were going to jump out from behind—first a few inches, then all the way. Leaning in, Evie looked around the dark office and flipped on the light. She didn't enter but stared inside.

The room was smaller than she remembered. Maybe it was the additional desk and chair. Maybe it was that the blinds were down. She strained to look through the cracks to the campus green, crowded with business-clothed students sitting at picnic tables and sauntering on the winding, concrete paths. Some of those people would be her students.

She leaned against the doorjamb. She looked at the pictures on the wall, and when she shifted her eyes back to the hallway, Sandy Perlman was next to her.

"Welcome to the team," he said.

"Thank you. I'm really looking forward to it."

"You should be."

Evie dug into her purse for nothing. His sarcasm flustered her.

"I'm kidding," Sandy said. "I'm glad you accepted."

She looked up. "You are?"

"I don't want to teach at night!"

Evie put her hand on her hip. "Very funny."

"Glad to see you have a sense of humor. You never know what's going to happen here, so we're all pretty laid-back and adaptable. Did you have trouble finding the office?"

"Not at all."

"If you want the desk on the other wall, I can probably slide it over there," he said, gesturing.

"So you're a tour guide and a furniture mover? I mean, thank you, it's great."

Sandy smiled and revealed white, straight teeth. Evie reached into her purse and retrieved her water bottle, but left the apple. An apple was way too cliché. All of a sudden, her stomach churned.

"We might not bump into each other too much this summer," he said. "My classes are in the morning and afternoon." He checked his watch. It was stainless steel and clunky with a blue face. Its size made his hand look small. "I have a meeting in twenty minutes, but we can talk about the curriculum until I have to go."

"Sure." Evie sat at what would become her desk, her chair, her space. It was better than a country-club membership. It meant she would be okay.

Sandy sat at his desk and tilted back in his chair. "Don't be nervous about the students. These people all choose to be here, and most of them pay their own tuition. It might not seem like a lot to some people, but . . . well, you don't find too many trust-fund babies at County." He clamped his lips. "Sorry, I didn't mean anything by that. I'm just glad to be out of that environment."

"You taught somewhere else before this?" Even though she knew nothing about him, Evie had assumed Sandy Perlman was a couldn't-get-a-job-at-a-real-college, frustrated academic—although a handsome one.

He looked at her and squinted as if trying to remember if he left his oven on. "Yes, but at a college on the East Coast. In New Hampshire. Aah, you've probably never heard of it." He clasped his hands behind his head.

"Try me," Evie said before she could stop herself. Why would he assume she would be unfamiliar with an East Coast college? She grew up in Delaware. Although twenty-six years near Chicago had left her with a distinct Midwestern twang.

"It's called Dartmouth. With a *D*."

Evie stared at him, unsure if his sarcasm was the result of her transparent speculation on his professional tenure, or if he thought she'd never heard of Dartmouth.

"I'm kidding," he said, shaking his head and holding up his hands in surrender.

"So you didn't teach at Dartmouth."

He patted his desk like a bongo. "No—I'm kidding that I think you've never *heard* of Dartmouth."

Evie scanned the shelves and desk for photos, a glimpse inside more than the office. She saw one photo of Sandy and a young woman she assumed was his daughter, on his desk in a plain, black frame. Evie pointed. "Your daughter?"

Sandy nodded.

"She's beautiful. And obviously very smart." Evie mentioned the multiple hoods adorning the young woman's graduation robe and hoped the Dartmouth gaffe was erased.

"Yep. That's Rachel. She's starting Kent Law next fall. Taking a year off to find herself first." He chuckled. "I'm proud of her. You have two kids, right? How old are they?"

"Twins. Sam and Sophie. They're almost eleven."

Sandy's eyes widened. "Young 'uns."

Evie shrank at her desk. She wouldn't defend or explain.

"It's nice," he said. "You have all the good stuff ahead of you."

"I hope so."

Sandy stood from his desk, stretched, and almost touched the ceiling. "Why don't you walk with me to the meeting? It's a Social Science meeting—a wild and crazy group." He rolled his eyes around and did a mediocre Steve Martin impression.

Evie picked up her purse. Nerves overtook intrigue.

"Where's your armor?" he asked.

She looked at him, deadpan.

Sandy ran his hand atop his spiky, peppered crew cut. "You have to lighten up, Ms. Glass, go with the flow. It's just American History at County College, not life or death."

Evie laughed from deep down, glad to know she still could.

Chapter 18

EVIE STARED AT THE COUNTY College contract in her hands. *Evelyn T. Glass* would be employed as soon as she signed it. Part-time and temporary, for now. According to Sandy, there was potential. Potential with medical and dental benefits. The college paid more for an eight-week summer job than she would have received from Nicole in that time. Of course, if Nicole were there, Evie wouldn't be worrying about who'd watch the kids two nights a week, what a judge would rule about Nicole's insurance claim, and whether she'd be packing up the kids and moving in with her parents and eating early-bird dinners before the start of the next school year. But all that worrying would have to wait until after soccer. The kids deserved her full attention, even if she sometimes faked it with nods and smiles and extra quarters for the concession stand. "Let's go, guys. Hustle," Evie yelled. Sophie and Sam ran into the kitchen from different directions. "Get the leash, I'm bringing Rex."

"Why?" Sophie asked.

"Because it's a nice day, that's why." Evie also wanted a point of conversation other than the absence of Nicole.

"Why are you so dressed up?" Sam asked.

"I'm not dressed up." Evie hadn't thrown away her Minnie Mouse sweatshirt, but had folded it and tucked it in the back of her closet so it wasn't easy to grab and go. Laney was right. Evie did feel better wearing jeans and a long-sleeved, red, thermal T-shirt, a long, beaded necklace from the Days of Dating, and hoop earrings. Her jean jacket had been cleaned, and she also wore one of Laney's hand-me-down knit scarves. It had only taken Evie an hour to create today's casual soccer-mom look.

With one collapsible chair slung over her shoulder, Evie pulled out her sunglasses. Sunglasses made her feel glamorous and served as a handy tool in the dating days. If she met someone outside, she could give him a surreptitious once-over. Today she hoped the dark plastic lenses hid her trepidation. Trusting Nicole had left Evie feeling like a loser on *Are You Smarter Than a 5th Grader?* She didn't want anyone to know why Nicole moved out, so there Evie was again, making excuses for the truth. She did not want "I told you so" or the finger-wagging that would come along with admitting that her intuition had led her astray. She did not want to explain that while she was livid, she didn't hate Nicole. She couldn't explain it to herself; how was she going to explain it to someone else?

As the kids and Evie walked onto the soccer field, Nicole was waiting.

"Where are you sitting?" Nicole did not wait for an answer and sat, pushed the stroller wheel lock with one foot, and flung open a blanket with the other. "I didn't want to miss the game."

Still standing, mouth agape, Evie stared at Nicole on the ground. "Make yourself at home," she mumbled. "You always do." Her nostrils flared, then she scratched her nose to disguise evidence of disgust. Maybe giving Nicole the sports schedules was a bad idea. Evie did it for Sam's and Sophie's sakes, but when was she going to allow herself something for her own sake?

Sophie skipped over with Isabel and asked, "Can I buy popcorn?"

"Did you say hello to Nicole and Luca? " Evie said without taking her eyes off the field. Teaching good manners could be a bitch.

Without a word Sophie stepped to Nicole and hugged her. Evie cringed. But when Sophie hugged Luca, Evie smiled.

"It's fifty cents," Sophie said.

Evie dug out quarters from her pocket and tucked them into Sophie's palm, closing her fingers around the coins and squeezing. "Be careful with your money so no one takes it from you."

Unfazed, Sophie and Isabel ran toward the concession stand. It was commonplace for Sophie, and even Isabel, to see Nicole and Evie together. It was all they remembered.

"You haven't returned my calls," Nicole said.

"I can't believe you expect me to."

"I thought you'd change your mind, for the kids' sake."

Evie turned to see if anyone was within earshot. For the first time she was glad that the duo made the other moms uneasy. They'd waved from a comfortable distance, but did not approach. Evie looked back at the soccer field and spoke in a raised whisper.

"For the kids' sake I gave you their sports schedules. For the kids' sake I didn't walk away when you sat down. For the kids' sake, I won't tell them you want the money their father left them."

Evie removed her sunglasses and cheered loudly for Sam, raising her arms above her head. Luca clapped and Rex barked. Evie led Rex with his leash closer to Luca in the stroller so he could pet the dog. "You messed this up. I ignored *everything* everyone said about you and let you into my home. I even *liked* you."

"Then why won't you share Richard's money with Luca?"

Evie turned away from Nicole. Was this girl stupid? No, she'd schemed her way into Evie's family—twice. Evie turned back. "It's not Richard's money. This policy belongs to Sam and Sophie. I'm not saying anything more on the subject."

"I only want enough for Luca to start a college fund."

"I know how much you want. It's in all the legal documents. Go home to Iowa, Nicole. I'll let the kids web-chat with Luca. If they remember to ask."

Nicole twirled her hair enough to start a small propeller plane.

Evie put on her sunglasses and looked to the soccer field. She blinked back tears and felt as though a soccer ball were lodged in her throat. Crying would ruin her bitch vibe, so she coughed to feign a case of spring sniffles. Evie was over it. Over Nicole. Over Luca. Over the family cookie nights and sparkling refrigerator shelves. She was done.

— Chapter 19 —

EVIE PREFERRED BEING SERVED, EVEN if it was just deep-dish pizza. Nothing was better than a meal she didn't have to bake, roast, nuke, serve, or clean up. Add a bottle of wine, subtract the twins and going-out guilt—and it was a perfect night. Or it would have been perfect if Laney hadn't insisted on inviting Beth and Alan, and if Evie weren't obsessing on how to behave when they showed up, now that she knew their secret.

Evie stabbed an olive on the group's appetizer plate, popped it into her mouth, and washed down the saltiness with a sip of cabernet franc. She cleared her throat, wanting to make an announcement before her new nemesis arrived.

"I got the job at County College."

"We know!" Laney said. "That's why we're here, to celebrate."

"I wanted to tell you!"

"Alan told us," Herb said.

"How did he know? It hasn't been announced yet."

"Because Sandy told me."

Evie twisted in her seat, saw Alan and Beth, and then turned back to Laney.

"Oh, stop it," Laney said. "Whatever is going on between you— and I'm not asking—it's time to put it aside. We're celebrating." She scooted around so there was enough space in the U-shaped booth for the five of them.

Evie did not want to celebrate with Beth or Alan. But that's exactly what she was going to have to do. Laney had coordinated the dinner, and Evie couldn't forget that Alan was the reason she'd known about the job in the first place.

"Thank you for telling me about the job." Evie nodded toward Alan but didn't look at him. "And for putting in a good word."

"All I did was mention your name," Alan said.

"Twenty times, I bet," Laney said.

"No, only about ten."

Everyone but Evie laughed and held up their glasses, so she acquiesced. They clinked and drank. The wine was warm on Evie's throat, coating her apprehensions.

"So what did they say?" Beth asked. "Tell us everything." She used her extrasweet Beth-voice, the one she used with customer-service reps when she was trying to get her way.

"Nothing to tell, really," Evie said. "Excuse me, I'm going to go to the ladies' room."

"Laney doesn't understand why you're so angry," Beth said over the roar of the hand dryer when Evie stepped out of a stall.

"No, she does not. And I'm not going to tell her."

"I think she's afraid to know. It takes a lot to make you angry."

"Laney would probably combust."

Their absentminded laughter echoed off the tiled walls.

"Are you really going to let the fact that we're here ruin your celebration? Can't it be the first step with us?"

Evie shrugged. She was so mad at Beth. And more than that, she was hurt. But this was Beth. This was still Beth. Maybe Evie could shuffle her feelings and expectations until she found a comfortable combination. After all, nothing in her life was as she'd expected.

"Time for pizza?" Beth asked.

"Time for more wine," Evie said, walking back to the table a few steps ahead.

She heard Beth mumble, "Whatever works."

"So, who is this Sandy person who told you about Evie's job?" Laney asked.

Damn. Nothing gets by Laney. Well, almost nothing.

"A history professor," Evie said. "One who has been there for a long time and now has to share office space."

"Sucks for her," Laney said.

"Sandy's a man," Alan said. "Alexander. Alexander Perlman."

"A may-an!" Laney hollered, louder than she should have, even at Antonio's. Part wine, part enthusiasm, equaled a whole lot of Laney-itis. "A *Jewish* may-an."

"He was very nice to me," Evie said. "I'm sure the last thing he wants to be is my tour guide and babysitter."

"I've met him. He's handsome," Beth said, attempting normalcy. Evie looked at her, wanting to be annoyed, but she wasn't.

"Of course he's handsome," Laney said, even though she'd never met him. "If he wasn't handsome, Evie would've already mentioned him."

The dim lighting camouflaged Evie's flush.

"So it's pretty exciting that you got the job and you'll be working with Sandy. It's just what you wanted," Alan said.

Evie wanted Alan to shut up. A bathroom treaty with Beth was one thing, but chitchat with the cheater was another. Alan glanced at Evie over his glasses while moving plates around on the table to make room for the waitress to deliver the deluxe veggie deep-dish pizza. Evie knew he felt her disapproving vibe, and she was fine with that.

Garlic and spices overwhelmed Evie's senses, her appetite re-placed with a swirl of queasiness. "It's fine. I'm just not sure how I'm going to swing it." Evie shifted in her space, eight eyes upon her.

"Swing what?" Herb said. "It's a job. You don't swing it, you just do it."

Laney opened her mouth to speak, but Evie put up her hand like a crossing guard. "Herb's right, which is one of the reasons I ac-cepted. Another is because Alan really went to bat for me." She looked right at him and he nodded once. "And of course there's the 'I really need a paycheck' reason. But without Nicole around, I don't know how . . ."

"What? You don't know how you're going to be normal?" Laney said.

Herb glared at his wife.

Evie didn't want them fighting because of her. "Lane, she was my free babysitting. Tonight my kids are at your house, but I can't do that for eight weeks. I know Sam and Sophie aren't babies, but if I'm going to be teaching a class from six to eight, twice a week, it means I'll be gone for longer than that. I can handle the at-home stuff—the planning, the reading, and the grading—but the logis-tics of being gone that long aren't easy to figure out."

"We'll all help you," Laney said. A chorus of "Of course, don't be silly, we'd be happy to" and "Whatever you need" relieved Evie's anxiety, or should have. She felt a cold spot in her stomach that hadn't been warmed by pizza, wine, or kind words.

Beth lifted her glass. Evie allowed Alan to pour her a drop from their second bottle.

"Here's to Evie," Beth said.

"Here-here." Voices rose to meet their glasses.

"Ooh, and let's not forget about the cute professor," Laney said.

Evie's cheeks warmed but she furrowed her brows as if she'd forgotten about him.

Laney put her head on Herb's shoulder and looked up, batting her eyes. He kissed the top of her head. Between their bickering and flirting, Evie got marital whiplash. But whatever they were doing, it was working. The solid marriages that surrounded her served as good examples to Evie and her kids. No matter what else had happened.

Laney popped up her head and reached over to Alan. "Why don't you see if the professor is single."

"Stop," Evie said. "He's a colleague. It wouldn't be professional. Plus, I'm not dating anymore, remember? Men are out of sight and out of mind."

"How about when one's *in* sight?" Laney asked, then took a slug of her wine.

Evie didn't know. She just prayed she would not see Sandy Perlman anytime soon so she wouldn't find out.

Chapter 20

"I'D HAVE MOVED UP THE court date if I knew you'd visit," Evie said. The click of her seat belt served as punctuation.

Lisa shut the car door and Evie pulled away from O'Hare's congested Terminal 1, zigzagging around the waiting cars, hoping for no traffic as they headed north on the tollway.

"You don't need a lawyer, but I didn't want you walking into that courtroom alone. And my fee is much less than that of anyone you would hire anyway." Lisa looked at the floor by her feet.

"Your *fee* is in the backseat."

Lisa turned and reached back for her Tupperware container of chocolate-chip cookies. "Want one?" Lisa garbled the words with half a cookie in her mouth.

"Nope. I've sworn off the stuff."

Lisa chewed and stared at Evie.

"What?"

"What what?" Lisa said.

"What are you thinking?"

"Right now? I'm thinking you *still* make the best chocolate-chip cookies. In general though, you know what I'm thinking. I'm not sorry that this *thing* with Nicole is coming to an end. She has shattered your life *twice*."

"Oh, is *that* all?"

Lisa held out half a cookie. Evie shook her head, gripped the steering wheel so tightly she felt the pebble grain of the faux leather. She just drove.

After twenty minutes of silence, Evie coasted down Bayberry Drive. The lawns were still brown from their winter's nap, yet daffodils, hyacinths, and tulips heralded the arrival of spring. Evie obeyed the twenty-five-mile-an-hour speed limit even though no neighbors were outside and all the kids were in school. Hers included.

"Home sweet home," Evie said. And she meant it.

Evie took Lisa's hand and jerked her, almost in an awkward dance move. "Bring your stuff to my room," Evie said with a bubble in her throat. "I love it when we have sleepovers!"

"And I love your haircut!" Lisa said, gently withdrawing from her sister's grasp. She patted the bottom of Evie's bob with one hand and tapped her suitcase handle with the other. Lisa had her priorities, and one of them was haircuts.

Evie knew another of her sister's priorities was *her*.

The courthouse steps did not resemble a grand marble staircase like the ones on prime-time detective shows. Instead, they mimicked baby steps, with wide treads and short risers, and just enough space for one lane of pedestrians going up and one lane coming down. There wasn't room for the gobs of reporters and hordes of bystanders reflected in those ripped-from-the-headlines episodes. Thank goodness. Evie did not like the idea of an audience, although she knew the courtroom would not be private. Family members commonly fought over even meager inheritances and battled wills with the departed in an effort to keep a grip on the past, and it all happened in plain view. But no matter the venue, she needed to go forward, to get through the piles of paperwork, the legalese and verbal roughhousing, so that she and Sam and Sophie could move on.

Evie ascended the steps without holding the banister. Lisa had okayed the outfit Laney had chosen, so Evie donned beige pumps last seen at Yom Kippur services three years before. She landed on each tread on the ball of her foot to avoid having to balance on the three-inch heels.

Evie had been in court only once before, and the corridors were no more welcoming this time than when she had arrived to finalize the divorce. Directories and framed portraits lined the white walls. Her heels clicked with each step on the marble floor. Tall wooden doors separated the regular world from the world of judges and lawyers and gavels and permanent decisions.

On Divorce Day, Evie realized the power of the court system was not unlike that of the religious system into which she and Richard had married. She walked into court as a married woman and sat across the aisle from the one person in the world from whom she wished to be legally severed. There were words and signatures. The judge asked if they were sure this was what they wanted. It hearkened back to saying vows and exchanging rings. The gavel banged. Evie left the building as a person with a new marital status: divorced.

Today Nicole was at the far end of the hallway, wearing a gray skirt, white blouse, and pumps. She stood with a white-haired man in a dark suit clutching an accordion file as if it held top-secret information. A stroller was noticeably absent. It would have been inappropriate to bring Luca to the courthouse. Still, Evie hadn't seen him in weeks and hoped to catch a glimpse. Babies always made her smile. Who was minding Luca? Maybe Nicole's mother had gotten off the pathetic train long enough to watch her grandson before she packed them up to go back to the trailer park.

And then, Beth rounded the corner pushing Luca in his buggy.

Evie's heart pounded. Beth walked toward her and, without stopping, reached out and tapped Evie's arm. "It's almost over."

Evie grabbed Lisa's arm as if it could stop her from fainting from uncertainty and panic.

"What the hell was that?" Lisa asked.

"I guess they're best friends now." Evie's heart ached. She knew her friendship with Beth had changed, that it might be unsalvageable, but she never thought . . . well, she never thought a lot of things.

"I'm going to ask her what's up," Lisa said.

"No, stay here with me."

"She is right though. It's almost over."

Evie looked at Nicole and her sister yanked her back. "Stop looking at her."

"I can't. You're not going to go all Miss Manners on me and tell me staring is impolite, now are you?"

"Hardly. But you're not taking your eyes off them. It looks like you care."

All Evie cared about was what Beth was doing at the courthouse. Evie swallowed hard and focused her attention on Lisa's open-toe pumps and pointed with her chin. "Should you be wearing those in April?"

Lisa lifted a foot and turned it side to side. "Open-toe is the new black." She glanced at Evie's feet. "Oh, um, sorry."

Evie laughed. "At least I didn't wear my Crocs."

"Thank God for small favors and clearance racks."

Evie laughed and clamped her hand over her mouth rather than risk impropriety in public.

The door to the courtroom opened. It was ten o'clock. Evie knew this didn't mean the judge would be on time, but she could sit, breathe deep, relax. Nicole walked toward the door. The white-haired man was nowhere to be seen. Reaching the doorway, Nicole touched Evie's arm. She jerked it away. Nicole looked at the floor and kept walking. Nicole had been solicitous at a few soccer games over the past few weeks, but here in the shadow of justice she withdrew her hand and tucked it into her pocket.

The courtroom was brown with varying shades of 1970s amber. The wood on the bench, tables, and the chairs' armrests was clean but dull. Evie and Lisa sat in the second row, Nicole several rows back.

"When your case is called," Lisa said, "we'll stand up and go right in front of the bench."

"I did that last time," Evie said.

"That's common for divorces. The judge doesn't want any distractions, and most people have a hard time lying when they're face-to-face with a judge. At least in civil cases. I guess we'll see if the norm holds true for Nicole."

"Will we be up there together?"

"You and Nicole? No. She's the plaintiff and the burden of proof is on her. She has to prove that the life insurance was meant for Luca too. I'm guessing that's what's in that snazzy folder."

"Okay." Evie wrung her hands. They'd gone over all of this since Lisa's arrival three days before, but now it was real. It was also public. Family court mimicked the family dysfunction with everyone in one room—mothers and fathers, some children, extended family, and a multitude of strangers. No matter why they were here, they were all reduced to a docket number. Most likely the defendants and the plaintiffs in the room were lost in their own dramas, not interested in Evie's. She exhaled, feeling a little nauseous.

Everyone stood as Judge William Henry walked into the courtroom. He sat. Everyone else sat. The whispering resumed. The clerk shuffled papers and handed a stack to the judge, who leafed through the pile looking through trendy horn-rimmed glasses. Evie didn't think judges should be trendy. She tapped her foot and her leg bounced. Lisa put her hand on Evie's knee to both comfort and still her. "It'll be over before you know it," Lisa whispered into her sister's ear.

"That's what I'm afraid of," Evie said without looking at her. Evie wondered if the people around her could hear her heartbeat.

A woman in the row ahead of them turned around issuing a silent reprimand. The room was abuzz with the squeaking of chairs, the rustle of papers, and an undercurrent of dismay. Evie just stared at the woman. Who appointed her hall monitor? Evie and Lisa were not the only ones whispering. Evie, tempted to stick out her tongue, just stared until the woman surrendered and turned around.

"Now why can't you do that with Nicole?" Lisa asked.

"Do what?"

The woman shifted in her seat.

"Look like you mean business."

"I did mean business when I kicked her out."

"Right."

The woman turned around again and pulled out the big guns. "Shh. Please. I don't want to miss it when they call my name."

"Sorry," Evie said.

"You're such a pushover," Lisa said.

"No, I'm just trying to be considerate. Now shh."

The clerk called the first case. Evie listened as an aunt fought for custody of her niece and nephew against their father. Could someone who wasn't a parent win custody? Nicole wanted the twins' money—did she want Sam and Sophie too because they were Richard's kids? Could she sue for visitation rights? Or the house? What if she told the judge it was *her* house and she didn't want to leave?

Evie whispered her fears to Lisa, who smacked her hand. "Don't be ridiculous."

Evie wasn't being ridiculous, she was being smart. During the second case she witnessed a minor become emancipated. The third, fourth, and fifth cases were updates for the judge—siblings who'd been in a car accident and were awarded settlements, a father defending himself against paying child support, a grandmother granted custody of her grandchildren because her daughter was a drug addict. Evie, who realized she'd dug her nails into her palm, unclenched her sweaty fists and looked around the courtroom. No sign of Beth.

The lawyers were neither savvy nor slick. They were either overweight or overtired. Some wore wrinkled jackets. Most were men, with worn, hard-sided briefcases. Fluorescent lighting made everyone look a little jaundiced; even Lisa's skin had a yellow tinge, which of course coordinated with her broken-plaid St. John suit and Louboutin pumps.

The woman in front of them appeared before the judge alone. She handed a stack of papers to the clerk and stood with her feet more than shoulder-width apart. Her body language tried to say impenetrable force—instead Evie thought it said, "I have *feminine itch.*"

Evie etched the stance in her mind. She did not want to stand in front of a courtroom and look as if she were riding a horse. She had nothing to be ashamed of but was embarrassed nonetheless. This all seemed like a chair fight on *The Jerry Springer Show.* Nicole had the requisite tattoo and the crowd *was* a little dicey, so the image worked. Distracted, Evie watched the woman at the front of the room and wondered if today was the day Evie's latest course would be set. She gulped. She'd focused so much on Nicole's actions, she sometimes lost track of the bigger picture: selling the house, finding a full-time job, changing their lifestyle, and explaining to the kids why things were different—again. Evie's pulse quickened as she noticed no one was standing at the front of the courtroom.

"Case FC-1016-P. *Glass vs. Glass,*" the clerk said.

"That's us," Lisa said.

Evie wanted to turn to the crowd and say, "Chat amongst yourselves." She had listened to an hour of personal tribulations, financial woes, and family drama, but wanted no one hearing hers.

Lisa and Evie walked to the bench, jacket sleeves brushing together. Evie squelched her instinct to touch Lisa by taking a step to the left, leaving a foot between them.

The judge peered at the paperwork on his desk and motioned at the clerk. He tapped the papers in front of him.

"Will the plaintiff please approach the bench?"

Evie stared at Lisa. Lisa shrugged. This was not criminal court where both sides had to alert the other to evidence or witnesses. Evie could rally a town of character witnesses, she was sure of it. But Lisa said it wasn't necessary. Evie should have followed her instinct and brought reinforcements.

The judge did not lift his eyes until Nicole was standing to the left of Evie.

"This case is dismissed," Judge Henry said, looking at Nicole.

Evie turned to Lisa as the judge addressed them all, shifting his gaze between Lisa, Evie, and Nicole.

"The plaintiff has withdrawn the petition."

Evie was not sure what had happened. She wanted someone to speak English.

"Thank you, Your Honor," Lisa said. She grabbed Evie's sleeve and led her down the aisle in an almost-run. Lisa pushed open the door with her body, and when the door closed, she slumped onto a chair against the wall. "You won. Your kids get their money."

By that time Nicole was in the hall. Evie fancied herself rather bright, but she was still confused. She walked over to Nicole.

"What just happened?" It was a demand, not a question.

"I'm going home, Evie. You win."

Was this a joke? A trick? Nicole wasn't going after the kids' money but she was taking Luca away from them? Evie's neck muscles tightened in a precursor to a tension headache. She rolled her head around for relief.

"Why?"

"It doesn't matter why. I told my mother we're coming, and

she's fixing up my old room for Luca. She got what she wanted. You got what you wanted." Nicole swallowed hard.

Evie did the same, imagining the secondhand smoke that would ravage Luca's lungs while they shacked up in Super Granny's double-wide, even though she didn't know if Nicole's mother smoked *or* lived in a double-wide.

Lisa led Evie away.

"I have no idea what just happened," Evie said.

"Maybe I can explain."

It was Alan.

Sitting on a bench between Alan and Evie, Lisa took the lead.

"I'll tell you what happened. She chickened out. She'd have had to pay the lawyer whether or not the funds were awarded to Luca, and he probably told her she wasn't going to win."

"That's only part of it." Alan looked at Evie, who refused to meet his glance. "Do you want to know what happened?"

"Yes."

"Beth invited her over—"

Evie put her head in her hands.

"I'm not finished," Alan said. "Please listen."

Lisa kissed her sister on the cheek and walked toward the elevator.

"Beth invited her over to convince her it was wrong to try to take this money from your kids."

"How?" Evie tried to reconcile the image. Beth and Nicole talking about her. Beth defending Sam and Sophie. And Nicole listening.

Alan looked toward the window across the wide, marble hallway. Evie glanced over and saw Beth.

"You'll have to ask my wife how. But before you do, I have something to say."

Here it comes, Evie thought.

"Beth is probably one of the best friends you'll ever have. If you're willing to throw it all away because of something that happened twenty-five years ago that is frankly none of your goddamn business, you're more judgmental than I ever thought possible." Alan paused, his brow sweating. He put his clenched fist on the seat between them and lowered his voice to a whisper. "I'm tired of Beth apologizing and feeling guilty for being honest. It's how we met. It wasn't ideal. But it happened. Get over it. And you need to think about something else. One day you'll struggle with a choice you're not proud of. One day you'll do something you never thought you'd do. Are you absolutely sure you don't want Beth standing by your side when that happens? I would if I were you."

Alan should have been a lawyer.

Evie and Beth sat alone on the bench for what seemed like an hour, but was only thirty seconds.

"I'm sorry," they said in unison.

"I was really shocked," Evie said. "But I shouldn't have been so mean. A little mean, maybe . . . for a minute . . ."

"I should have told you sooner."

"Or never mentioned it at all."

"Yeah, well, there's that too."

"What did you say to Nicole? And where's Luca? And why were you here with him? I thought you totally traded me in. Which I would understand after how I behaved."

"For Nicole? Nah. She's too skinny." Beth winked. Beth was size four when she was bloated. "I can tell you the whole story another time—but Luca, I just wanted to make sure that Nicole could focus today, and I took him so she could do what she had to do."

"You did it for me."

Beth tapped Evie's shoulder with her own. "Of course I did it for you, silly. And I did it for us. Now let's go celebrate."

"Celebrate what?"

"You *won*."

Nicole had said the same thing, and the words echoed in Evie's ears.

Beth took her hand and they wrapped their fingers together like little girls.

"You'll have college tuition for Sam and Sophie, money to help with expenses, you got the job at County, and Nicole will take Luca back to Iowa. It's everything you wanted."

Getting everything she wanted made Evie a little queasy.

— Chapter 21 —

"How come we don't live near any family besides Nicole and Luca?" Sophie asked, tucked in for the night, lying on her back but up on her elbows. The night-light glowed on one wall, but it was bright enough for Evie to see her daughter's head tilt in curiosity.

Evie knew Sophie's questions stemmed from a few days with Lisa and from missing Nicole and Luca. The kids didn't like when the two moved out, and they never wanted their Aunt Lisa to leave. Still, Sophie's cuteness and innocence exacerbated Evie's sense of guilt.

Guilt? Evie saved their college funds and their home. She got a job. What did she have to feel guilty about? And why do children know exactly the wrong time to ask a question?

"Hey, what am I, chopped liver?" Evie said.

Sophie fell back onto her pile of stuffed animals and giggled. "I don't like chopped liver!"

"You know what I mean!" Evie tickled Sophie's side.

"But Aunt Lisa lives far away in Washington, and Grandma and Grandpa live far away in Florida, and all those other people live in faraway other places."

"All what people?"

"All those cousins and everything, the ones that came here."

"Well, most of them live in Delaware, sweetie. You know, where

Aunt Lisa and I grew up. I moved to Chicago to go to college, and then I went to graduate school, and that's where I met Daddy. And he grew up in Cleveland. So that's where his whole family lives."

"Mommy, I don't want to go to California or Delaware or Cleveland."

Evie leaned her body over Sophie's and propped herself on one elbow. "What makes you think we're moving?"

Sophie shrugged and buried her head and mumbled.

Evie snuggled down next to her daughter. "What makes you think we're moving, Soph? We're not going anywhere, I promise."

Sophie looked at her. "Really? But Nicole and Luca left, and I know you needed her money for the house. What are you going to do without Nicole's money for the house? What happens if you don't pay for the house? Will the police come and—"

"Sophie!" Evie touched her face. "We're fine. I don't know what you heard, honey, but we're fine. I'm sorry if any grown-up talk worried you. It did help us to have extra money when Nicole was here, but now I have that job at County College, remember? And now, some other things have worked out. We're going to be fine."

Evie sighed, relieved she wasn't lying. She had deposited the insurance check that very afternoon, with Beth and Alan by her side.

"Who will stay with me and Sam when you work at the college?"

"Sometimes Laney and sometimes Beth."

"Why not Nicole?"

"That just didn't work out the way we wanted it to, that's all. Do me a favor, Soph. If you hear grown-ups talking and it upsets or worries you, just tell me. Sometimes—no, lots of times—grown-ups say things they don't mean or wish they hadn't said."

"Why do grown-ups do that?"

"I wish I knew."

Evie poked Sophie in the side and she giggled.

"Do you think Nicole will be at the game with Luca this weekend?"

"I don't know."

Evie was beginning to think it would be easier when they were gone.

"I miss Luca," Sophie said.

Or maybe not. Evie tucked the blanket tightly around Sophie and kissed her head with a loud smooching sound. "I know, sweetie. Me too." Then Evie headed to Sam's room.

"Good day, kiddo?"

"Yeah."

"It's fun to have Aunt Lisa here, isn't it?"

"Uh-huh. She told funny stories about Daddy."

"Oh, she did, did she?" What could she have told them that Evie hadn't?

"She told us all about when he was going to propose to you but had no idea what kind of ring to buy, and how she had to help him over the phone because that was before the Internet or e-mail or anything."

"Yeah, the Stone Age."

Sam laughed. "And she said I look just like him when I stick out my tongue when I'm doing my homework." He curled his tongue over the left side of his upper lip.

"Absolutely. I've told you that."

"I know but . . ."

"But you believe it now that Aunt Lisa said it."

Sam flashed a toothy smile and batted his eyes. Evie laughed, took his shoulders, and touched her nose to his and then sat back.

"That's okay, it's always nice to get a second opinion."

Sam nodded. His smile softened but remained. He closed his eyes, and Evie could almost see the images of Richard that Sam saw on the insides of his eyelids. Richard in bed bouncing each child on one knee; Richard in his grubbiest clothes building a sandbox in the backyard with toddler twins playing with sand on the grass; Richard coaching; Richard growing tomatoes in the bathroom during his infatuation with hydroponics, teaching the kids how to tell when they were ripe and harvesting a bucketful even though he didn't like tomatoes.

Evie searched her son's face for sadness, the corners of his eyes for tears. Sam resembled Richard not only with the sandy blond hair streaked by sunlight, even though there was little sun in northern Illinois, and the way the hair fell over his eyes, but the way it didn't seem to get in the way and was never deliberately swept out of the way. Sam clasped his hands behind his head the way he'd seen Richard do a million times and opened his eyes, still dry.

"You're a lot like Daddy," Evie said, sitting up. "All the best parts of him and the best parts of me are mixed together in different ways in you and Sophie." Sometimes it was hard to remember Richard's best, but when that happened, all she did was look *into* Sam and Sophie instead of *at* them. Evie held her left arm round as if cradling a large bowl. With her right hand she stirred with an imaginary giant spoon. "And that—is forever. No one can take that away." She tucked in his covers under him.

Sam stretched and crossed his arms on top of the quilt. He looked relaxed, yet resolute.

"You look just like him when you do that," Evie said.

Sam nodded and whispered, "I know."

Chapter 22

Evie ransacked the Everything Drawer in the kitchen desk.

"I can't find them! Where are they? How am I supposed to leave without them," she muttered.

Evie knelt and unzipped every zipper on Laney's vintage Coach briefcase and dug her hand inside each pocket, sloshing around. She grabbed the organic-cotton tote bag Laney had given her and turned it upside down. Out rolled a water bottle, an apple, and a plastic bag of cookies. She'd leave them in the bag if it wasn't appropriate, but faculty members got hungry at meetings, didn't they? Evie stood, huffed, put her hands on her hips, tapped her foot, and looked around the room. Sam and Sophie stared—horrified amusement on their faces.

"What are you looking for?" Lisa said. "Maybe we can help you find it."

"My sunglasses. This is the worst time of day to drive without them. I'll have to hold my hand up like a visor the whole way to County, and when I get there, I'll probably have a headache. Great for my first department meeting, right? I am *so* buying cheap ones tomorrow and putting them in every room of the house and in the car."

"Mom?" Sam said.

"What!"

"You're wearing them." His gaze focused above her eyes.

Evie touched the top of her head. "Jeez. Now I'm going to be late."

"You're not going to be late," Lisa said. "You gave yourself extra time, remember?"

"Chillax, Mom. You'll freak everyone out," Sophie said.

Lisa put her arm around her sister. The touch was firm, encouraging, and familiar. "She's right, Sis. Chillax."

Evie blew two audible breaths and walked to the table. "Thanks for the reminder, Soph." Evie looked at Sam. "And thanks for finding my glasses."

He chomped a cookie and smiled with a full mouth. Evie smiled at the laid-back manner as she reached over to hug him. "I should be home before bedtime."

"We'll be fine," Lisa said.

"If there are any problems, call my cell."

"We'll be fine." Lisa pushed back her chair and stood.

"I know, but . . ." Evie shrugged. "You never know, so just call me if you need me. If it's an emergency. I left the college number by the computer, and someone will come and get me."

Lisa put her hands on Evie's shoulders and turned her toward the living room.

"We'll—be—fine."

"I know, but—"

"Go!" the kids yelled.

Evie saluted without turning back and touched the top of her head one more time.

She drove south toward County College and rearranged her mental priority list, pushing family to the bottom and work to the top—just for a few hours.

She'd stop in her office before the meeting. It was five o'clock. Sandy probably wouldn't be there; his classes were in the morning and the afternoon.

Stopped for a red light, Evie glanced at the passenger seat and patted the container of oatmeal raisin—no risk of chocolate smudges anywhere they shouldn't be. When Evie looked ahead, the late-afternoon sun pierced through the middle of the windshield. She squinted and slid sunglasses from the top of her head to the bridge of her nose. Even still, the view was so bright it hurt her eyes.

Evie parked, then walked up the well-worn path on the grass hill and through the metal security gate onto the campus green. This route offered a view of Sandy's office window. The blinds were raised.

She entered the building and walked down the hall. Evie knocked. The door was unlocked.

"You don't have to knock," Sandy said, looking up from his monitor.

"I don't want to disturb you. You must be busy."

"Thank you, but it's not necessary. Just catching up on paper-work. And besides, this is your office now too."

Evie laid her tote and briefcase on the floor by her desk, took out her water bottle and the container of cookies. She felt out of place and in denial. Both she *and* her cookies belonged at picnics, not faculty meetings.

Sandy pointed. "Sharing?"

"Oh, um, sure." She removed the lid and walked to Sandy like a waitress, not a colleague. She was getting it all wrong before she even started.

Polite as usual, he reached in and took two cookies. "Did you make these?"

Not sure of the right answer, Evie opted for truth. "I did." She leaned on Sandy's desk and then stood straight. "I shouldn't have brought them. That wasn't very professional, was it?"

"Are you kidding? We need sugar and caffeine at these meetings. You'll see. These cookies might just save the department."

Polite, handsome, and diplomatic. Evie stepped to her desk and sealed the cookies. "I know your daughter doesn't live here. Do you have other family in the area?"

"No. And this year her boyfriend trumps both her mother *and* me for Passover."

"Ouch. Need another cookie?"

Sandy smiled at her. "Definitely later. And next time."

She looked at the time, stacked papers on the desk, gathered the briefcase strap and tucked it inside. Grabbing the tote, cookies, and water bottle, Evie headed to the door.

"You have time," Sandy said, tapping his watch.

"I want to go a little early. The new person, you know. I don't want to be late."

"You want to make sure you get a good seat. In the back of the room."

Sandy rose from his chair but left his jacket hanging on its back. He grabbed his keys. Evie turned the doorknob and opened the door. Sandy put his hand above her head and pulled the door wide. She walked through first and they broke into a familiar stride. When Evie tilted up her head to meet his gaze, she felt eye to eye even though her kitten-heel sandals only made her five foot six.

"It must be hard not seeing Rachel as much as you'd like."

Sandy nodded. "I'm used to it, but splitting time between parents is never easy for a kid. No matter how old they are or how long they've been doing it."

"I know."

Sandy's eyes questioned her, but he said nothing.

"I'm divorced."

"I figured." He pointed to her left hand. "No ring."

Evie added *observant* to the Sandy list. *Oh, no. I am making a list.*

They were the first ones in the conference room.

"Are you sure I can't interest you in another cookie? You could set the trend, make me look good." She lifted her voice at the end of the sentence, grinned wide, and batted her eyelids like Jessica

Rabbit, then stood straight wishing she hadn't attempted cuteness instead of professionalism.

Sandy chuckled, a deep, husky sound that suited him and soothed her. "Thank you, but no." He patted his stomach.

For two beats Evie's eyes lingered on the winter-tanned hand against the starched white oxford. She looked up at him.

"Can I help you with something?" he asked, raising one eyebrow and adding thought lines to his forehead.

Busted. Being caught staring should have embarrassed her. Instead, it raised the stakes. If Evie was going to end up fired for flirting, she might as well enjoy herself.

"No, you can't help me. That's not what I meant. You did help me. I mean, thank you for walking with me. I appreciate it." Evie wiped sweat from the back of her neck with a napkin, then shoved it into her tote bag even though the trash can was well within two-point range.

"No problem," Sandy said, jingling his keys and chuckling. "If there are any cookies left over, you could leave them in the office. It would be nice to have some cookies to go with my coffee in the morning."

"Oh, I don't know about leftovers," Evie teased. "My cookies are delicious."

"Indeed they are," Sandy said with a half smile. He tipped an invisible hat and backed away to his chair.

For that moment Evie had forgotten about the two kids, sister, widow and baby, pile of bills, endless housework, and a shedding dog—and she'd also forgotten about the new faculty members and administrators she'd meet in ten minutes.

It was the good kind of forgetting she had almost forgotten.

At the meeting, Sandy took a cookie and placed it on a napkin at his place, like a preschooler at snack time. As the men and women walked into the room, they introduced themselves to Evie and followed Sandy's example, each taking a cookie. She figured they were just being polite, until none were left. Cookies were always a common denominator.

After the meeting, Evie waited in the hall for Sandy, leaning against the wall the same way she had waited for her friends after high school algebra.

"Thanks for the cookie thing," she said when he walked out the door.

"No problem. I can't reciprocate though. I don't cook. Or bake. But if your desk wobbles or you want to hang something on the office wall, I'm your guy."

"Tour guide, professor, and handyman?" Evie laughed.

Sandy bent toward her and looked from side to side. "I wear flannel shirts in the winter. Plaid ones," he whispered.

Evie shook her head and laughed. "Your secret's safe with me."

When Evie walked into the house, the kitchen was spotless, the sofa cushions fluffed with the decorative throw pillows placed, not thrown. Sophie's and Sam's backpacks were packed, zipped, and by the door. The alphabet magnets on the fridge spelled *Lisa rockS*. Who was this woman and what had she done with Lisa?

"Homework's all done?" Evie said.

The kids nodded.

"All went well?" Lisa asked.

Evie removed the empty Tupperware from her tote and shook it. No noise meant no cookies. "Better than expected."

"Why does Aunt Lisa have to leave tomorrow?" Sophie asked, clinging to Lisa's arm like a barnacle.

"I have to go back to work, sweetie." Lisa kissed the top of Sophie's head. "But that's tomorrow. Maybe we can persuade your mom to let you guys stay up a little later tonight since my flight is in the morning."

Evie put her hands on her hips and glowered at the trio, but they just scowled back, aware she was faking.

"Get a deck of cards," Lisa said. "I'll teach you Texas Hold'em. And how to shuffle like a pro."

"Awesome!" Sophie said.

"Cool!" Sam said, and started rummaging through the Everything Drawer for a full deck.

"Gambling, fabulous!" Evie laughed.

"Hey, I have to pass on the skills. Can I help it if I spent my summer after college in Atlantic City?"

Evie just shook her head. She loved watching Lisa with her kids. Her sister would have been a great mom (aside from the gambling instruction), and she'd always wanted kids, but it never happened. Evie had not cornered the market on loss, and she knew it. There were many ways for a life to be rerouted.

"Take a bubble bath and read a book. We are A-O-K." Lisa pointed out of the room, and Evie obeyed, hurrying up the stairs. Maybe Lisa understood more than Evie gave her credit for.

Evie checked the clock. It would be at least thirty minutes until Lisa had bilked the kids out of their allowances. Evie grabbed a magazine and a candle from her bedside table and locked the bathroom door. Then she opened it, but just a crack.

Without Nicole *or* Lisa in the house, Evie settled into her newest morning routine. Walking downstairs, sleep still in her eyes, she knew the creaks would not stir the kids, and that the expected noise on the eighth and third steps resulted only in Rex's repositioning himself on the landing. But Evie still tiptoed though the kitchen on a coffee quest, forgetting no one was below who would wake from heavy footsteps.

The gray sky stretched the early hours and tricked her for a moment into thinking it was a lazy day instead of a typical suburban

Saturday with a basketball game at ten. Evie liked the company of friends and the comfort of Lisa. When Evie was honest, she knew she'd even liked having Nicole in the house. But when Evie opened her e-mail without turning on any lights, she also enjoyed having no one looking over her shoulder.

She looked at her class syllabus online. After reading the textbook, preparing lectures and assignments, grading tests and term papers, she'd end up making about eight dollars an hour. She drew a big zero in the air with her index finger. Eight dollars was more than zero dollars. She didn't need her bank account to grow—not yet. She just needed it to stabilize.

She walked away from the computer and poured another cup of coffee. It almost overflowed. Lowering her mouth to the cup on the counter, she sipped until she saw a white ring of china. Then she opened and shut the freezer. Twice. "I am going to eat a bowl of Cheerios or oatmeal or something else healthy to start my day," she said to herself aloud.

She grimaced at the yellow box and the O's that tasted like their cardboard container and pulled out a few sugar packets.

As she scooped, chewed, and swallowed while staring at the monitor, Evie's stomach flipped. *I have a job. A real job. A job that feels more real than selling scarves, silver picture frames, and embellished serving spoons at Third Coast.* She might have gotten the interview because of Alan, but the name on that contract was *hers*. It would be *her* name on the paychecks. She put her bowl in the sink and sat back at the computer and stared.

Accepting this job had been the biggest step. They were back on track and staying there. The kids would see their mom doing something she loved that *didn't* revolve around them. *That is a good thing.* Evie would exist outside the realm of motherhood and suburban matriarchy, even if just for two hours at a time. At County she could be Ms. Glass or just Evie. She could use her maiden name even though she was clearly no maiden. No matter what they called her, she would be judged on her performance and that of her students, not by whom she chose to marry, divorce, or live with.

To everyone she met, Evie would be normal. She laughed. All she'd wanted for so long was a normal life, a husband, two kids, and a dog. The picket fence was there too, albeit in need of Tom Sawyer. And now she was on the cusp of redefining normal, not for her nosy neighbors, potential colleagues, students, or her children— but finally, for herself.

Evie sat on the bleachers and wished she'd swiped one of Beth's tush cushions. She waved at the Bunco moms and the library moms and the soccer moms impersonating basketball moms. Then she turned her back, positioning herself with a view of the gym door. Between Monday in family court and Saturday on the basketball court, Nicole might have packed up Luca and their Lakewood life and driven back to Iowa. But if she hadn't and was coming to the basketball game, Evie intended to be prepared. She had twitched when Nicole referred to Evie's house as *home;* but anticipating Sam's and Sophie's grief over losing Luca was worse than twitching. It made her inside ache and her outside sweat, so she was uncomfortable *and* unattractive. Great way to start a new job and a new life.

Evie looked at the court and smiled at Sophie. Evie sipped her coffee loudly, warding off an internal, suburban symphony of *I told you so's*. She forced away the thoughts of Nicole with each dribble of the ball. Nicole was going to start over in a place she'd thought she'd never see again, in a situation that would once have been unthinkable.

Evie winced, herself and Nicole somewhat interchangeable. Also unthinkable.

The ref blew the whistle, Evie nodded once at Sophie, and Beth and Laney walked through the door with Sam.

"Here she is," Sam said. He looked at Evie for permission to return to whatever he was doing before he became a tour guide.

"Go ahead," Evie said.

And off he went.

"What are you doing here?" she asked. "I thought you were spending the day with Herb."

"Beth said you didn't sound good when she talked to you this morning, so this is a 'friend-tervention.' Now, where is *she?*" Laney said, looking around.

Beth shook her head. "I didn't say anything about Nicole. I said you sounded down and that maybe we should come and sit with you at Sophie's game."

"Yes, you did," Laney said. "But *down* implies *annoyed*, and *annoyed* implies the widow, er, Nicole."

"Since when?" Beth said. "It's over, Lane, let it go."

There was that word again, as if Evie had beaten Nicole in combat, when there hadn't actually been any. Nicole just gave up. If it was a win, it was empty, because Evie's insides twisted with loss she didn't understand.

Beth pulled out three bleacher cushions from her tote bag. "Get up," she said. Laney and Evie lifted their bottoms. Beth set the cushions on the wooden seats and motioned for Laney and Evie to sit. Once a cushion was tucked under her, Beth put her elbows on her knees, her head in her hands.

"So, what's wrong?" Beth looked at Evie with squinted eyes of curiosity and closed lips of sincerity.

"Nicole showed up at soccer last week, but not this week," Evie whispered. "So I'm thinking she may have left. I didn't return any of her calls this week. I just needed to be alone, but I didn't think she'd leave without saying good-bye. To the kids, I mean."

"She didn't leave." Beth pointed with her chin. "There they are."

Evie swung around. Laney turned as well.

Evie looked back at Beth and touched her hands. "Thank you," Evie mouthed.

Sophie was on the bench, but spotted Luca and Nicole. Evie's basketball-playing daughter smiled so wide her cheeks must have ached.

For one moment, nothing mattered but that smile.

Nicole didn't look at Evie. She wheeled Luca to the far end of the bleachers and perched on the corner of the first row, looking ready to run away.

"That was weird," Evie said.

"The farther away, the better," Laney said.

"Knock it off," Beth said. "Can't you see that Evie wants to talk to Nicole?"

"She does?"

"I do?" Evie said.

"Of course you do." Beth nudged Evie's elbow in an upward motion. "Go ahead. You wanted to say good-bye."

"No, I wanted *her* to say good-bye to the kids."

"Let your kids see you go over to them. Say your piece. Make peace."

Beth was right. Discarding the past meant more than ignoring it. It meant facing it and moving forward. Evie leaned forward and shot up her hand as though she were hailing a taxi on Michigan Avenue during rush hour. She stopped short of putting two fingers in her mouth to whistle—she had gotten enough attention lately.

Nicole looked around as if she thought Evie might have been motioning to someone else but grabbed the stroller handle.

Beth scooted a bit and made space for Nicole to sit next to Evie.

"I hope you don't mind that we came today," Nicole said.

"I know the kids will be glad to see Luca."

Nicole turned the stroller toward the court and Luca clapped.

"He looks so big," Evie said.

"I know. I'm constantly amazed that I can put him to bed one night and the next morning he seems to have grown. It was the same way with Lucy."

Silence.

"How's the sleeping going?" Evie said, diverting the conversation away from Nicole's dead daughter. Evie was sympathetic, but it couldn't sway her.

"Yeah, he seems to have gotten a few new teeth so I guess that was just a bout with teething."

"I hated those!"

Nicole laughed.

"When are you leaving?"

Nicole shrugged. "Soon I guess. But I'd like to spend some time with the kids before that. If that's okay with you? I wanted to take a bunch of pictures so I could show them to Luca every day."

"Sure," Evie said.

She tapped her feet. They watched the game and cheered for Sophie in unison. Evie checked the game clock. One minute to halftime. Beth and Laney were focused elsewhere.

"Why did you back off?" Evie whispered.

"Why did I what?" Nicole turned away from the noise of the court.

"Why did you drop the lawsuit? I know Beth talked to you, but she didn't tell me what happened."

Nicole played with her fingers. "Beth and her husband helped me with a budget and financial plan for me and Luca; they showed me we'd be okay. And we had some long talks about family and friendships. And trust." Nicole looked at Beth, who smiled at her and nodded. "I still don't believe what you said about Richard. I'll never believe it, and since he's not here to defend himself, I'm not going to think about it anymore. There's just so much one person can handle."

Evie silently agreed.

"No matter what he did or didn't do, Richard was good to me," Nicole continued as if she'd memorized a speech. "After Peter and Lucy, Richard was the first person who made me feel good about myself." Nicole grabbed Evie's hand. "You were the second."

Sophie ran to Luca. She hoisted him out of the stroller with a grunt, carrying him like a sack of flour back to her teammates. He didn't seem to mind.

Evie's gaze followed them. "The kids will miss him so much." Evie realized she'd said it aloud.

"We'll miss them too. And you." Nicole fumbled with the diaper bag at her feet. "Maybe we can get webcams or something, you know, so they can see each other."

"Maybe."

Evie knew it wasn't the same. Her kids had web-chatted with her parents, but the novelty wore off fast. Lisa and Evie never got into the habit and talked on the phone like in good old days of land-line cords they could twirl around their arms. But maybe it would be different. The kids would want to see how Luca had changed and grown, they'd want to hear him talk and see him walk.

So would Evie.

"It's not the same," Beth said. She scooted closer to Nicole. "Sorry, my ears perked up at *webcam*. It's good but it's no substitute for the real thing. We're web-chatting with Cody while he's in Paris," Beth said to Nicole. "Not the same as sitting across the table from him at dinner."

Laney looked at her watch. "I've got to go meet Herb. I promised him I'd be home for lunch. Are you coming with me, Beth? Didn't you have something to do?" She tugged on Beth's cotton sleeve.

"Yes, I'm coming. See you tonight, Ev."

Laney bent, cheek-kissed Evie, and squeezed her shoulder. "Remember what Beth said. Grudges cause wrinkles."

Laney acknowledging there's a benefit to forgiveness? Pigs must be flying somewhere, Evie thought.

"Bye," Nicole said.

Beth waved at Evie and Nicole.

"She doesn't like me much," Nicole said.

"Don't mind Laney, she just can't hide anything. She doesn't even try."

"Does she know what happened?"

Evie nodded.

"And that I'm going back to Iowa?"

Evie nodded again.

"Then why can't Laney let it go?"

"She likes wrinkles."

Nicole looked surprised. "Why would she hold a grudge against me? I fixed it. I stopped it. Is that why you didn't call me back all week? I wanted to apologize again. I am so sorry, Evie. Not for wanting what was best for Luca, but for going behind your back. And I'm sorry I threw it in your face that you needed money."

"I trusted you when everyone told me not to. I invited you into my home. I feel betrayed *and* foolish. That sticks with someone. Especially the second time."

"You don't have any reason to feel foolish." Nicole put her hands in her jeans pockets and looked Evie in the eye. "All I wanted was a family, and I did everything to mess that up. I know that now. I've lost my family twice. Four times if you count the fact that I'm hundreds of miles from my mother. I had a real family growing up. I had a real family with Peter and Lucy. I had a real family with Richard, the twins, and Luca. And I thought *we* had a real family."

"So did I," Evie said, her throat vibrating.

"Are we okay?"

"Sure." The word was easy to say with Nicole heading to Iowa. Sophie walked over with Luca and handed him to Nicole. "His nose is running, it's gross," Sophie said as she turned back to the court.

Nicole pulled a crumpled Kleenex out of her pocket, wiped the baby's nose, and shoved the tissue into the side pocket of the diaper bag. "Guess I better get this guy home for his afternoon nap."

Evie looked at the clock and wondered where Sam was; he hadn't gotten any time with Luca. Nicole buckled a yawning, runny-nosed Luca into his stroller and handed him a bottle filled with water. He sucked and batted his eyes slowly. He'd be asleep before Nicole was out of the parking lot.

"I'll call you later so we can make plans to get together. Will you answer the phone?" Nicole asked.

Evie nodded but she wasn't sure.

Chapter 23

"I CAN'T BELIEVE MY KIDS agreed to sleep at your house," Evie said, walking into her kitchen from outside, with Beth and Laney behind her.

"They've slept over before," Laney said, ignoring the significance and opening the fridge and then shutting it.

"You deserve some time to yourself," Beth said.

"And they're having fun camping out in my basement. Jocelyn and Jordyn have it all under control."

"They've got one up on me then," Evie said.

She and Beth walked into the living room and each snuggled into a corner of the couch, leaving the middle for Laney, who stayed in the kitchen.

"I'm thrilled they wanted to sleep over," Evie added. "Maybe more for me than for them." That was hard to admit. "But, I'll probably be up all night worrying about them."

"Don't do that to yourself," Beth said. "Your kids are comfortable enough at Laney's to wake someone in the middle of the night if they need you. But they'll be fine. Be positive."

Positive, schmositive. Evie kicked off her shoes. She knew *fine* could end without any notice.

"Do you have anything sweet?" Laney said.

Evie heard the freezer door slide open.

Laney gasped and yelled, "Where are the cookies?"

"No cookies," Evie yelled back into the empty airspace. "Trying that new thing we talked about—healthy eating?" She patted her stomach, aware the take-out burgers and fries she'd just consumed weren't part of that plan. "Don't worry though, I've already started thinking about Passover desserts!"

"I don't want matzo-meal pancakes, I want cookies."

"You love my macaroons," Evie shouted. "And my *mandel brot*."

"This is true. But, I want something now, not later." Laney walked into the living room. She looked like a disappointed four-year-old—or, an annoyed almost fifty-year-old. "You've purged the house of all the cookies?"

"Pretty much."

"I'll find something," Beth said, trading places with Laney.

Evie heard the fridge open and close again. Being home alone with her friends wasn't much different from being home alone with her kids.

"What did you find?" Laney said. "I'm starved."

"Cheese and crackers," Beth said. "I'll make up a platter."

"Of course you will," Laney said.

Beth replied with a "Ha!"

Laney turned to Evie. "I don't want to ruin our fun, but when's that widow of yours moving? I know she stayed longer at Sophie's game than you expected."

"I wanted her to see Sam."

"So, she saw Sam, and then what?"

"No, he spent the whole time watching the boys' team. We're going to see them tomorrow."

"You're kidding me," Laney said. "I thought she was leaving."

"She is. I think. I don't have any details. I don't want any details."

"That's for the best," Laney said.

"No, it's not!" Beth appeared under the arch that separated the kitchen from the living room, one hand holding a tray like a wait-ress, the other hand on her hip like an irritated best friend.

"I said she could see the kids before she left, and I said we'd keep in touch. Other than that, I didn't make her any promises. I don't trust her. She knows that."

"Good for you," Laney said. "She has made a lot of bad choices. People *don't* change. She's proof of that."

"People can learn from their mistakes," Beth said, holding the tray in front of Evie, then Laney, then placing it on the end table. Beth constructed a cheese-and-cracker sandwich and popped it into her mouth whole and sat on the floor facing her friends.

"Nicole hasn't learned," Laney said. "You can take the girl out of the trailer park, but you can't take the trailer park out of the girl."

"Nicole grew up in a nice small town, Laney, not a trailer park," Beth said. "You're making a lot of assumptions."

"We assumed she was married *once*. We assumed she moved in with Evie just to help her out and because she was lonely. So, please don't defend her. You know what they say, the best indicator of fu-ture behavior is past behavior. And I assume you have a good rea-son for knowing so much about her that we don't know?"

Beth looked away from Laney and didn't answer.

"Don't get your granny panties in a bunch," Evie said. "I'm not saying I can ever trust her again."

"Trust can grow over time," Beth said. "People learn from their mistakes, Laney. You've learned from yours with Herb."

Laney threw a cracker at Beth. She caught it and tossed it back.

Evie didn't know if she could ever trust Nicole, but as her friends played combat crackers, Evie pictured a small town, haystacks on the sidewalk, one traffic light—actually, no traffic light. She envi-sioned Nicole holding Luca and walking up rickety, wooden steps to a double-wide trailer and Nicole's mother opening the door.

Nicole was thin from smoking instead of eating and smiled to reveal summer teeth—*some are there, some are not,* an inappropriate dentist's joke Evie had learned from Herb.

She was finished with Nicole, but hoped these assumptions were wrong too.

When Laney left to check on the kids at her house, the door clicked shut and the sound echoed in a moment of cavernous silence.

"I know she means well," Evie said to Beth, who insisted on staying and getting Evie's pot of coffee ready for the next morning. "And I agree with her a lot of the time, but she can make it worse when she's so . . ."

"Unforgiving," Beth said, counting scoops. "With Laney, there's no wiggle room."

Evie nodded. "There *is* no universal right and wrong. I've learned that."

Beth shook her head while pouring the water into Mr. Coffee's tank.

Evie slid her ring off her finger and spun it on the counter.

"Can I ask you something without you getting angry at me?"

"I don't know. Can you?"

"I guess we'll find out. Think about this, and be honest. Do you still want Nicole and Luca in your life?" The coffee job complete, Beth searched the kitchen for busywork and walked from cabinet to sink to counter.

The constant activity gave Evie the heebie-jeebies. "Sit. You're making me nervous."

Beth sat and folded her hands, then started twirling her thumbs, like on the day their friendship tumbled like a block tower that was now being rebuilt.

"I look at Nicole and see poor choices and bad judgment and

selfishness," Evie said. "I was starting to see good things—and then she ruined it."

"So why can't you focus on the good parts?"

"Like with you and Alan? That's totally different. We've been friends for years. And you didn't try to take away my children's security."

"I know it's different—and I'm grateful it's different. But Nicole is leaving. Is that what you really want?"

"Absolutely!"

"You want your kids to grow up without their brother?"

"No, but I want Nicole to leave, and I can't have both."

"People can change, deep down. No one is just a collection of her mistakes. And that includes Nicole." Beth smiled. "You have to trust *yourself*. Can you do that?"

Evie didn't know. Although she did know she was worn out from counting pennies, rebuilding her family, and doubting herself.

"If your gut is telling you to forgive her," Beth said, "or that you want to work toward that, you should. I'm not saying *forget*, but you have good instincts, you just have to listen to them. You can be really, really angry with someone and still move forward with them instead of without them." She was almost pleading.

Evie shooed Rex from the bed and folded down the comforter. She smoothed it across the bottom third of the bed, tugging to make it even on both sides. Knowing she would kick it between the mattress and the footboard as soon as she got into bed didn't matter; the routine was better than a dose of NyQuil. She patted the bed and Rex jumped back up, curling at the bottom like a kitten instead of a one-hundred-pound, muscular Lab. She wiggled under the lighter cotton quilt, maneuvered the pillows, and lay on her back.

Then her side. She pictured a softball game, a field covered in daisies, silently recited a recipe by memory.

Evie thought about her job, her syllabus, her students, her wardrobe, her colleagues. She thought about Sandy Perlman.

Evie sat straight, and Rex's head popped up as if he knew what she was thinking.

Sandy Perlman would be alone on Passover.

Chapter 24

SAM AND SOPHIE POKED AT each other even though the minivan had rear bucket seats specifically designed to help avoid such things. The bickering was a welcome respite from pondering moral turpitude.

"We'll be there in a minute," Evie said.

"Why aren't they just coming over?" Sam asked.

"Because it's a beautiful day. And because it's the Spring Festival."

"Can we go out for dinner?" Sophie said.

"You just ate lunch."

"I know, but that way we can be with Luca all day long."

Evie's stomach tightened.

"There they are." Evie looked across the parking lot to Nicole's car. The trunk was open and Evie spotted a jumble of suitcases. Her stomach tightened again. "Get the blanket out of the back, Sam. Soph, grab the water bottles for me."

Evie didn't want the kids to see suitcases. She hadn't told them Nicole and Luca were moving.

Nicole shut the trunk as the twins rounded the minivan. A woman Evie had never before seen stood next to Nicole.

Everyone in Lakewood knew everyone in Lakewood. Newcomers were usually married couples or young families; this woman looked older than Evie. Much older. She must have stopped by

Nicole's car to ask for directions or for a neighborly chat. But then why were they walking toward Evie together, their stride and sway in sync?

Mousy-haired and starchly dressed, the woman looked like a White House–age Nancy Reagan. She also looked familiar, as if Evie had met her before or passed her a hundred times without being introduced. One of this woman's hands helped Nicole steer Luca's stroller onto the grass and to the edge of Evie's blanket. Nicole and Nancy Reagan brushed hair off their faces at the same time, with the same sweeping motion.

Iowa's Mother of the Year.

Sophie threw her arms around Nicole's waist, then reached out and touched Luca's hand. Sam picked up one hand in a casual, teenager-like wave.

"Sam, Soph, this is *my* mom," Nicole said.

Evie looked at Nicole and raised and lowered her eyebrows. The twins, almost eleven, straddled childhood and adolescence and mumbled hello.

"Say, 'Nice to meet you,'" Evie mumbled.

"Nice to meet you," the twins said in unison.

Nicole's mom stroked each twin's shoulder and smiled wide.

She has all her teeth. They were white and straight and accented by light pink lipstick.

"I've seen your pictures," she said. "You look much more mature in person. At least *twelve*."

The twins beamed and looked at Evie. She nodded, and they ran to the giant blowup slide, which conveniently emptied in front of the pony rides.

Evie stood and put out her hand.

Nicole gasped. "I'm so sorry, that was so rude. Mom, this is Evie. Evie, this is my mother, Margaret."

"Call me Peg. It's nice to finally meet you. I've heard so much about you. Seems we have quite a bit in common."

This was going to be good. "Really?" Evie said. "How so?"

She was polite, not sarcastic. This woman was sturdy Iowa farm stock with a firm handshake, proper grammar, and good dental hygiene, but coming to Lakewood had to be a big deal. Evie should make a good impression even if Peg was here to scoop up her daughter and grandson and take them away. *Take them home.*

"Oh, Nicki didn't tell you what I do for a living, did she?" Peg shook her head and grimaced with maternal disappointment.

"No, she didn't," Evie said, looking at *Nicki.*

Nicole smiled and rolled her eyes the way Sophie would have.

Peg slid her hand into her jacket pocket and pulled out a business card and handed it to Evie.

MARGARET H. SMITH, PH.D.—PROFESSOR OF AMERICAN LITERA-TURE, UNIVERSITY OF IOWA.

She probably didn't live in a trailer.

Evie rearranged her perceptions and stared at the distant conglomeration of play equipment. Sam giant-stepped up the sliding board. Sophie scaled the climbing wall. Evie monitored the appropriate risks and moderate challenges enjoyed by her kids. Anytime they played, she smiled.

"How about if I take Luca over to the twins?" Peg said.

"Are you sure you don't mind?" Nicole said.

"I am here to help, aren't I?" Light sarcasm flitted through the air.

Nicole nodded.

"So, would that be helpful to you, Nicki?"

"Yes, Mother."

Peg swiveled the stroller and walked quickly toward the corner of the park.

"You didn't tell me your mother was a college professor." Evie sat on the blanket. Nicole did the same.

"You never asked."

Evie had not asked. Evie had assumed. "So I really don't understand what's been going on. You said your mother couldn't take
time off to come to the funeral."

"She couldn't. It was finals week."

"You said she didn't approve of your marriage because Richard
was Jewish. Is she really that narrow-minded?"

Evie had been that narrow-minded as well. She'd lectured Lisa
for the year she was engaged to what's-his-name, saying it would
never work because of their cultural differences. Three years later,
Lisa and no-name divorced because they were too much alike. They
were both workaholics.

Nicole stretched out her legs and crossed her feet at the ankles.
She pointed her toes as if imitating ballet and then flexed. "She
doesn't approve of anything I've done since I got pregnant in high
school. I'm not exactly a daughter she can brag about."

Evie leaned back on her hands, stunned. Her parents would
never have turned her away. She would never turn away Sam or
Sophie. "I don't know what to say."

"It's no secret that I haven't lived up to her expectations. That's
why I moved away. After Peter and Lucy, she wanted me to go to
college and start over. I didn't want to do it. I had been a wife and
mother; I didn't want to be a sorority girl. I couldn't be. So I moved
to Chicago and went to cosmetology school."

"She didn't understand that you needed a new life?"

"Not really. She had my brother and me in her late thirties,
worked two jobs, went to grad school. She always said it was for us,
but she did it for herself. She was never around." Nicole nodded and
shrugged in surrender. "But now I understand why."

"So, she was thrilled with your choice to go to beauty school—
which you did for *yourself*."

"Not half as thrilled as when I told her I was dating a man
twenty years older. She figured out pretty quickly that he was mar-

ried." Nicole looked down, away from Evie. "She didn't talk to me for months. Even on the anniversary of Peter's and Lucy's deaths. Or on their birthdays." Nicole looked back at Evie with a forced smile. "I thought the fact that Richard had a Ph.D. and taught at Pinehurst would make her happy. I thought they'd have a lot in common and she would realize that I'd done okay for myself even without going to college. Then I thought when I had Luca, she'd want to be a grandma again."

"But she didn't, did she?"

Nicole looked right at Evie, with a gaze stronger than any Evie had seen on Nicole's face since Richard died. "I hadn't done any of the things she'd planned for me. And when she wanted to get back into our lives, I told her it was too late."

"It's never too late." *Of course, until it is.* "Why did you tell me she didn't like Richard because he was Jewish?"

"I didn't want you to like her," Nicole said.

Evie didn't like Peg. Nor did she want to be like her. Peg had been so grief-stricken, so bitter, so cemented in the past, she had been without the capacity to let go in order to move on. Nicole had to live hundreds of miles away and become a widow the second time before her mother would accept her—flaws, faults, funky family attachments, and all. Evie would never let that happen. She would not become the next Peg Smith.

"It's okay," Nicole said. "We've been having long talks, and I think we've come to an understanding."

That was probably a good idea considering Nicole was moving in with her.

"She understands that I don't want what she wanted for me," Nicole continued. "And I think I finally understand that it's okay for her to wish things were different as long as she can just accept that they're not. She doesn't have to like it, but if she loves us, she'll learn to deal with it."

"So things are good between you?"

"They're better. We even talked about Lucy." Nicole scooted closer to Evie, almost invading her personal space.

Evie leaned away, boundaries intact.

"She was glad I got a job, that's for sure," Nicole said. "Unemployment is not high on her list."

It hadn't been high on Evie's list either.

"I renewed my cosmetology license," Nicole continued. "I'm going to cut hair again and manage the front desk at a really nice salon. Finding a babysitter for Luca is the only thing standing in my way."

"Why won't your mom help?"

"How is my mom going to help?"

"Look, I know your mom is a professor, but maybe the university has child care."

"Why would Luca need child care in Iowa?"

"Because you're *working*? You can't take him to a salon, there are too many chemicals, it's not safe, and there are so many sharp tools. It's dangerous!"

Nicole grinned. "I'm working at Hair Expressions in *New Meadow.*"

"*Our* New Meadow?"

"Is there another New Meadow?"

Evie exhaled a breath she didn't realize she was holding in. New Meadow, just a few miles east of Lakewood, was a post–World War II town built around the old Amtrak line that ran from Chicago to Minneapolis. The town was filled with classic bungalows, apartment complexes, and newer town-house subdivisions named after Native American tribes.

"Oh, that would be a bit of a schlep."

They chuckled.

Evie released her public reticence, put her hand on Nicole's arm, and left it there. "I didn't want you to go. For Sam and Sophie." Evie remembered she had wanted to be careful. "But if you're not leaving, why is your mother here? What were all the suitcases in the back of your car?"

"Mom took the train. She said she's going to start acting like a mother and a grandmother. She was on sabbatical this term and changed her plans to help me move and to spend some time with Luca. And hopefully to get to know you and the twins."

"What made you change *your* mind about leaving?"

"My mother."

"Your mother convinced you to stay here?"

"My dad left us with nothing. He took off and left a wife and two kids and he never turned back. I never wanted Luca to think Richard abandoned him and left him nothing. My mother pointed out that not only did I have Social Security, but Luca would never think that if I didn't let him think that. She admitted she fueled our bad feelings about my father. I don't blame her, but she's right. It's different. And she's putting all the money she had saved for me to go to college into a fund for Luca. He'll be okay."

"Yes, he will," Evie said.

"Your kids will be fine too, you know."

"I know." Evie's throat softly closed and kept her voice from cracking.

"And my mom and I are going to be okay too. She's offered to watch Luca while I find a babysitter."

Evie's wheels turned in a million directions, mimicking the inside of an elaborate clock. "Why wouldn't she help you before now?"

"I didn't ask her before now."

It wasn't easy to ask, Evie knew that.

"Do you think you might consider letting me see the kids sometimes? You know, with Luca?"

"Okay," Evie said.

"Just okay?"

"Yep, *just okay.*"

Evie thought about Beth. Beth and Alan moved somewhere no one knew their story in order to start over. No one who Nicole met in New Meadow would ask if Richard was married when she'd met him. They'd know she was a widow with a baby, and they'd learn about Sam and Sophie and probably about Evie. Nicole would leave out the details that no longer impacted her life and that might affect her future.

If Nicole was lucky, one day she would have a friend whom she trusted with the truth.

When the troops arrived at her feet, Evie reached into her purse and pulled out dollar bills.

Peg shook her head and reached into her pocket and corralled the twins and Luca for an ice cream run. "Last one to the ice cream truck is a rotten egg," Peg sang out. The twins took off running. Maybe she would figure out the mother thing *and* the stepgrandma thing.

"I'll watch Luca," Evie blurted. "When you go to work." Evie spoke before thinking it through. Why not? She loved babies. More important, she loved *Luca*.

"You will?" Nicole's eyes grew wide, and Evie saw a thin ginger border around the green. She had noticed it the night Richard died, when Evie hugged Nicole and they ended up nose to nose, but without a haze of tears Nicole's irises looked like peridot rimmed in gold.

"Well, I guess I should say, if our work schedules mesh. I need someone to watch the twins too."

"You got the job at that college?" Nicole said.

Evie nodded. "And I'm going back to Third Coast."

"Mazel tov." Nicole grinned at her command of universal Yiddish. "When do you start?"

"I'm going back to work at the store after Passover. Just a few hours one or two mornings while the kids are at school. I start teaching in June, but that's at night. Once your mother leaves, we can coordinate our schedules."

Nicole nodded.

As if she held a flipbook, Evie scanned the future. Rickety images emerged and bled into one another. She and Nicole and the
three kids together—in the park, on the bleachers, at the kitchen
table, on birthdays, for holidays. Nicole would care for the twins.
Evie would care for Luca. It wasn't what Evie had planned twenty,
ten, or one year ago—but the pictures in her head slowed her pulse.
This was about choices. Evie had chosen to accept the job at County,
and now she chose to keep Nicole in the fold. Nicole had chosen to
stay near them. It could work. This time she and Nicole would
choose to be on the same side of the picket fence, and to stay there.

Sam and Sophie ambled to the blanket, cones in hand, with an
ice pop for Luca. Peg lowered herself to the blanket next to Nicole.
Sam pulled off the white paper wrapper of the ice pop and twisted
it around the stick. He hesitated, and instead of handing it to Luca,
he knelt and held it at his brother's lips. Luca licked the green Bomb
Pop, smiled, licked it again, and shivered. The April sky teased
them into believing it was spring, but the wind off the lake reminded them all that steady, warm breezes wouldn't blow in until
summer.

"We're going to babysit for Luca while Nicole goes to work,"
Evie said.

Sophie clapped and bunny-hopped in a circle, her smile wide
and bright enough to dissolve any of Evie's suppressed uncertainty.

Peg crossed her arms. "Do you think that's wise?"

"Yes," Evie and Nicole said.

"I'm just here to help," Peg continued. "You two know best."

"And when I start teaching this summer, Nicole will keep an eye
on you guys. How's that sound? Remember, that's two nights a
week." She said it as much for Nicole and Peg as the kids. "So you'll
have lots of time with Luca. And Nicole. I guess we'll have a lot of
time together."

"Like a family," Sophie said.

"Not *like* a family, Soph. We *are* a family," Evie said.

"Daddy would like that," Sophie said.

Evie hadn't added Richard into the equation, but Sophie's emphatic tone convinced her.

Sam looked at his feet and kicked the grass once.

"You okay, Sam? You want to sit with me?" Evie patted the blanket, away from Nicole.

"No, I'm fine." He looked up. "I just think he—Dad—would think it was weird. Good weird, but weird. None of this is normal, you know."

Evie jumped on his words, her own tinged with defiance. "This is going to be normal for us. And that's all that matters. Now, which one of you is going to give me a lick of ice cream?" She smacked her lips loud.

Sam and Sophie laughed and drew back the hands that held their cones. Evie hadn't expected the twins to share their ice cream. Their lives, their hearts, their home, their mom, yes—but their Rainbow Cones? No way.

Chapter 25

THE GRANDFATHER CLOCK CHIMED FIVE times and then the doorbell rang. Nicole and Peg were on time.

Evie held the front door open with her foot as Nicole, with Luca on her hip, stepped inside. Peg handed Evie a plastic-sleeved, over-size bouquet of pink, yellow, and orange gerbera daisies.

"Luca *and* flowers," Evie said, kissing the not-quite-toddler on the head. "What a great combination."

Nicole and Peg pulled off Luca's jacket in tandem. Peg took Luca and stood him on the floor, holding both his hands. He raised his leg to walk, but Peg was not ready to go anywhere.

"Happy Passover," Nicole said. "I knew we couldn't bring food, so I hope these are appropriate."

"I told you they were appropriate, Nicki." Peg shook her head.

Evie grabbed Nicole's hand on instinct and squeezed. "Thank you, they're beautiful. I'll put them in a vase. Do you want to introduce your mom to everyone? They're in the living room."

"Do I have to?" Nicole muttered.

"I heard you, Nicki. I won't embarrass you, I promise."

Peg and Luca baby-stepped toward the sound of voices.

"Take a deep breath," Evie said, letting go of Nicole's hand.

Nicole nodded and put her purse on the floor by the bench. Then, she leaned and peeked into the dining room. The lights were dim, but the crystal goblets sparkled. Bubbe's Passover dishes—Lenox Daybreak, with its gold flowers—"popped" against the white linen tablecloth. Bubbe would have kvelled. The middle of the table was crowded with candlesticks, Elijah's cup, a soup tureen, bottles of Manischewitz wine and Kedem grape juice, seder plates, and stacks of matzo.

"Wow," Nicole said. "It looks beautiful."

"Thanks. Just don't ask me where all the kids' art supplies are." Evie cocked her head toward the hall closet. "Open that at your own risk."

Nicole walked into the room. She touched the back of each chair as she circled the table, set for sixteen. Evie knew Nicole was hoping Luca would handle the grandma introductions.

"Is the table usually this big?" Nicole asked.

"I have all the leaves in. I haven't done that in a long time, but it's a holiday. My family and friends are here, and I just decided—why skimp when I can make lots of work for everyone?" Evie grinned, jostled the chair at the head of the table, and patted the pillow. She picked it up and pointed to the handprints scattered across the pillowcase. "Ever since the twins were little, they've done this at the end of the night. It was Richard's idea." Evie found the tiniest prints and outlined them with her index finger.

The smallness of the handprints, coupled with the grandeur of the tradition, choked her. Evie flipped the pillow from front to back to front to back to front again and plopped it onto the chair, pounding it into the seat much harder than necessary.

Everyone sat in the living room, so the sofa, chair, and folding chairs were filled. With several conversations and a White Sox game on TV, it was boisterous. The way it should be.

"So, this is *liver*?" Nicole said, nodding at the bowl.

"Chopped liver. Try it on a cracker," Evie's mother said. Shirley took a Tam Tams cracker from the basket and put a spoonful of chopped liver on top.

"It's like pâté, dear. Have you ever had pâté?" Peg said, placing a dollop onto a small plate as if she were teaching everyone how to use a spoon.

Evie seethed. It was her holiday, her house. Any wisecracks would be hers too.

Nicole remedied the situation by ignoring her mother. "I thought you couldn't have crackers on Passover," she said, eyeing the small, hexagon-shaped cracker.

"It's matzo so it's fine."

"But liver?"

"Trust me, it's good. Richard loved my chopped liver."

"Mom!" Evie stomped her foot.

"Your mother has a point, Evie," Peg said. "If Richard liked it, Nicole should try it."

Shirley smiled. "Thank you, Peg. I knew another mother would understand."

Evie and Nicole had apparently been demoted and demotherized.

Nicole bit the corner of the cracker. She placed the remainder on a plate and dabbed her mouth with a napkin. "It's good."

"You don't have to say it's good," Lisa said. "I don't eat it, and she's *my* mother. Sometimes mothers are troublemakers."

Nicole smiled. Evie knew her sister had just initiated a truce with Nicole.

"I'm going to tell you something, Luca my man," Evie's dad said. He leaned out of his chair and reached to the floor. Luca looked up at him, mouth open. "Chopped liver is good. But women?" He blew a raspberry and Luca giggled. "Smart kid." Bob built a tower with the primary-colored blocks and handed a red one to Luca, who gently placed it on top.

Beth and Alan walked into the living room, arms full of

Tupperware cake carriers filled with matzo-made goodies. Laney, Herb, Jocelyn, and Jordyn followed with foil-topped plates. Evie wanted to set the table and lead the seder and host her family and friends on a holiday, but she quaked at the expense. Everyone cooked to help with the cost and to show off a little.

"Let's get all that in the kitchen," Evie said. "Sam? Take their jackets, please."

Sam stood and everyone laid their light spring outerwear over his arms. Herb put his jacket on Sam's head like an Indian headdress, and Sam marched out of the living room and up the stairs. Sophie motioned to the girls to sit with her on the floor by Luca.

Laney and Beth followed Evie into the kitchen and placed the containers and plates on the counter. The trio swatted Alan and Herb into the living room.

"How's it going?" Laney asked.

"I told my family to behave, and so far so good." Evie poked up her eyebrows for a temporary lid lift. "Same goes for you."

"What? I haven't done anything."

"Yet."

Beth laughed and winked at Evie. Friends back in the fold of understanding and acceptance. Pointing at Beth, Laney tore the tops off her plates, revealing carrot *tsimmes* and potato kugel. Beth's famous matzo-meal rolls, often mistaken for hockey pucks, were displayed in one of her favorite Longaberger baskets with a blue-and-gold-striped liner.

"Why aren't you scolding *her*?" Laney asked.

"She's always nice," Evie said, basting the brisket.

Laney mimicked her, and they all laughed. Beth stared at Evie, who fixed her gaze on a baking pan sizzling with roasted vegetables.

The voices in the living room melded into white noise, an unobtrusive backdrop for cooking. Evie stirred the chicken soup and turned off the burner but didn't turn around. If Beth was still staring at her, this wasn't going to work. Evie counted to ten in her head and looked over her shoulder. Beth and Laney were counting Haggadahs.

"How many do we need?" Laney asked.

"Sixteen." Evie turned to the stove and stirred, waiting.

"I think we only need fifteen," Laney said.

"Oh, no, sixteen," Beth said.

Evie left the spoon swirling and turned from the pot.

Laney rattled names and counted. "Fifteen. Are you counting the widow-mama twice?"

"Very funny."

Laney licked her forefinger and gave herself a tick mark in the air. "Laney, one. Evie, zero. You only put a cup out for Elijah the Prophet, you know, not a whole place setting."

"I know," Evie said.

"I'm going to put a book on each chair." Beth recounted sixteen Hagaddahs.

"What am I missing?" Laney said.

"I invited Sandy Perlman to the seder," Evie mumbled.

"I get to meet the History Hottie? Woo-hoo!" Laney shoved Evie's shoulder. "So it's official? You're dating?"

"I am not dating him. Or anyone else. He has no place to go, what was I supposed to do? Plus, he knows Alan."

"Well, he accepted your invitation."

"He's just a busy man with no family here."

"And no friends?" Laney asked.

Beth and Laney looked at each other.

"You're kidding, right?" Laney said.

"Look, I never thought I'd invite him, but it just happened."

"Fancy that. Doing something you never thought you'd do. Like, let's see—*teaching college*." Laney threw her arms in the air. Drama was never far from her reach.

"We're proud of you," Beth said. "For getting the job and for inviting Sandy tonight."

"Just because I invited him to seder and can admit he's handsome doesn't mean I *like* him."

"It means you're baaaaack," Laney said. "Although do we know if this History Honey is single? Because if he's off-limits, this is much less fun for me, and you may just have to tap into the coed population."

"He's divorced."

"Are you sure?"

"Yes, Lane, I'm sure." Evie was not wrestling morals with Laney with Beth in the room. "Now how about I concentrate on brisket instead of my imaginary love life?"

"If you must," Laney said.

Evie's mom walked into the kitchen. "Can I help?"

"We're all set," Evie said.

"I like you-know-who's mother very much. Did you know she's a college professor?"

"Yes, Mom, I know—and can you just say Nicole's name please."

"I agree she's not so bad, Evelyn, and that baby is a cutie-pie. Even the mother is nice, and well-spoken, although she could do with a bit of a makeover. I guess fashion doesn't matter much in Iowa. But are you sure you can be happy in this situation?"

"What situation?" Evie pulled her mom next to the refrigerator, hoping the hum would drown out the ridiculousness. "The situation where my kids have to grow up without a dad or the situation where I do what's best for them—which includes you-know-who and the baby?" Evie smiled.

"You're right," Shirley said. "But why did you invite them to the seder?"

Evie lifted the lid on the pot and fanned the steam toward her nose for a quick chicken-soup facial. "Aren't we supposed to let anyone who is hungry or needy come and eat? Isn't that how we are supposed to behave on this holiday" She thought more about Sandy than Nicole.

"You're right," Shirley said. "But they're—"

"It doesn't matter that Nicole isn't Jewish."

"It used to matter very much."

"That's true," Evie said. It was easy to dismiss Nicole as the shiksa, but the truth was, Evie hadn't been fond of Richard's Jewish mistresses either.

"If she was Jewish, you'd have some common ground," Shirley said.

"We do have common ground. Our kids." Evie wiped her hands on a towel and puttered with the soup bowls. "Nicole's going to watch the twins when I go to work, and I'm going to take care of Luca when she works."

"Just be careful," Shirley said with a tsk-tsk-tsk. "People don't change too much, you know."

"I'll keep that in mind." Evie thought of Beth. And then, Evie thought of herself.

Sophie skipped into the kitchen. "When are we going to start the seder? I'm hungry." Her declaration was answered by the doorbell.

Laney poked her head back into the kitchen. "I think Professor Preppy is here."

Sandy held a box of Bartons chocolates in one hand and flowers in the other. His mother—or his ex-wife—had taught him well.

In one motion Sandy stepped into the foyer and leaned toward Evie with an unexpected hug, his arms as warm as if the heat were turned on in his car. Evie reached around him, her arms gliding on his lightly starched shirt. Sandy squeezed with gentle strength, swayed, and stopped. She patted his back and they both released their arms to their sides. Her cheeks burned. She'd blame it on a hot kitchen if anyone asked why her face matched the fuchsia horseradish set out for the gefilte fish.

"Thank you," Evie said, gathering the flowers and the box Sandy pushed into her arms. "I just want to warn you, this is *not* going to be your ordinary family seder."

"Good." He put his hands in his pockets. "Ordinary's boring."

Sandy winked and Evie's temperature spiked from smoldering to five-alarm blaze. She looked at the floor, and with his finger under her chin, Sandy tipped up her face, leaned down, and kissed her on the lips. The soft, quick kiss was not a cousin—*or a colleague*—kind of kiss. Sandy stepped back, smiling. "Want to introduce me to your family?"

Evie stared at him. *He wants to meet my family? After one kiss and a box of Passover candy?*

"Your family *is* in the living room with your friends, right? Shouldn't we go in so I can meet *everyone?*"

"Oh, right. Everyone. In the living room. It's Passover. Right!"

Evie knew he enjoyed flustering her and just shook her head on the way to the living room, listening to Sandy chuckle behind her. Uncertain of her ability to mutter a coherent sentence, Evie nodded at Alan, who introduced Sandy to the crowd. Laney smiled so wide her eyes were almost closed. Herb shook Sandy's hand. Beth hugged him. Nicole stood and shook his hand, then introduced him to Peg. She and Sandy would have a lot in common.

Not too much, Evie hoped.

She watched Sandy cup Luca's cheek, a tender gesture unmarred by his usual wicked humor. Beth scooped Luca from Nicole's arms and sat on the couch with him, head-to-head, chattering, motioning with their hands. Sandy and Peg stood and chatted, her arms folded, his stance more open and welcoming with his hands by his sides. Evie whispered to Sophie, who clapped twice.

Everyone stampeded into the dining room, do-si-do-ing to find his or her assigned seat. Kids interspersed with adults. Family intertwined with friends. They scooted chairs into position, unfolded napkins, and opened their Haggadahs to page one.

The commotion filled Evie's ears almost as much as it filled her heart.

Nicole put a whole chocolate-chip macaroon in her mouth. "These are so good," she mumbled.

"Use your manners, Nicki," Peg said.

Peg should take her own advice and she should take it back to Iowa, Evie thought.

"Oh, she's fine. It's the blessed season of macaroons," Lisa said.

"Really?" Nicole asked, taking a chocolate-dipped one.

"No, hon, not really," Shirley said.

Lisa rolled her eyes. Evie laughed, treating herself to *her* last macaroon of the evening. Or at least of the hour. She held the plate out and thrust it toward Peg, a peace offering to sweeten her up.

Peg took a plain one and popped it into her mouth. "Mmm," she said—with her mouth full. "You were right, Nicki, these are delicious. May I have another?"

The power of macaroons.

Evie stepped back to get a better look at the innards of the dishwasher, willing it to have space for a few more plates.

"We'll have to run two loads, maybe three," Evie said, eyeing the counter.

"I'll stay and help you," Laney said, burping a Tupperware container filled with brisket.

"Me too," Nicole said.

Sandy stood in the kitchen doorway. "Count me in."

Evie waved a white napkin in surrender. "Lisa and my parents are here. You don't have to stay—they do or they won't have a place to sleep."

"I'd love to talk to you about your time at Dartmouth," Peg said.

"It was a long time ago, but sure."

Nicole shook her head, but smiled. That mother and daughter had a long way to go, but at least they'd gotten started.

Evie looked at the kids sitting at the kitchen table playing Trouble. The click of the center plastic bubble was inaudible after Evie pushed SCRUB on the dishwasher control panel, although it had been a nice change from the whistles and beeps of video games.

Luca balanced on Jocelyn's lap. Laney watched her. Evie watched Laney. Nicole watched Evie. Beth entered the kitchen, balled up tablecloth in her arms.

Evie's happy-family trance was broken.

She balanced containers and opened the fridge, scanning the shelves for space. She rearranged some of the leftovers, and a small relish plate appeared. So much for nibbling on olives, gherkins, and sour tomatoes after the gefilte fish and before the soup. Evie swore next year she'd make a list more detailed than the one stuck to her fridge that said, *Don't forget anything.*

She would also let Nicole reorganize the kitchen. Again.

Organized or not, making handprints on the pillowcase was something Evie never forgot—not even the first year she and Richard were divorced. She had gone to Beth's without the kids, then fashioned a second night of Passover, makeshift seder, and dinner for three, with preschool Haggadahs, rotisserie chicken, frozen potato pancakes, and Bartons chocolate-covered raspberry-jelly rings that served as both a fruit and dessert.

"Is it time?" Sophie said.

"I guess it is," Evie said. "Put a plastic cloth on the table."

The kitchen crowd exchanged looks. Sophie opened a cabinet and bent to the floor, pulling out a plastic basket filled with art supplies. A rolled, stained vinyl cloth lay on top.

Evie walked to the dining room and returned with the Passover pillow and pulled it out of its case. She handed the pillow to Lisa, who wrapped her arms around it the way she did when she was sixteen, sitting on her bed and talking about boys. Evie wondered if she'd twirl her hair or tap her fingers, but Lisa just looked at her. Evie flattened the pillowcase and pointed to a few spots that would work. The handprints overlapped slightly, the design becoming abstract art, beautiful but unrecognizable. Evie took out a small, noisy plastic bag from the side drawer and revealed three small plastic paint bottles. This year she opted for metallic instead of primary, jewel tones, pastels, glitter, puffy, or iridescent.

"I want silver," Sophie said.

"Do you want gold or copper, Sam?" Evie said.

"Gold."

"It's copper for Luca then."

Nicole gasped.

"Do you not want him to have paint on his hands?" Evie asked. "I'll make sure he doesn't lick them." Evie averted her eyes from Lisa and her parents and winked at Nicole.

"It's not that," Nicole said, her eyelids fluttering. "It's fine. No, it's perfect."

It had been months—maybe years—since anything in the Glass home had been perfect. But Nicole was right.

Sam and Sophie both stuck out their palms, and Evie squeezed a glob of appropriate-color paint onto each one. The kids rubbed their hands together, coated their fingers, and pulled apart their hands with a thwack. Evie pointed to Sophie and to the pillowcase. Sophie placed her hands, counted aloud to ten, and pulled them off. Shirley turned on the water and waved Sophie to the sink. Sam followed suit.

Nicole held Luca facing Evie and gave her his right hand. Evie put the copper paint on three middle fingers. Nicole stared at Evie. So did Luca. She rubbed the paint on his hand and held open his fingers, guided them to the pillowcase, and pulled them off without a smudge. Luca's palm print was solid, the fingers and thumb outlines sharp in some places and muted in others. Evie breathed deep.

"Good job," she said.

Luca squirmed and smiled wide, exposing two top teeth, two bottom teeth, and a mouthful of saliva. Evie threw her head back and laughed, then out of the corner of her eye she watched Lisa examine the newfangled heirloom.

Evie changed her mental channel, rinsed the rest of the dishes one by one, and placed them on a patchwork of old kitchen towels. The sound of the water obliterated the voices behind her, but Evie daydreamed a modern Norman Rockwell scene. She looked straight ahead and out the window so as not to break the spell. *It is such a pretty picture.* Then she shut off the faucet and turned around, which is when she saw, and heard, *reality.*

Laney was talking to Herb, her voice like a Charlie Brown adult's. Evie's parents sat at the table reading the newspaper, turning pages in time to Jocelyn's and Jordyn's slap of playing cards. Sophie's head disappeared into the freezer. Peg held Luca, who had chocolate all over his face. Rex licked something off the table leg, then the floor, then himself. Nicole dug in her diaper bag and emerged holding questionable, crumpled baby wipes. Laney took them and threw them away. Beth organized Tupperware by size, color, and contents. From the living room, Alan hooted and hollered something about a home run, and Sam belched his rendition of "Take Me Out to the Ball Game." Then Evie watched Lisa pop the last homemade macaroon into her mouth, without asking if her sister wanted it.

"Hey!" Evie joked. "That's the one I wanted!"

Sandy belly-laughed. The sound was becoming familiar.

Evie turned away again, closed her eyes, and let the sounds of domestic chaos weave under and over her thoughts. *This is my normal.* She smiled, feeling warm and content, as though she were relaxing in front of a roaring fire with an old friend.

Or perhaps, with a new one.

Acknowledgments

COUNTLESS HANDS AND HEARTS HAVE helped me reach today, but there are people I must mention by name, without whom my journey would not have been possible, or nearly as much fun.

Many thanks to Jason Yarn, my agent, for his insight and expertise, and for answering all my questions all the time. Boundless gratitude to Brenda Copeland, my St. Martin's editor, whose enthusiasm for *The Glass Wives* and confidence in me not only humbled and challenged me, but transformed me from a writer into an author. Heartfelt thanks also go to Laura Chasen, editorial assistant extraordinaire, for paying close attention to every detail, for quelling my nerves, and for risking her life to hail me a cab.

My critique partners, Pamela Toler and Christina Gombar, spent years reading chapters as many times as I rewrote them without complaint and always with insight. My earliest readers may not recognize *The Glass Wives* as the manuscript they read, but make no mistake, their feedback was crucial. Then there are later readers, workshop companions, those who answered questions or offered extraordinary moral support. Julie Asregadoo, Jami Bernard and the Ducklings, Annmarie Lockhart, Linda Oltman, Rebecca Flowers, Debra Lynn Lazar, Tina Ann Forkner, Kelly O. Levinson, Holly Root, Keith Cronin, Kristine Asselin, Janna Qualman, Julie Wu, Jeff Gold, Magdalen Braden, Adrienne Kress, Priscille Sibley,

Alice Davis, Kathy Calarco, Sandra Kring, Brenda Janowitz, Lori Nelson Spielman, Julie Kibler, Eric Schlanger, Fern Katz, and Manny Katz (even though all his ideas were somehow edited out).

I've made many friends through my Women's Fiction Writers blog, the Women's Fiction Writers Alliance, and The Debutante Ball, where Kerry Schafer, Dana Bate, Kelly Harms, and Susan Spann are my 2013 Deb sisters. The sense of community these writers has provided has been a blessing.

These amazing authors and editors taught me more about writing and publishing than can be found in any book: Erica Orloff, Steve Mills, Meg Waite Clayton, Randy Susan Meyers, Karen Dionne, the members of Backspace, and last but not least, Book Pregnant—my BPeeps—my tribe.

Renee San Giacomo lovingly handed me a shovel and told me to dig deeper. Whitney Finkelstein believed all this would happen long before anyone else, even me. My sister-friend, Judith Soslowsky, has read in between the lines of my life for thirty-three years and has always understood the work as well as the reward.

For the opportunity to come into the lives and hearts of readers—in the past, present, and future—I am forever grateful.

My parents', Sarah and Michael Nathan's, and my brother David Nathan's unconditional love provided the foundation on which I have built my life (many times, in many places).

My wonderful children, Zachary and Chloe Gropper, have been enthusiastic about my writing career since that Sunday in 2006 when my first essay appeared in the *Chicago Tribune* and we filled the back of the car with newspapers. You are now both remarkable adults with whom I am honored to share this and every journey. I love you, and believe that for all three of us, the best is yet to come.